A CRY FOR HELP

A CHRONOLOGICAL HISTORY OF
A BLACK COMMUNITY IN NORTHERN NEVADA

BY HELEN TOWNSELL-PARKER

Copyright © 2010 Helen Townsell Parker
All Rights Reserved

ISBN 1452814279
ISBN-13 9781452814278

DEDICATION

This book is dedicated to my Grandparents;
Big Daddy and Mama Helen.

I miss you both so much!
I did this in REMEMBRANCE to you.

I am so proud to be your Granddaughter.

Now, your works have been 'Documented!'

I LOVE YOU!

Your Granddaughter,
Helen Jr.

It is a privilege to participate in an astounding historical evolvement of a Northern Nevada community called Black Springs (aka Grand View Terrace). It is located just north of the heart of Reno. While perusing through the documents, that are many, placing them in chronological order, it shows how God's path is very straight yet narrow, it is extremely wide. Its width is due to the various roads that intersect along the journey. There are many reasons why so often the journey takes on alternate routes, it could be for rest; service to a stranger; or a life lesson. This is a collaborative attempt to unfold the tenacious efforts and accomplishments of this little but mighty neighborhood.

C. John Harris

Everyone has expressed that I need to write. My peers have stated I have this gift, so here I am, writing. I would have preferred relinquishing the information and someone with adequate writing skills could perform the task. I asked Carol, her reply, 'You need to'. I approached John his response, 'You need to write it'. Therefore, I am attempting to write about my discovery on what I consider very important history. The documents put into picture a story of growth within a little community called Black Springs, Nevada along with the residents' struggles to acquire what every other neighborhood had.

The story will speak of my grandparents, Ollie and Helen Westbrook, who were by all means pioneers in accomplishing their goals. They never stopped striving to make their community a place that their selves and others would call home.

I hope you will enjoy the journey.

Helen Townsell

CONTENTS

Acknowledgments

Introduction

1	Discovery	1
2	Arizona	11
3	A Partner	15
4	The Phone Call	19
5	Nevada Historical Society And The Media	23
6	The History Begins	37
7	The History Continues	41
8	Black Springs Cry For Help	57
9	An Effort To Rebuild	81
10	The P.O.W.E.R. Of Youth	95
11	Chronology Of The 1970'S	103
12	Chronology Of The 1980'S	211
13	Chronology Of The 1990'S	247

ACKNOWLEDGEMENTS

I'd like to recognize Christopher John Harris for all the dedication and hard work he put forth to help make this book possible. Although he did not want the title, to me, he truly is The Executive Editor.

Thank you, Cuz.

I'd also like to thank my sponsors and everyone who believed in this journey; the encouragement to continue; all those who gave of their time to support me; and gave finances to help a dream become a reality.

THANK-YOU ALL!

First Baptist Church of Black Springs, under the leadership of Reverend Don Butler

Rev. & Mrs. Don Butler • Jeff Townsell, Dad • Carrie Townsell, Mom

Aunt Lenora Holmes • Uncle & Aunt Skaggs • Uncle Rudy Townsell

Christina, Lucille & Jr. Townsell (all cousins) • Maurice Townsell, Brother

JoJo & Suzie Townsell, Brother/Sister-in-law • Butch & Jan Townsell, Brother/Sister-in-law

Julia Young, Cousin • Dana Lobster-Harris, Cousin • Jennie Parker, Step-Daughter

Andy & Carol Gordon, Brother and Sister in Spirit

Ceola Davis, Founder and Editor of Ensoul Magazine, the 1st Black Magazine in Reno

The Dalton's, Founders of 'Our Story' • Thurman Carthen Jr., Dear Friend

John T. Drakulich, Dear Friend • Candy Fife, Dear Friend • Lucille Adin, Dear Friend

Bertha Mullins, Dear Friend • George Hardaway, My Black History Teacher in High School

Jo Ann Newbury, Dear Friend • Chuck Folt, Dear Friend

INTRODUCTION

"Can you imagine what it would feel like to have a Park, Fire Station, Recreation Facility to be built on Streets you had paved serviced by Water and Sewage lines you made possible while sitting in the House your Husband built on a Street named for you?"

(Reno Gazette Journal—October 7, 1990)

This book is about fifty-years of Documented History, of a once small but mighty Black Community located North of Reno, Nevada, once called Black Springs, Nevada.

"Like any family who wants to settle down, first came the steady jobs, and then came thoughts of buying a house and starting a family. This did not prove to be easy in the "Mississippi of the West." In 1954, an African American could not buy a house, get a mortgage, a construction loan or purchase property. But that did not deter the Westbrooks. They found the one man who would sell property to blacks—Mr. J. E. Sweatt. Mr. Sweatt didn't care who bought the land as long as they had cold, hard cash. The property that he was selling was north of town. It was called Grandview Terrace and was later known as Black Springs. The Westbrooks bought their acre of property with no electricity, water, sewer or paved roads . . . such a deal. But their journey had just begun."

(Nevada Intelligence—October 2000)

CHAPTER 1
DISCOVERY

My grandfather, 'Big Daddy' as he was called, expired on July 28th, 2005. After the funeral preparations and services were completed, I became still. While glancing around my grandparents' home as well, as the tool shed, I immediately realized the project that laid before me, sorting and clearing out what I had inherited. Now, keep in mind this is 50 years plus of documents and items. Big Daddy was quite a pack rat and grandmother, bless her heart, kept things organized and under control. Mama Helen's, that's how we referred to her, death, preceded Big Daddy on January 13th, 2003. They lived in earthly bliss for over 52 years. It was obvious Big Daddy's spirit went with her. He was present only in body. He felt his home was no longer a home. Why, as he stated, "Mama's not here".

Anyhow, I had my hands full. I began to thumb through some paperwork in the house. All personal information about them, their house insurance; medical records; birth certificates; marriage certificate, etc. I sorted through all of it. There was quite a bit that had to be perused and determine what to retain as valuable memorable information for future generations to reflect upon. As you could imagine, there were numerous trips to the dumpster. There were in the midst of the accumulation canned foods and boxed foods that had been stored for years upon years; they had amassed quite a collection. There were even record albums of Billie Holiday, Ella Fitzgerald and tons of what I mused as old time music.

I felt weird browsing through my grandparents' effects. After all, they were very private people when it came to their personal belongings. You just didn't go rambling through their possessions. I surely would have been chastised as a kid, teenager or even as an adult had they been

A CRY FOR HELP

present. Sensing their loving spirit, you can imagine why I felt weird. After about six months of going through the house organizing and finding needed information, I decided it was time to tackle the shed. When I opened the door I gasped. Before me stood multiple boxes, office styled file cartons as well as packing boxes, stacked on top of each other reaching as high as the ceiling. Of course, after catching my breath, I became very curious as to the contents. From observation, I could see some of the boxes would be hard to access. They were blocked by other objects that needed relocating. So, the reachable files I began to open and discovered more documents. Every box I was able to get hold of all contained paperwork and documents. I thought to myself, what have I gotten into and what the hell is all this Mama Helen and Big Daddy kept.

I began reading some of the documents and newspaper clippings. To my astonishment, they were all about Black Springs. I read a couple of articles from each box and everything seemed to pertain to the area. You know, growing up in Black Springs and reviewing the contents jogged some memories of events from the past. I began to smile, as I am doing right now and asked myself, what have I discovered?

I took a box into the house and began reading. There was so much in just one box. I knew then I needed help getting the boxes out of storage from under and behind piles of my grandparents massive collecting.

A neighbor of mine, Hosea, is who I called on. Hosea and his family grew up in Black Springs. He still resides there. Hosea is considered one of the neighborhood's repair people. A man with incubus habits yet very dependable in doing odd jobs and performs them with great pride. That's why the neighbors call upon him, he is very trustworthy and does an excellent job. So, I solicited his help to clear out the shed in April of 2006, he agreed to the task. It took three days to clear out the storage, which netted 30 file boxes stacked neatly on the porch waiting for perusal. I was very overwhelmed by the undertaking that was before me. Every box was full of papers not booklets not binders but individual sheets of documents and articles stacked on top of each other. Knowing I can't discard anything until a thorough review of each document is done based upon earlier findings. Therefore, I thought,

DISCOVERY

what do I do? How do I begin? Who can I ask to help? What have I gotten into? Thanks Mama Helen and Big Daddy!

    I glanced at Hosea as he seemed to glare at me with a smirk of a smile and I said, "What the hell am I gonna do? How do I do this?" He replied, "Pick up one box at a time, take it into the house and start reading until you finish the last box. Take your time." I looked over at Hosea and mumbled, "You're right." I stooped to pick up a box and Hosea retorted, "Here I'll do it for ya. How many you want me to bring in for you?" He brought three boxes into the den and there I began sorting paperwork which was covered with dust. As mentioned, these papers had been stored in the shed, some for over 30 years. The recent years like 2000 and up were in the house. I had to wear a mask to protect myself from the dust spewing from the papers. The floor was layered with dirt, I even found mice droppings, bugs, spiders and at the end of the day I would be covered with dust.

    I first had to figure out how I was going to organize this information. The system was to sort by year, month and finally day. While sorting, I discovered many duplicates. There were also news articles and out of curiosity, I read some of them. They were always informative and interesting. Some spoke of how Black Springs was an all Black community, the only place Blacks could buy property; a ghetto, slum, etc. I was shocked to read that. I started reflecting on my childhood trying to visualize living in a ghetto or slum. I thought to myself, I always had nice clothes, a bed, roof, food, toys, great Christmases so I couldn't relate to these news articles. This was society saying I grew up in a ghetto-slum. I rather felt they were terribly mistaken.

    I recall the stories my parents and grandparents told about how they would haul water from town daily because there was no running water in the house. I distinctly remember using an outhouse and Lord, how I was always scared going to the outhouse by myself. However, I don't remember, even to this day anything negative about my childhood while growing up in Black Springs.

    Nevertheless, I couldn't help but interconnect with the information I had read. So much excitement began to arise in me through reading

A CRY FOR HELP

and looking at old pictures with everything bringing back memories. Finally, I couldn't take it anymore. I shared with my mother, father, brothers, neighbors, and the church almost everyone who had a part in this community as to what I had come across. They all seemed to be excited. From their reaction I invited those who lived or grew up in the community to help go through the paperwork. Even though there was shared excitement, no one had or would take time to help. I continued with my journey. It was as if I had to do this. I had no choice. I made the findings and now had to act on it. There was a reason my grandparents left all of this to me, for me to discover. They knew I would not just throw their life accomplishments, struggles, determination their story away. They knew I would investigate and stay on it no matter how long it took to tell the story. They knew. I didn't, but they knew. Therefore, I sorted and sorted and sorted papers. I finally eliminated a host of duplicate paperwork, you see my grandparents made multiple copies of everything. Their reasoning was to keep all residents informed of the community's undertakings.

I recall one day that it began to rain. I still had about 20 boxes out on the porch. I panicked and thought, 'Oh my God!' The rain would damage the documents. I ran outside, low and behold, there was Hosea already on top of it. Right when it started raining he said he was sitting at home saw the rain and thought about all those boxes exposed on the porch. He ran, got a tarp and when I arrived outside Hosea was already covering the boxes. He was yelling, "All this work you've already done, can't let it stop now with a little rain." He went on, "This is all about Black Springs, and this is my home too." I thanked Hosea repeatedly. I appreciated him more than he knew. I offered him a beer and to come in out of the rain, he accepted. When he came into the house, he glanced at all the work already done and laid out he stated, "Better you than me. I don't know if I could have done all this!" I answered, "I know. I cannot believe I'm doing it, but Mama Helen and Big Daddy left it here for me for a reason. I don't know why yet, but I'm sure I'll find out." Hosea downed a couple of beers, we shared some memories and he left.

I went back to my sorting dedicating at least 4 hours daily until completion. It took about 2 to 3 months before every single piece of paper had been sorted by year. They went back as far as 1956. I was so glad

DISCOVERY

it was finished, at least the first portion. Next, I would start sorting them by month, after that by category. There was the Black Springs Volunteer Fire Dept.; water; roads; community center; P.O.W.E.R. (People Organized to Work for Equal Recognition); Black Springs General Improvement District; tutoring; and tons of letters to city, county and federal government officials regarding Black Springs. This should take another couple of months. All news articles went in a pile of their own by dates.

I continued to educate myself on the many experiences of the growth of the community. Many of the articles touched me very deeply. I read what my grandparents, my parents and neighbors had to endure mainly because of their skin color. It gave me memories, insights to just how strong and determined they all were to make a home, a community, and boy did they ever. My grandparents left behind them a provocative legacy; it will be passed down from generation to generation. Not only have Ollie and Helen Westbrook gone down in history for their great accomplishments, but also included the entire Black Springs community.

After discovering more and more information, I asked Skeeta (Dana Lobster-Harris), for help. One reason was, unlike me, I knew she was a very fluent reader, understood what she read and would be a very big help to me. I had also, come across information and pictures about her father, who passed on September 18, 1986, as well as signatures and petitions that were from her parents. You see her father, William Lobster, was the Fire Chief for the Black Springs Volunteer Fire Dept. That is why I thought she would help, after all her family was apart of this history. She did come out one Saturday afternoon and worked with me all day into the night. Can you believe with the two of us on one box we barely got through it? We were too busy reading and reminiscing about what we were discovering.

Skeeta appeared as excited as I was. We made plans to meet every Saturday with an endeavor to complete the task. Skeeta worked, I did not, so that did make a difference for the time she could contribute, as I continued to share my excitement with people. I asked Skeeta if she would take a box home hoping her and John, Dana's husband, could go through it and I would start taking boxes to my apartment. You see my son and I inherited the property. I chose to let my son and his family live

A CRY FOR HELP

in the house and I kept my apartment. At home, I sorted through papers at my leisure so to speak. So much time had gone by and this was taking forever.

I then spoke with the pastor of First Baptist Black Springs. I shared with him all the information I came across. This I did due to the information found regarding the church, thinking he might want to have it. I asked him if any of his members could help in assisting sorting through documents; just give me one day a week. To this day, there has been no response. He did ask, when done would I give him everything pertaining to First Baptist? I agreed, but it was a bit upsetting that yet again, no help. I then made up my mind I was going to complete this project with or without any help. Therefore, I continued to sort, read and try to organize all this valuable history.

Finally, I got it down to about ten boxes. Remember, I started with thirty. I had made a huge improvement, realizing that about two of those boxes were personal information regarding my grandparents. They had kept every receipt, paycheck stub, bank statements; anything that had to do with money transactions. So now, I'm down to eight boxes sorted by year and month but not by day. However, I was still finding duplicates even when I thought I had gotten rid of them all.

I continued sifting my way through the paperwork. I began to see the boxes diminish, I was happier. This turned out to be quite time consuming. It had now been close to two years. Sometimes a couple months would lapse before resuming. But it would become the top priority once again. I dedicated a few weeks and hours upon hours daily reading and organizing paperwork. I became very hypnotized.

I constantly shared my discoveries with anyone and everyone who would listen. Even when they showed no interest, I started sharing the discoveries, they became attentive. It was exciting watching their faces and expressions as I shared some of the contents. There would suddenly be a spark in their eyes as if to say, 'I remember that', and suddenly an outburst of reminiscence was re-lived between us through the experiences I was reading. One neighbor in particular, Mr. Carthen, there was a news article in the Reno Gazette Journal showing him

DISCOVERY

cleaning up his property. Of course, all remembered that occasion and it sparked up about a two-hour conversation of reminiscing.

Now down to four boxes, although this was a great accomplishment, I could see the back porch, there was still much more to do, there were all the boxes at my house. There were only four boxes, but three of those boxes had nothing but single sheets of documents. There were some packets of ten paged reports, but there were far more individual documents, all communications between the Westbrooks, who represented the Black Springs Community, and governmental officials, also a partial box of news articles about Black Springs. We will get into detail about the findings a little later.

Months and months go by thinking and expressing how, 'I need to complete this project.' I think about it constantly. My conscience says, 'do this Helen, do this.' I want to but I'm lacking incentive. As a result, I keep the boxes nicely stored in my apartment and storage closet kind of out of sight out of mind theory. Yet, it is still on my mind. I'm thinking if I could just get someone to assist me. I still needed help, so who? Everyone I previously approached stared at me with that, 'I feel for you, but I'm not volunteering my time' expression. 'This is your journey. I wish you well, but I'm not doing it.' I felt alone and at a standstill, a roadblock. What am I to do? I need to think this out.

Then, I met this woman named Madeline. She had and has such a positive lively energy that spreads all over you when you come into her presence. I love her energy. She never concludes with anything negative. She responds only to the positive. I don't think Madeline has a negative bone in her body and she is very intelligent. I mean, this woman has it going on!

I became acquainted with Madeline while working. My mother, who also works with us, had spoken about Madeline and commented that once I met her, I would really like her, she is very intelligent. As I said, I love her energy.

While working together, Madeline and I began to talk and I shared my project with her. She was quite interested in what she heard.

A CRY FOR HELP

She asked to see what I had. So we planned to get together and she would look over a few of the documents and share her views on the next steps to take. A couple of months went by and our schedules did not permit us to meet. We finally said, 'this is it we are going to get together' so we did. Madeline came over one morning for coffee and looked over the documents. I was very animated; for the second time someone had come over to help go through the documents and see what I had discovered. My stomach was doing things a stomach does when you're eager, tossing and turning. She did call to say she was running late. The knock finally came. I was scared she was canceling when she called, it has happened on previous occasions. However, she had called and was on her way. She's here! I am so excited I want to start right in on the paperwork, but I must be hospitable, do the greeting and make one comfortable, offer coffee and coffee cakes, and after all, this was her first time to my place. I showed her around while discussing items of interest to her like African art; you know the woman type thing, checking out ones surroundings, their style in life.

With all the preliminaries over it's time to get down to business. There were already four boxes out ready for working. I showed them to Madeline, she looked at the boxes and said, "Girl, you've got your work cut out for you!" Then she began to instruct on how to organize them. I began telling her about all the history discovered as she was very interested in what I was saying. She listened attentively, but made it clear that she helps by instructing not doing. After sharing the findings with Madeline, I was able to persuade her to read a letter my grandfather had written back in December of 1968. As she began to read it, I could tell her plan was to scan through it. She recited the title aloud, "**A Black Springs Cry for Help**" I heard a "hum". I thought to myself, 'Yeah, read this and it has to affect you.' The first paragraph Madeline sat down. Suddenly her attention had left me, her continued expressions of 'I can't stay long' all disappeared, and she was definitely in the moment, nothing else mattered but reading that letter. Her facial expressions told me what I needed and wanted to know. That the letter in itself was most powerful just as prevailing as little Black Springs, for all I read, this letter was the root and start of it all.

By the time Madeline completed "the letter", her mouth was wide open. She was in awe from what had just been read. The first time

DISCOVERY

I read it, I was the same way. When finished she looked at me and said, "Oh my God! Girl, your grandfather was extremely intelligent. I could just picture him standing before the County Commissioners reading this letter with such dignity and grace." She went on to say, "I don't even know your grandfather, never had the pleasure of meeting him, but through this letter I feel I already know him personally. Girl, this is news worthy. This needs to be in the Nevada Historical Society." She continued, "This is something of news, call CNN, call Oprah. Have you! Are you trying to apply for a grant to display items in the community center? You get this information out. Let people know how your community is still suffering and ask for little things to complete the community and you will not need a grant. Donations and other opportunities will start coming your way faster than you can imagine." She compared Black Springs to the ninth Ward in New Orleans, mainly because it dealt with a community of Blacks being over looked by the city officials. As she said, "It took years to get what we got. Why not complete this community?"

I didn't mention that another reason I asked Madeline to my place is she's a grant writer. I needed help in how to write a grant and she was going to help me. I wanted a grant to have a display case built to share articles and items in the Westbrook Community Center for all to see. I also wanted to open another access road in Black Springs as well as a nice sign at the entrance. Therefore, Madeline was there to assist me in how to get started and which grants to apply for.

After reading the letter, Madeline's thoughts were very different from previously. She suggested I contact all these people. All I could do was sit and listen very amazed at what I was hearing. I thought to myself, Madeline has lost her mind. No way is this that news worthy. I am not contacting those people. They are not interested in our little story. I thought she was making too much of it. Yeah, I felt it was very important to us who lived through it, but Oprah, CNN, Nevada Historical Society. Yeah, right. I wrote down everything she said. She even suggested doing a play about it next year during Black History month and having someone recite the letter. She called it young Chautauqua, it's where kids memorize the speech and recite it.

A CRY FOR HELP

By the time Madeline left, I was overwhelmed with all she said. I did not know what to think. I started calling people to get their reactions. I called my mother and she was thrilled. Oh, Madeline also mentioned she could see this in a movie and I needed to start writing about what I had discovered. I asked her if she was interested in writing about it. I told her I have all the information. She smiled and said, "No Helen. You need to write it." She concluded, "I know that was a powerful speech Ollie wrote."

I told my dad and brothers they listened and showed a little excitement but went on as to say, 'Here she goes again with another one of her big dreams.' Not negative, but not positive either. Somewhat of a 'let us see reaction.' Others I shared it with seemed interested but still no offers of help just advice on how I should or could do it. I was a little discouraged by that, but it was not going to stop me. So, I pressed on determined to complete this project, yet still did not know where to start or should I say how to finish.

I maintained the same process. The four remaining boxes I would organize by year, month, and day like the others in chronological order, that way I could continue following the growth of the community. The boxes were still full of papers, but very well organized. I was extremely happy and satisfied with that. Reading it again, you find out more with each perusal. Still, I had not grasped what Madeline had told me. I just could not imagine the dreams that had awakened my thoughts would ever happen. It would be nice, but unimaginable. Once again, I sat on the discovery. I was sitting on a history.

Months went by. Madeline would ask me on occasion what progress has been made. "None," I reply. "I'm just not feeling it." She retorted, "Girl, you've got some serious history there." I recoiled, "Help me then." However, she really did not have the time to commit.

I had gone back to work pretty much all of 2007 for a Harley production company traveling around putting on Harley or Classic Car events. I had to give the project a rest. I needed time away.

CHAPTER 2
ARIZONA

While at an annual car show in Arizona, my dear friend, Andy and his wife Carol Gordon who live there, I would visit. We would get together and reminisce. I've known Andy since I was about 12 or 13 years old. He first came to Black Springs as a VISTA worker in 1969. There is a lot more to say about Andy.

While in Arizona we went out to dinner at a beautiful Italian restaurant, it was on Super Bowl Sunday, 2008. It was hard to converse, there was a sports bar connected and the game was intense. Twice Carol got up to go check out the score. We were not fans, but with all the excitement, curiosity got the best of us.

During dinner, I began to share with Andy and Carol as to what I had found. All the documents describing the work, accomplishments, all the set backs, disappointments, struggles, etc. the community, Black Springs had gone through; Andy's work as well as the constant contributions and determination everyone put forth just to have a decent place to live and raise a family. I told them how my grandparents had saved everything; they saved the history of the processes of growth in Black Springs, Nevada. They could sense the passion in my voice. I spoke uncontrollably as if someone, (my grandparents), were talking through me. They saw my enthusiasm and they too became very excited.

Carol then began to share some very profound information with me. She told me my grandfather was very pleased with what I was doing and wanted me to keep up the good work. She expressed that my grandmother was standing beside me during the renaming dedication ceremony of the Black Springs Community Center to the Westbrook Community Center, on October 6, 2006. Carol shared other insights

A CRY FOR HELP

with me, I knew some things she revealed could not have been known. I was in awe. I can't share everything with you some things are not to be shared, but I knew from the messages Carol had delivered that night, I had to get back to Reno and find a way to complete my task. I must complete what my grandparents had started. I had a new goal, a new purpose.

Carol and I began talking. She stated this story needs telling. Carol shared with me how 35 years ago when she and Andy met, he told her all about his experiences in Black Springs, this was a movie, a book it was a story that needs telling. Carol went on to say she was a screenplay writer. Now, I had tried to solicit her skills a few years ago about writings I have done. She was more than happy to look at them, but I never pursued the plan. I was to make copies of my writings send them to her and let her see what she could do. Well, I agree with her that I need to write about this. I thought, wow a movie. She also informed me that she was taking some film classes. I thought aloud, "Carol you can write and film your own movie, all about Black Springs." We did not laugh it off either. Andy kind of chuckled while saying, "Oh you guys," but did not dismiss it.

He drove listening, not making many comments at all. Andy's the type of person, that if you believe in a dream, go-for- it, and he will be there to support any and every way he can.

Carol and I continued sharing ideas. I shared with her all the things Madeline had purposed and we were both excited. I told Carol I would stay in touch and now I needed to go home to resume the project, the history of Black Springs and my grandparents.

Before I parted Carol said, "Let me know when you're ready to start and I'll be right with you!" How can you turn down an offer like that? A screenplay writer and producer voicing what everyone else is saying, "You got something here!" Yet that other thought was still there. Who can I get to assist in putting it all together? Who will want, who can give 100% with Carol and I on this. Carol lives in Arizona, moreover she's in school and I need someone local who had time to share, a lot of time.

ARIZONA

In the meantime, back from an awesome visit with a positive shift in energy, I shared with everyone what Carol imparted to me. My entire experience in Arizona I shared with friends and family. My mom became emotional when I shared with her about her parents, my grandparents, what Carol had shared. I updated Cousin John all about Arizona and the insights from Carol.

John's name is Christopher John; he is married to my childhood friend, Dana (Skeeta) Lobster-Harris. Our families, Skeeta's and mine, adopted each other a couple of generations ago as relatives. We consider ourselves' cousins; therefore, John is my cousin-in-law. Throughout the story you will here me refer to him as John or Cuz. That is our lingo.

What I shared with John was enough to spark his interest. I asked John would he just read the letter that Big Daddy had written. I gave him the letter and he glanced at it, thumbed through the letter and sat it down. My thought was, 'He is not interested either.' I was so excited ready to do this but felt like I struck out again. John showed no reaction. I sometimes can sense John's insights but was not sensing any interest on his part in my joy.

I had errands to run and asked John to ride with me. I thought about leaving him at my place, maybe he would read the letter, but I didn't want to force my joy on anyone. You have to feel what I felt to be a part of this. John went with me, I mentioned he could bring the letter with him and read it in the car. He said, "NO, when I read it I want to give it my full attention." "Okay", I said disappointed, but knew he would read it. When John commits to something, he will do it.

Completing the errands, we returned to my apartment. I had left it alone asking John to read the letter by moving on to another subject. Originally, John came over to assist in putting together information needed to apply for a grant. I explained I had a deadline, March 29th, to submit the application. I was at my computer surfing the internet for information regarding the grant. I asked John a question. There was no response. I asked again. Still there was no response. I had my back to him so I couldn't see what he was doing. I just knew he was not responding. I turned around to see why there was no response. John was standing in

A CRY FOR HELP

the den reading Big Daddy's letter. I said no more. I knew once he finished, I would have his help. John was extremely intense in what he was reading. He stood in one spot frozen to the literature, he was in awe. The facial expression said it all.

I had completed my findings on the computer and I sat awaiting John's completion of the letter. When he finished, he looked up at me with a gleaming, glowing smile and said, "Oh my God!" His mouth stayed open as he stared at me in amazement. He was awe struck from what he had read. He said, "I feel every bit of what Big Daddy was saying. You would not know he didn't graduate high school and had a sixth grade education." He went on, "I knew Big Daddy was very knowledgeable and intelligent. I would consider it an honor to help. When do we start and what do we need to do." We made plans on what was needed, when we would start and how much time we would spend on it daily, etc.

We started the next day. John was at my place at 8 a.m. the next morning until 6 p.m. that evening. We continued this schedule everyday, Monday through Friday, nothing under eight hours daily. Our plan was to re-read documents, label the outside, put them in envelopes, and note the contents.

CHAPTER 3
A PARTNER

John and I made an agreement to complete what began two years ago. I finally had someone who I knew, if he committed to a project, would definitely see it through. I knew of his intelligence and knowledge of organization. I witnessed his excitement, and for the above reasons believed in his dedication to completion along with accuracy. I HAD A PARTNER!

We decided to dedicate a lot of time, for there was a bundle of work ahead of us. We began the next morning at 8:00 a.m. I had coffee ready had put a card table up in my living room, pulled out the boxes along with paper and pens for notes. I waited for 8:00 a.m. I knew John would be there. He is a very punctual person. I believe it would disturb him terribly if he were late. Sure enough, at 8:00 a.m., there was a knock on the door. Might I add it was a happy enthusiastic kind of a knock? Although I knew it was John, I still looked through the peep hole; there he was anxiously waiting for me to open the door. When I opened the door, he was all bubbly ready to go. He saw the table, coffee, boxes, paper and pens and commented, "Oh, you are ready for me," as he chuckled. We got ourselves a cup of coffee, sat down and began to discuss how to proceed.

I explained to John, that I had everything in order by year and category. We agreed to start by sorting the years. We had piles of documents spread over the entire living room, which is small. There were papers on the couches, coffee table, end tables as well as the card table, on the floor and in the den. The only place there's no documents was the pathway for us to walk.

A CRY FOR HELP

We were enthralled about the adventure we were about to undertake. I was so keyed up my heart was beating fast, I had little tingles in my stomach. Every time I spoke, I would articulate with such joy. My joy was that I had help, a PARTNER. I had someone who shared my enthusiasm. Someone who had the same goal I had which was to get this history out there for everyone to see and read about, especially the residents of Black Springs. You see, there are still some residents from that time who experienced so much of everything you will read. I wanted them to see, re-live in memory their struggles, accomplishments and successes in completing important goals. It is something, they should be proud.

Anyhow, it took a couple of days, maybe more to sort the first box. Actually, it took about four days. Once we had everything sorted in piles, and thought we were finished, I remembered three more boxes in the storage closet. We thought we were finished, all this paperwork already all over the place, yet there were more boxes. At the end of each day, we would leave everything as is. If someone came over, we would have to sit around the documents or go into the bedroom to visit. We were not moving those documents. John agreed, all the info would stay right where they were.

I pulled out the three boxes from storage. One box was nothing but pamphlets regarding the water system, community center, by-laws, etc. they were manuals that was great. Another box was church information. I remember this once I glanced inside; this box was from earlier sorting. The third box, as you may guess, were individual papers again. We thought all had been finished, but we had one more box to go through and sort. A little bummed out, we got busy. I did the sorting and decided John would start placing the piles already stacked by years in order by month then date. That way we would have a chronological order of every document. As I sorted and added to stacks, the majority of paperwork was from 1969 and up. This was great, because it did not interfere with what John was doing. It took about two days to complete that last box. This time it was the final box. We had finally completed a very big task. It took a total of five days to get everything sorted by year from me. John had sorted from 1956 to 1969. Now, 1969 was the biggest stack. Yes, it was a very enterprising year. Although there was

A PARTNER

paperwork back from 1956 to 1968, there was not much documentation, but there were some important documents. As I said before in 1969, things started happening. Things took off like a skyrocket. We continued putting everything in order by month and date. This took another four days. Then the brief reading began. Then we had to put all documents in 8 x 10 envelopes listing the year and contents on the outside.

Through all the sorting, we would sometimes see a news article or document that would grab our attention and stop sorting, and start reading and discussing it. Then we would say, 'get back on track, we will read about everything soon enough.' The day came, sorting was completed and the reading officially began.

CHAPTER 4
THE PHONE CALLS

John and I were reading, page by page, the documents we would pick up. We would discuss the contents, and how we would organize the information for adequate retrieval. Now, the fun started. But first, phone calls must be made. Knowing what we had, it was time to share this news with a few people. On February 11th, John called the Northern Nevada Black Awareness Society. There was no answer, so he left a message, leaving my name, phone number and the type of information we had discovered regarding Black Springs, asking if they would return the call at their earliest convenience. He was sure they would be interested. We did not stop there; I asked John if he would call the "White Society." He laughed replying, "Okay, but you mean the Northern Nevada Historical Society." Not resting, he called.

John relayed to me how excited the receptionist was to hear what he shared. I heard him say, "I would like to speak to someone about the historical documents of Black Springs that we have found." The receptionist placed him on hold; she went to find the person he needed to speak with, Mr. Eric Moody. John told him of our discovery, and Mr. Moody was interested in what documents we had. We scheduled an appointment for Thursday, February 21, 2008. That would give us plenty of time to complete our enveloping and detailing of the contents for presentation.

I called some of the current board members in Black Springs to setup a time to meet with them regarding the discovery. We met with them Monday, February 18th, at the Carthen's home. The Carthens are long time residents of Black Springs. They moved there in 1956. Mr. Thurman Carthen is currently Chairman of the Water District, his wife, Mae Ella Carthen, Treasurer; Roy Moore, Vice Chairman; Shelly Moore, Secretary; Danny Carson, Member.

A CRY FOR HELP

John and I shared with them the information. We were able to show them the work we had invested time in and stressed the work yet to do. We also informed them of the meeting scheduled with the Nevada Historical Society in the Research Department, and invited them to join us. They expressed their approval and encouraged us on what we were doing. They never knew such records still existed. They thought any records might have been lost after my grandparents had past on. They could rest easy knowing, that the records had not been lost. Now, we had proof of everything this community endured just trying to survive and make a living while raising their families. All the doors that were shut in their faces were unbelievable, now to actually read and see the pictures of their journey was breath taking.

I contacted Carol the next day. I e-mailed her about the meeting with the Nevada Historical Society and about the meeting with the Board of Black Springs. We setup a time to call and discuss everything and where to go from there. I spoke with Carol again on February 12th. First order of business was the introduction between John and Carol. I had told Carol about John, they had never met or spoke to each other. John just knew her through what I had shared.

We began informing Carol on who we had contacted. She congratulated us on a job well done. Her first suggestion was that I e-mail Oprah and tell her about my news. I was not real convinced of that. Carol was not the first one to say that. Madeline and John said the same thing. As unbelievable as it was for me, I did it. Carol also began to talk about what questions we wanted to ask the Nevada Historical Society. She suggested we ask what they're looking for from us by turning over the documents. She also stated they could preserve the documents, and everything would be recorded, it would be history. She expressed how this could really open doors to projects we were trying to accomplish, such as the original reason we did this, to justify why Black Springs deserved or was entitled to grant money in order to display the history we had. Carol also asked us, "What is it you want?" I asked, "What do you mean by that?" She said, "Do you want a documentary, book or a movie?" I could not stop smiling and neither could John. I was quiet for a moment then blared, "All the above."

THE PHONE CALLS

Carol stated the documentary would be a little harder because everything had to be totally accurate, but a movie, although it is based on a true story, you can spice it up a little. Then she said, "As far as a book goes, Helen you need to start writing about all of this." John urgently agreed. He began co-signing for Carol saying, "I told her the same thing Carol. See Helen I told you. You need to write a book." I told both of them, "Okay, I will write it." I was willing to make copies of everything and send it to Carol so she would be able to write the story. I would be available for any clarification she may have needed and if I did not have the answer, I would find it.

Carol also wanted us to focus on one sentence for the title of our project, the book, or movie. John and I did not have to think long. As soon as we hung up, we looked at each other smiling. John picked up Big Daddy's speech and said, "Here's our title. 'Black Springs Cry For Help'." I totally agreed. That was it.

Carol also said she wanted all the old photographs we had of Black Springs along with current pictures. She said at some point in time she would be coming to Reno to interview the Black Springs Community. We told her when ever she's ready to let us know, we will make arrangements.

Carol left us with a couple of tasks to complete before our next meeting. We already had completed one of those tasks. On February 13th, I e-mailed Carol stating we agreed on "Cry for Help."

Chapter 5
NEVADA HISTORICAL SOCIETY AND THE MEDIA

On February 19th the last piece of paper had been placed in the envelope and labeled for our presentation. John and I just looked at each other, both with huge grins on our faces feeling satisfied in completing a mighty task.

If you recall, July 2005 is when my grandfather passed. Some time in August or September of 2005 I had discovered the documents; over two years would elapse before totally organizing this history, the legacy and growth of a community. My grandparents were awesome. No one knew how diligently kept the records were. Most of them, even down to the news articles, were in pristine condition. I was proud to be apart of their ancestry. I had to spread their words, accomplishments, struggles and determination to press forward only to look back at where they had come from and where they were now. Wow, what a legacy to leave behind for review.

The day had come to meet with Mr. Moody of the Nevada Historical Society. John and I were fully charged. I called Roy and Shelly Moore and Mr. and Mrs. Carthen the day before the meeting to remind them. They assured me they would be there. We felt like a little but mighty army going into the chambers to convince "the man" to once again listen to our story, too point out the historical significance. Yes, he did sound excited to get this information over the phone. Although we knew what we had, would he feel the same way after we presented our findings?

We were instructed to go to the Research Department and ask for Eric Moody. He was a gentleman of average height and weight with

A CRY FOR HELP

a close cut beard, sort of strawberry blonde hair, wore glasses, and very soft spoken. He greeted us with a smile, introducing himself with an extended hand. We all shook hands as we introduced ourselves. I expressed how excited I was to finally be there to meet him and show-and-tell what we had.

Mr. Moody directed us to the conference room where we all began to converse. The basic question from Mr. Moody was, "What precisely do you have?" John and I both seemed to chime, 'the history and growth of a small community called Black Springs.' We explained how we found documents supporting everything. We felt this was apart of the Northern Nevada history as well as Black history. It is a historical site. We have documented proof from the time Black Springs started settling in the community. He explained to us that it is only a historical site if it no longer exists. John went on to say, "It doesn't exist anymore. It's now called Grand View Terrace. So that does make it a historical site." Mr. Moody smiled, looked down at the table looked up at John and said, "You're right." Mr. Moody went on to inform us that he sat on the committee when Black Springs applied for a name change. He went on to explain that once the research was completed and the name change was granted, Black Springs was like wiped off the face of the earth, as if it never existed. He knew it existed because he has lived in Reno since 1968 and knew about it. He also reiterated there was very little history because there were no documents to substantiate anything about Black Springs. That's when he said those magic words, "Yes, I'm very interested in seeing what you have." John looked at him and said, "I know, you will be interested. I know you will want them." Mr. Moody did ask how we came across these documents. I explained how I found them and how long it had taken to put it all together. He expressed his appreciation that I didn't destroy what I had discovered, the fact that I was even interested in pursuing it. I told him I could not let my grandparents' work, the community's history to go in the garbage. It was all left for a reason and I was in the process of discovering why. We agreed to meet at the Westbrook Community Center in Black Springs for an in depth presentation.

Before we left, we invited him out to the car to see what we had. It was sprinkling outside when I opened the trunk. He saw the documents neatly organized in envelopes. He started smiling and responded,

NEVADA HISTORICAL SOCIETY AND THE MEDIA

"Close the trunk, you don't want the paperwork wet. Protect the documents." It was the first sign of emotional excitement I had seen from him since we had met. I knew then, so did John, that it was a done deal. We only had to follow procedures.

The community center was called the Black Springs Community Center. After my grandfather's death, I went on a campaign to have the center renamed the Westbrook Community Center. The reason being the documents and all I had read, my grandparents deserved the community center to be named after them. Although the community did get involved and backed all the projects, the Westbrooks were the initiators and pioneers at getting things started and following it through. They would report back to the community regarding community issues. They would call upon the community for support in filing petitions, writing letters, and attending Commissioner's meetings. They took time off work to go present their cases for a better community, the right to have what every other American community had. They were the true pioneers of Black Springs not from my perception, but from facts.

In the process of setting up the meeting with the Nevada Historical Society, I also contacted KNRV, Channel 4 News regarding the discovery. I contacted them regarding a letter I found in 1969 addressing an issue pertaining to another access in and out of Black Springs. In February 2007, there was a fire at the front entrance, the only way in and out of Black Springs. The community was blocked in that day. School buses, people needing to get to work, no one could get in or out. The news media was there. I complained as well as other residents to the County Commissioner about this issue months prior to this incident. I, Roy and Shelly Moore and my mother, Carrie Townsell attended meeting after meeting asking that another road be opened.

There was a dirt road that had been open although bumpy, it was an emergency exit. Someone, that no one will take responsibility for doing, placed big boulders there so you could no longer use the exit. This happened after a news report from Channel 4 regarding the issue had aired. The County Commissioner finally did have the boulders removed, rather moved over enough to permit access for emergencies. They have all the infrastructures being placed for the new developments on the

A CRY FOR HELP

south and north sides of Black Springs which is everything a community has when being built, although our community had to seriously fight for. The road, that for all the years I've lived in Black Springs was only partially paved and that lead to the freeway, stores and Lemon Valley, was suddenly paved, which everyone in Black Springs was happy to see. Then one day, boom, boulders went up on the other side of the emergency dirt road exit we had. On top of that the people built a deep trench to where you would damage your vehicle if you attempted to drive over or down it.

We tried to inform our Commissioner, all of a sudden it was private property and she couldn't do anything about it. It was basically thrown back in our laps to deal with and once again, a hurdle to jump. We had what I felt was very good ammunition to take to the news media for a follow up story based on the fact that Black Springs has been looking for another way out for years. It was also a way to announce the documents and information we had discovered, a growth of a community.

So, we contacted Channel 4 news and spoke with Liz Wagner. She's the same reporter who reported on the issue in February 2007. She was surprised to hear the problem had not been resolved, instead worse. She thought by now the boulders were removed and we had a paved road. She was especially concerned for the elderly who lived on the lower part of Black Springs if an emergency occurred. Who would get them out? I told Liz I had a letter from 1969 showing and proving how long Black Springs had been looking for another exit.

Like I said, all the new developments already have at least two ways to enter and exit. The Black Springs community has been there since 1952, asking for help in 1969 regarding another access road and to date nothing but 'I don't know'. Anyhow, Liz asked if we could meet on February 25th, 2008 at my apartment. That made sense, because all of the documents were there.

John and I were very ecstatic. I passed the word around to all the family members and friends. I spoke with Roy Moore, the Vice Chairman on the Board of Black Springs; he planned to be there. Roy is who Liz interviewed regarding the roads in February 2007. Channel 4 News

NEVADA HISTORICAL SOCIETY AND THE MEDIA

would once again re-address our issue and announce the news of the possibility of the documents being donated to the Nevada Historical Society. Who would have imagined little old Black Springs would be going down in history? Big Daddy and Mama Helen would be so proud. I knew they were watching over everything. It had been confirmed back in Arizona.

The day arrived; we were set for Liz Wagner of Channel 4 News and her team. I was so worried, rather nervous, I began to perspire. John was just sitting there all calm saying, "I don't know why you're so nervous." I had to put my sweat suit jacket on to hide the perspiration. When Roy arrived John and I took time to discuss some of the issues going on. I gave Roy paperwork concerning the Westbrook Community Center as well as pictures of a neighbor's yard that needed cleaning up also he was able to look over the documents that we had for Mr. Moody's and News 4's review.

Finally News 4 arrived, right on time. I opened the door and there was this big smile on Liz's face, you could tell she was very excited, that made me excited. She extended her hand and we introduced ourselves, around the room introductions preceded. That alone, made me feel great and very comfortable. This was fantastic.

Liz and her crew of two started setting up for the interview. In the meantime Liz and I got acquainted; I showed her the boxes full of envelopes with the history. She asked questions about the contents and how I came about all of this information. I told her my story. She also spoke with Roy, remembering him from last year, expressing how happy she was that he was present. She went next to John and spoke extensively with him. John began telling Liz about the history of Black Springs. He got into detail about some specific subjects, especially the water rights that Black Springs still to this day own. Liz was very interested in hearing about all of this.

It was time for the cameras to start rolling. Because of the time to mingle and talk, I felt at ease with being interviewed. Liz and I sat on the couch with the camera men right in front of us. John and Roy, my rooting team of comfort, were standing in the den. It had begun;

A CRY FOR HELP

Liz wanted to know how I discovered the documents, down to the letter about the request on behalf of the Black Springs community for another access in and out 40 years ago. The following may be reviewed at the Nevada Historical Society.

May 21, 1969

John Bowden
State Highway Dept.
Carson City, Nev.

Dear Mr. Bowden:

This is a request that something be done <u>immediately</u> about the state property that turns into the Black Springs area off old 395 entrance to Main Street.

I have contacted Mr. Bill Sinott, also John Bowden and Ralph Colleta, about the entrance way. I was informed that there is some 150 or 200 feet of State property we want paved, <u>now.</u>

We were informed last summer by Ralph Colleta that there was enough State property between the paved new 395 lanes, and State property line, for a frontage road from North Street through to the Lemmon Valley enter change.

We want that frontage road, because it gives us two outlets for this community.

Yours truly,

Mrs. Helen Westbrook
Outreach Center Worker

LEW

NEVADA HISTORICAL SOCIETY AND THE MEDIA

This next letter is from 1970.

March 5, 1970

Senator Howard S. Cannon
Senate Office Building
Washington D.C.

Dear Sir:

The Black Springs Civic Improvement Club, is requesting your support in a Frontage Road connecting Medgar Avenue or Westbrook Lane, to Highway 395 North on the Four Lane Freeway.

John Bowden, Nevada State Highway Department, stated that there is enough State Land joining the highway and Black Springs to have a Frontage Road. It was suggested that the Black Springs Civic Improvement Club get help from the Federal Government.

There are times the one road we have is impossible to travel. We are concerned about our children getting to the School Bus. This Frontage Road would be a very easy entrance and exit for the School Bus Service.

Thank you for your consideration and concern.

Sincerely,

Helen Westbrook
Community Organizations
Coordinator

Cc: Senator Alan Bible

A CRY FOR HELP

I explained in detail how I found the boxes of papers, sorted them, read them and came across the letters. I went on to say how surprised I was to discover how long ago this request was made, and to date nothing. It sounded just like what I had come up against with the present County Commissioners, nothing.

After that discussion, Liz wanted to view some of the documents in the boxes to know what type of information and its pertinence. She asked me to read a couple documents explaining what they were. The first document I pulled out was what? Yes, the letter my grandfather wrote in December 1968, 'A Black Springs Cry for Help.' Liz asked that I read portions of it. I read the first paragraph where he introduces himself and speaks of his journey. I read about the no running water. I then picked up the white envelope containing the information about P.O.W.E.R. (People Organized to Work for Equal Recognition). I explained how special and personal that organization was to me. It was the youth group of Black Springs doing their part in contributing to the betterment of the community in which we lived. We wanted the same opportunities other communities had for their youth: a playground, swings, merry-go-round, slides, basketball courts, Community Center, baseball field and water.

I then picked a clipping up from a news paper called The Sagebrush, which is no longer in business. Its title was 'Black Springs one of the most intriguing parts of Nevada history a Historical Site.' This just touched on the history we had found. I told Liz I could go on and on if they had time to stay and listen. During the entire interview I could see the interest on Liz's face, she wanted to know more.

Our interview was over, I felt very good about it and was reassured by Liz, the camera men, John and Roy that it was a good interview. I was just glad it was over. It was now John's turn. They focused the camera on him.

John explained to Liz how, through his readings, he had discovered how the little but powerful and dynamic the community was. How the people came together from nothing and became a viable community. He explained his interest in helping the community. One way was by fighting to obtain another way in and out of Black Springs as well as

NEVADA HISTORICAL SOCIETY AND THE MEDIA

share the history. He explained how well-deserving Black Springs is to get the recognition and how privileged he was to be a part of this project. He completed his interview with, "this is not just Black history but Nevada history and everyone should be aware of it".

Liz's assistant kept pointing at his watch. Liz knew it was time to go as well, they had another appointment scheduled. She had no idea the interview would take so long because she didn't realize just what was entailed until she got here and began talking to us. She didn't even get to interview Roy. We told her about our meeting with the Historical Society the next day, she asked if they could come to that. We all said sure. I mean for such a big event who's going to tell the news media no. We told her what time and informed her that the meeting would take place at the Westbrook Community Center. She assured us they'd be there and the cameraman who kept Liz on schedule guaranteed me a little more time. Liz told Roy she would interview him the next day, he was fine with that. We said good-bye. Funny thing about It no one wanted to leave. We could have stayed there all day long talking about the documents.

When everyone left, John and I just looked at each other with these huge smiles on our faces. It had been a very successful interview with all the preparation in getting my apartment ready, setting the files on the coffee table neatly in the boxes for all to view. Everything had gone as God had planned. I knew everyone would be at the Westbrook Community Center the following day. My God! It had been a perfect morning. I just knew Big Daddy and Mama Helen were there and proud.

John and I usually go out to rejoice after a successful completion of a project. So we celebrated by going to Twin Dragons, a Chinese restaurant in Reno and had lunch to discuss what we had just completed. We could hardly eat for talking about our experience and what had just happened.

The next morning John was at my place about 9 a.m. to help load the boxes to take out to Westbrook Community Center. I called and talked with Roy to ask if someone could make coffee, I was bringing donuts. Roy was more than happy to make sure a pot of coffee would be there along with cups.

A CRY FOR HELP

When we arrived, the Pastor of Black Springs First Baptist Church was standing in the parking lot as if there to greet us. We saw him from afar and immediately wondered why he was there. We pulled up got out the car; I spoke to him and gave him a hug. I mentioned that I was unaware he would be here. You see we had invited a few Board Members, Channel 4 News and of course the Historical Society. We immediately began unloading the car. We began setting out tables and setting up chairs preparing for the meeting. The Pastor helped in organizing chairs and continued talking, inquiring as to what was going on. He then expressed he was meeting a contractor regarding church business and he would not be staying for the meeting.

The Channel 4 team arrived. They were doing shots of the boulders that were placed at our emergency exit. Roy and I went and met them in front of the boulders to begin the interview. Roy explained how the same issue they had addressed last year was back, even worse. After the interview we went back to the Community Center, Mr. Moody was there already reviewing the files. Channel 4 came in with Roy and I, we continued walking and toured the inside while I explained Black Springs' history, showing them pictures and articles on the walls and explaining the growth of this little community.

We then introduced Channel 4 to the other people who were invited along with Mr. Moody. He had no idea the media would be there. We didn't feel it necessary to divulge that information. So Mr. Moody was a bit surprised but just smiled and continued to review the documents. Through all of my excitement, when I finally sat down, I asked Mr. Moody if he was interested in what we have. John spoke up and said, "He's interested. He's been waiting for you to sit down so he could talk to you about what's next." I just started laughing. I was so excited I didn't even hear them trying to get my attention. I had said goodbye to the news crew, thanked them for coming and found out when the interview would air on T.V. You see, I forgot to say, Liz expressed to me at the first interview that she had no idea the story was as big as it was, so instead of one day running it would run for two days on every segment. That's why I was so excited and lost thought for a second. But to hear Mr. Moody wanted what we had and was ready to make a deal was way beyond my imagination. I couldn't then and can't now

NEVADA HISTORICAL SOCIETY AND THE MEDIA

really explain how I felt. Only tears of joy could be expressed. I caught my breath, composed myself and said, "Let's talk." Mr. Moody began explaining the next step.

We set a date to turn over the documents with stipulations. We discussed whether or not we would give him the originals and we take copies because they have knowledge and resources to preserve documents. We agreed to give them originals. Mr. Moody then asked how we wanted them listed. We all decided to call it the 'Black Springs Community Collection', donated by Helen Townsell in memory of Ollie and Helen Westbrook. After all the Westbrooks were the ones who kept track and preserved the documents. They were also as I mention previously, the pioneers of the community. All stipulations were agreed upon by everyone present. Mr. Moody would write up the contract and get everything in order. Our next meeting with him would be March 3rd, to turn over all documents.

We went back to my apartment. I e-mailed Andy and Carol attaching a copy of the contract, called "Deed of Gift." Carol and Andy responded right away. They were so excited and happy at our success and said, 'this is fabulous.' Andy suggested that we might want to give Chuck Zeh a call to go over the 'deed of gift' agreement so it's clear what we really want to accomplish by this gift. I did as Andy suggested. I contacted Chuck Zeh through e-mail. I introduced myself and asked if I could meet with him. I explained it would be John and I, he replied asking us to call his assistant and schedule an appointment, he would be happy to go over the paperwork with us. I called and set up a meeting for the very next day. That was also when we were due to turn the documents over to the Historical Society.

We were at Mr. Moody's at 9:00 a.m. the next day as scheduled. He was running a little late his secretary explained. She suggested we go into the museum and look at some of the history on display. So we did and man, were we amazed at all the history of Nevada. We were even more amazed that Black Springs was about to become a part of it. Mr. Moody arrived about 9:20. He found us in the museum looking and awing over the history we were viewing. He came up explaining why he was late; his daughter had gotten sick on the way to school, threw-up all over him, his shoes and the car. John and I both told him to go clean-up, "we'll be here when you're done." I told him to take a breath and relax, we have time. He thanked us and disappeared behind a door only to reappear about five minutes later in a much better frame of mind. We laughed about the entire situation and continued our meeting.

Mr. Moody asked if we needed a dolly to bring in the boxes. We had to inform him that we didn't bring them. You should have seen the look of disappointment on his face. It just dropped. The smile was gone, everything. I apologized for the delay and explained to him that Andy, who I truly trust, advised us in getting legal insight regarding the Deed of Gift. I told him I just wanted to be sure of everything; too much hard work, sweat, tears and years had went into this I couldn't chance anything going wrong. I explained we were meeting with Zeh today and should have the documents there the same day or the next. I asked if I could have a copy of the contract to take to Zeh. Zeh was the VISTA worker, an attorney for Black Springs back in the day, so there was history there. Mr. Moody agreed and informed us that the form had been approved by the Attorney General, it was legal. Let me add the first time we met with Chuck Zeh we had a blank Deed of Gift. He informed us that until we had it filled out he couldn't advise us on it. We did sit and reminisce for about 30 minutes over some of the adventures building Black Springs into a community. He expressed the great respect he had for my grandparents and all their work and accomplishments. He said they were definitely pioneers of Black Springs.

He asked about my parents, Jeff and Carrie Townsell; spoke about Mr. Lobster, the Fire Chief at that time, John's father-in-law. He asked about Al Williams, if he was still as defiant as back then. He expressed how my grandfather and Al Williams were always at battle with each other.

He talked about his first night in Black Springs. How on the ride out there, he saw white things in the black of the night and thought it was snowing, only later to find out it was sagebrush. He spoke about spending the night at Andy's little shack with barely any heat and he slept on the floor. We all laughed at all of what was and is. Man, had there been one awesome journey in memory. Wow, what a journey.

NEVADA HISTORICAL SOCIETY AND THE MEDIA

So we all laughed at the fact that we expected an answer to a blank piece of paper. So that's when we had to go ask Eric Moody for the completed contract. He graciously gave it to us. We guaranteed him we would be back with the boxes. I assured him not to worry, we wanted to do this as much as he wanted too, just bare with us a little longer.

I delivered the paper to Mr. Zeh's, left a copy and retained one. I was told he was in mediation and would get to it later that day or the next. So that was done. I left both my home and cell phone numbers and went for a walk and to the spa waiting for Mr. Zeh's call. When I got home I e-mailed Andy and Carol and told them about the meetings. They were both glad I had gone to Mr. Zeh. As Andy stated, "He trusted him whole heartedly."

The next morning I called Mr. Zeh. I spoke with him personally; he assured me he would get to it after he finished checking his e-mail. He explained that the day before he had mediation and couldn't do it, but would call me back. I never received a call. John and I decided to turn over the documents anyhow. Something just didn't sit right with us. You see, when reading the documentation you will sense some difficulties the Black Springs Civic Improvement Corporation had with Mr. Zeh. We figured it may have had something to do with that. We can't say for sure, we were just speculating.

I called Mr. Moody that day, March 4th, and asked if we could bring the documents the following morning at 9 a.m. He said yes. I explained we still hadn't heard back from the attorney, but we were ready to move forward and I trusted through contract he would take care of the precious documents.

We met the next morning. John got a dolly and wheeled the boxes in. We took them to the research room in preparation to turn them over. We signed contracts and Mr. Moody explained the process of what happens next and what the end result would be. He then gave us a tour of where the documents would be stored and preserved. We were very impressed. It was so engaging seeing the documents that were already stored and preserved. There were huge metal sliding doors, all with long aisles with shelves and shelves of Nevada history. There were maps,

A CRY FOR HELP

documents, books, etc. all so neatly preserved. To think all of our documents, pictures, articles, and books would be among these documents. What we had, what my grandparents preserved was historical enough, important enough that the Nevada Historical Society wanted it. We were about to make history. I told Mama Helen and Big Daddy, "You guys have just made history." I felt their happiness through my happiness.

CHAPTER 6
THE HISTORY BEGINS

Everything is finally chronicled from 1952 to 2008. We are now going to be able to see how this little community called Black Springs came into existence. How it developed from shacks, dirt roads, sagebrush, no running water, no street lights, no sidewalks, nothing but a few Black families trying to purchase property, a place to build a home and raise their families. This was the place where Blacks could purchase property in Reno, Nevada. Yes, it was degradable but it was a start. Like grandfather said, "They were tired of traveling around trying to find a home." He tells the story of how he met this little old white man, J. E. Sweatt and they talked, he agreed to sell land to him and other Blacks.

Mr. Sweatt parceled off one-third acres of land and began selling. J. E. Sweatt's motto was, "As long as it's green, I will take it." He saw no color, only the color of money. The deal was made and in 1952, my grandparents purchased their first piece of property. I can imagine the joy they must have felt. After all those times being turned down, or given an impossible situation, the struggle was over. At least that part as I described before, the conditions of this land and you could say "this community" was unthinkable to us today.

At that time my grandfather worked as a construction laborer and my grandmother did domestic work. Prior to that my grandfather was a handyman in Stockton, California and grandmother once again was doing domestic work. Mama Helen and her daughter, Carrie, migrated from Tulsa, Oklahoma to Fresno, California and then to Corcoran, California where she met my grandfather. They moved to Stockton, California then to Reno, Nevada in 1952. They were able to stay downtown, on Sierra Street, in some apartments temporarily. You see, they were on

A CRY FOR HELP

their way to Canada or Alaska and stopped in Reno, liked the place and decided to stay.

Grandmother was about 5' 7" tall. I would say she weighed 200lbs, a beautiful woman and in every sense a fine woman. This lady was so unique. She believed whole heartedly in standing behind, in front and on the side of her man. She was a very strong, supportive, kind and gentle woman. Whatever she needed to be at the time, she could be. She had beautiful light brown skin with beautiful shoulder length soft hair. I use to brush her hair frequently, so I knew how it felt. It was always shiny. Mama Helen would have me oil her scalp then just brush and brush her hair. She would be sitting there with her eyes closed enjoying every single stroke. I would start from the scalp and glide the brush through her hair until it reached the ends.

Mama Helen was a woman who said what was on her mind and never backed down from any situation. She stood her ground and fought right along side my grandfather for Civil Rights, for justice and a right to live as an American without all the blocks, blocking their way just to live the "American Dream", just a right to be. Mama Helen had a very positive attitude. She walked with such grace but also with a little sassiness. She spoke and wrote with such eloquence. She was an activist for her community as well as Reno, Nevada. She was a wonderful woman. Read the luster in her words from the following document.

REMARKS BY HELEN WESTBROOK, PRESIDENT
RENO-SPARKS NEGRO BUSINESS AND PROFESSIONAL
WOMEN'S CLUB
PIONEER INN, RENO, FOR THE
ELEVENTH WESTERN DISTRICT CONFERENCE
SATURDAY, FEBRUARY 22, 1975

Good morning. I'm Helen Westbrook, President of the Reno-Sparks Business and Professional Women's Club. On behalf of the members, I welcome all of you to our city. We hope that you will have an enjoyable and enlightening visit.

THE HISTORY BEGINS

Women have always been vital to our civilization, but today . . . more and ever before . . . we are contributing to the social, cultural and economical progress of our ever changing society.

The road to our present status has not been an easy one. Throughout the years, we have had to challenge old saws such as . . . "Women are the weaker sex" . . . "A woman's place is in the home" . . . "Women shouldn't vote" . . . and so on.

The first emergence of women's rights in Nevada occurred during a legislative debate in 1869 . . . that being, a proposal to give the newly freed black males the right to vote. A Storey County Assemblyman suggested that the Suffrage Clause should not be limited to black males; it should include the women . . . all women. The Assemblyman's motion was suppressed, but again became an issue in the Silver State in 1910.

At the turn of the century, several women feminist staged allies and used every means available to them in order to campaign for their right to vote. Among the feminist leaders was Anne Martin, a native Nevadan and the daughter of a prominent Reno businessman.

Suffrage is one of my favorite topics; however, I want to give you a briefing on some of the activities that our chapter been involved in during the past year.

Our installation of officers was staged at the Sparks Nugget where we spent a profitable afternoon discussing various social factors which affect our community.

Over 100 persons attended our First Founder's Day dinner. We were all deeply touched as we experienced one of the successful outgrowths of our coordinated . . . and integrated effort.

Our children comprise one of God's most precious gifts to us. We constantly strive to establish activities which will provide our youngsters with entertainment . . . and at the same time, an early indoctrination of respect for the laws of God and man.

A CRY FOR HELP

Our chapter also gave two scholarships to youths in the local community in order to further their education ... a vital tool for providing today's youths with more socially acceptable and meaningful roles for when they become tomorrow's leaders.

Mabel Thomas, the Recording Secretary, and I had a very rewarding experience when we attended the National Convention in Detroit. Also, I have been elected to serve on the National Nominating Committee.

When our club was organized in 1972, we were prepared to meet the many challenges that would confront us. Each member is dedicated and has committed herself to the teamwork that is essential to achieve both the short-range and long-range objectives for which our programs and activities are designed.

As I address you delegates to the Eleventh Western District Conference, I take great personal pride in the realization that we are achieving our goals ... the betterment of mankind.

Thank you.

CHAPTER 7
THE HISTORY CONTINUES

We started in 1956 with the first Black Springs Volunteer Fire Department, and Mr. A. C. Jones was the fire chief. I had no idea we even had a Volunteer Fire Department at that time, after all I was only a year old. John and I later discovered that the Black Springs Volunteer Fire Department was the first all Black fire department in the entire state of Nevada. The history had begun.

Now, let me backup a bit. Here's a little history and archeology of the area. Man's presence in the North Valley dates back several thousand years when the Indians occupied the area. No permanent settlements were established however, because of the Indians' nomadic lifestyle. In the North Valley, the Indians found an environment favorable for hunting and camping – a warm, mild climate, a year-round water supply from playas and small streams, with a wide range of animals and birds. The most extensive campsite in the Valley was Black Springs.

The site was mostly destroyed when the water tank serving Black Springs was constructed. No sites exist in Black Springs which are listed on the National Register of Historical Places and the Black Springs area was opened to development in the 1920's when old US 395 was constructed.

In 1952, the Westbrooks moved to Nevada. Oh, what a day that must have been for them as well as the many other Black families. The total cost of their 1/3 acre of land was $500.00 and the history you're about to read will outline year by year the important issues. I'll give reference as to where you can locate documents for review. I plan to tell you enough to make you want to take that adventure, that leap into

A CRY FOR HELP

history about a little but mighty community once called Black Springs, Nevada and now known as Grand View Terrace.

The Westbrooks met a man, a land developer named J. E. Sweatt. Mr. Sweatt was probably 5' 1" tall as I remember, old and wrinkled, walked hunched over, always had a brim type hat on and you could tell it was expensive. He drove a big Cadillac and came around the neighborhood every first of the month stopping at every house collecting his rent or mortgage. Mr. Sweatt was the only person who would sell property to Blacks at that time. My grandfather approached him regarding property to build his home on. They made a deal. That is how the Westbrooks and many other residents acquired their property. Their monthly receipts were hand written in a small receipt book and they retained the pink carbon copy. They had every receipt from the day of purchase until the end which stated, "Paid in full".

June of 1956 is the year my parents as well as many other Black settlers began moving to Black Springs. At that time, there were 5 in my family. Strangely enough, my parents were on their way to Seattle, Washington. My dad's oldest brother worked as a merchant seaman and was going to help my dad get employment. They stopped in Black Springs to visit my grandparents and my dad decided to try his luck at the New China Club. It was one of the few casinos that allowed Blacks to gamble in. Anyhow, my dad's luck wasn't so lucky. He lost every single dime they had. As a result, both parents had to get jobs and we had to live with my grandparents until they saved enough money to move. Boy, did my dad hear it over and over and over again from both my mom and grandmother.

At that time, there was no running water. Families had to haul water from town. They used barrels, bottles, containers anything they could find to hold water. There was a gas station eight miles away in downtown Reno called Fosters, it was located on Sierra Street. The owner allowed the residents of Black Springs to fill their containers with water anytime they needed to with no charge.

My grandparents, the Westbrooks, had already lived in their home three years before there was finally hope of the community

THE HISTORY CONTINUES

getting running water inside their homes. In November 1956 a contract was drawn up for water service (original document on file at NHS). The name of the water company was to be "The Eugene Street Water Company" owned by J. E. Sweatt. Yes, you guessed it, the same man who sold or rented his properties to Black families. Like I said before, the only color this man saw was green.

Each household was asked for a retainer of $20.00 to help fund the project to basically dig their own well and secure water service. The breakdown was as follows, $5.00 service fee, $5.00 first month payment and $10.00 deposit.

My parents eventually rented a house (shack) in Black Springs for one year. In June of 1957 they purchased their home and land from an elderly black couple, Jimmie and Mamie Holliday, who had to move for health reasons, for $900.00. Their properties were adjacent to my grandparents. It was pretty neat. Many homes were shacks. Our home was the living room, kitchen and an outhouse when we moved in. There was myself, three brothers and my parents. I do recall bathing in the middle of the floor in a round tin tub. Imagine, we all bathed in the same water, but we were clean. Now reflecting it seemed like a primitive lifestyle that depicts the 1800's.

We found and read documents that in 1957, the residents of Black Springs went to Mr. Sweatt asking him to build a well so they could have water. He agreed and the process was completed. Think about it, no more 16-mile trips to haul water.

I'm not sure of the exact date, but between the months of January and June of 1958, Black Springs finally had running water inside their homes. No more hauling water from town. I can't even begin to imagine what that must have felt like. It definitely sounds like something on "Little House on the Prairie".

In February 1959 there was a letter to J. E. Sweatt regarding the condition of the unpaved roads along with the cost to bring them up to standard, i.e., Washoe County Engineering and Highway Dept. This was the start of a long battle in upgrading the dirt roads. They (the roads) had

A CRY FOR HELP

big rocks imbedded in them so much you could not pull them out but they rested high enough to drive over in your car. The roads had lots of potholes, so you definitely couldn't go fast, you would damage your car. Riding a bike you could duck and dodge the rocks and potholes. The residents of Black Springs use to get together and dig up dirt, put it in wheel barrels and go around filling in the potholes. When it would rain it was a mess, water would flow everywhere due to no drainage. I remember it being very muddy, so if you went from one house to another walking, you better have on boots or your shoes would be soaked with mud. The snow was about the same the only difference was trying to get up a small incline. From my house to exit Black Springs, my dad would load the trunk of the car with bricks and wood then back the car up to the end of the street which was a dead end street, to get a good start just to get up the incline.

Mr. Bufkin who lived next door always helped my dad. He was a lot older, but this man was very strong. He was a fair skinned man with a bald head that was as shiny and clean as "Mr. Clean". He always wore blue overalls and was always in the yard doing something. He was also a very religious man and was very well respected in the community. Also, other neighbors would always join in to help with any issues going on within the community.

November 15, 1962, an application to upgrade the water system with a March 24, 1968 completion date was submitted. Six years it took to upgrade the water system. I won't throw my opinion into this document as I'm trying to stay on track. But my God, six years, approved in 1962 with a completion date in 1968. What was the problem?

According to county dockets; in item 67-1121, it started out, "BLACK SPRINGS – SHACKS" it went on to say, "C. B. Kinnison, County Manager, reported that Mr. Stanley F. Cook of Black Springs, had contacted him and stated that if the County would condemn shacks located in the Black Springs area, he would remove them with his own equipment and then file liens against the properties to cover his expenses. After some discussion, on motion by Commissioner Streeter, seconded by Commissioner Cunningham, which motion duly carried, it was ordered that the matter be referred to the County Health Department

THE HISTORY CONTINUES

and the District Attorney's office for recommendation and report." This appears like demoralization which will always be met with an intervenient. This will become quite prevalent.

In March 1967, J. E. Sweatt is willing to deed away the title of the roads. He did just that. On *March 10, 1967* he was willing to deed the streets, in which he had ownership, "for free" with the condition that "all costs all responsibility of repair and upgrading to Washoe county regulations to said person." The cost was $96,000.00. The county said, "Not until there brought up to county specifications". Some of their concerns were the conditions of some residents' property which had to be brought up to code before the county would consider purchasing the streets. There were 17 residents in violation. Some of the violations were: inadequate sanitation, junk, weeds, hazardous, nuisance, vacant shacks and unsanitary premises, etc.

In *July 1967,* the first Outreach Center workers were formed. They would be the voice of the people of Black Springs regarding: clean-up of properties, education, housing, membership, hospitality, youth and special services; these were needs and desires of their community.

By *October 1967*, By-Laws were established for an organization called the E.O.B. (Economic Opportunity Board). This was established with the focus being on poverty areas, i.e. anti-poverty program, to involve residents in their community. There are the bureaucrats again with that word poverty. You know, I was 11 years old at the time, old enough to know poverty. I still can't recall growing up under the conditions so many of the documents I've read refer to.

We had only read up to 1967 and that it only dealt with the water. How can you have a community with no water? However, my grandfather wrote the speech in December 1968 that sparked a perpetual influx of growth. By now, you are getting tired of hearing about his letter. Just be patient I have to lead up to it, I do not want to get ahead of myself.

On *January 7, 1968*, numerous petitions were submitted to the Public Service Commission. The residents of Black Springs asked for help back in 1962, it is now January 1968 and the problem has gotten

A CRY FOR HELP

worse. Partly because there are more homes, people and the Eugene Water Company system, although inefficient, it did supply the community with running water in their homes. The residents realized their voice meant something. As stated by Mr. and Mrs. Albert Lee Williams, "We drink this water as we have no alternative. But we are very worried about the health of our children, how ever past complaints have not appeared to help as everything remains the same".

Another petition was for a child development center, 57 residents signed the petition.

In *February 1968*, there was a letter addressed to all outreach workers stating the new guidelines effective March 11, 1968. Weekly reports of all activities throughout the week must be submitted. The first documented weekly report was dated May 6, 1968 from Outreach Worker Helen Westbrook.

These are just some of the programs she started as well as services she provided for the countywide communities. All are documented on the Daily Activity Sheets: tutoring for all residents of all ages, parks and recreation, playgrounds, e.g. trees for parks and homes, community center, jobs, summer jobs for youth, Girl Scouts, Boy Scouts, swimming lessons, provided personal transportation for those who needed to get to jobs or job interviews and court appearances. Arranged for camping for kids, day camps in the summer when school was out, child day care, Head Start, 4H Club, supporting troubled youth, holiday gift baskets for the needy, clothing, clean-up and garbage removal, stood up for discrimination issues, marched for Civil Rights in Reno and attended many meetings regarding the improvement of Black Springs; her giving was extensive. When Helen Westbrook saw a problem, she didn't walk away from it, she would walk right up to it, address it and begin working on the solution, she was very strong minded and spirited. She felt with God's help, there was nothing she could not conquer and accomplish.

Boy, do I miss her. It's a pleasure and a privilege to read about my grandmother and grandfather, when you read about one you're reading about the other. Okay, I'm getting teary eyed, so back to the history!

THE HISTORY CONTINUES

Once again *5th February 1968*, "BLACK SPRINGS – SHACKS" appeared on the County docket item 68-166 it read, "Upon recommendation of Robert G. Berry, Chief Deputy District Attorney, on motion by Commissioner McKenzie, seconded by Commissioner Streeter, which motion duly carried, it was ordered that the Board reject the offer of Mr. Stanley F. Cook to remove shacks at Black Springs (Item 67-1121)." Two years later there would be some surprising outcomes.

On *April 6, 1968*, an article appeared in the Nevada State Journal headline reading; BLACK SPRINGS PROJECT . . . Commission Backs Plan to Request Federal Aid, where Robert Newquist, director of the anti-poverty board, told the commissioners that a grant would be available through the Department of Housing and Urban Development for a feasibility study of the area.

The Federal Government would provide two-thirds of the money, with the state providing the other third, he said. County cooperation is required to make the study a reality.

Newquist said that of 83 homes in Black springs, 32 are vacant and "should be condemned today".

However, he said, condemnation is not entirely the answer. One possibility would be to make a "model area" on adjacent land, in which streets would be paved, sewers would be installed and new low-cost housing would be built under the self-help method.

The existing area would be bulldozed off after residents moved into the model area. The bulldozed area could then be used for an industrial park, Newquist said.

The many facets of the project would have to be considered by the people who make the feasibility study, he stressed. It may be, he added, that an entirely different approach will be found.

"If we were to try to upgrade the community, it would be total bedlam for five years," Newquist continued. "That's why we want to rebuild from scratch."

A CRY FOR HELP

He said it would be about 18 months before the first shovel full of dirt could be turned in the project he suggested, if it is determined that it is feasible.

One of the problems would be obtaining the adjacent land, which is public land, from the Bureau of Land Management.

May 28, 1968, a lady named Ruth Cutten, who advised my grandmother on how to make Black Springs an incorporated town, responded to Mrs. Westbrook regarding the county commissioner's request and plans on the Black Springs study:

May 28, 1968

Dear Helen:

I told you last week on the phone that I would write out the information which may help you.

First about the property that Mrs. Orena Herron owns and how to contact her. She lives in a trailer home at 444 Yukon Street in Sun Valley – but doesn't have a phone. She has been working for Mrs. (Hazel) Erskine on Fridays, and told me she intended to continue working there unless she got a job at one of the hospitals. Mrs. Erskine's phone number is: 322-4972. You probably know the location of the Herron property on Main Street. I'll copy the description from the County Assessor's map on page 82-12, a portion of the J. E. Sweatt tract: Lot 6 of A section, parcel #126. The frontage on Main Street is 156.5 feet, by 278.34 feet. (Very little less than the number of square feet in an acre). She was asking $2,000 cash for it (net to her), about two months ago since she needed the cash, but said however that if she went to work on salary she might decide to hold it. By the way the well from which she obtained water, before her house burned and she left, is not "owned" by the Eugene Street Water Company! She said that the water piped to her lot was of very good quality and supply.

You said that your friend Mrs. Fleeter Turner, had property (located on the Assessor's map near the Herron property?) with a building already

THE HISTORY CONTINUES

on it; and that she would like to lease the land for a recreation area, etc. However plans to obtain a location for a "Center" of whatever nature must now come from a duly authorized source; and decisions are not mine to make. I was interested in getting "backing" for at least some kind of a play area for Black Springs' children and youths, from friends and relatives and anyone else. The time was "a way back when", even before Rev. Harris was appointed to head the Council of the Black Springs Out Reach Center. At that time he told me he didn't know of any lot for sale, but only that a woman owner had a place with a building (or two buildings?) on it and wanted $26,000. So I gave up on the idea until I learned about Mrs. Herron's lot.

In the interim you have been appointed to head your Out Reach Center. And now all of us can take encouragement for further plans to be made and achieved from the help which hopefully will be extended by the organization of the new Race Relations Center. During a recent telephone conversation with Maya Miller she expressed a hope that a child-care center be established at Black Springs. If this new organization succeeds and has the financial backing so necessary to that success – it will indeed have an important role to play in this County. For certainly Eddie Scott and Nancy Gomes wouldn't quit their jobs to work for it if it didn't. Nor would influential people like Dr. Rusco, and Maya Miller, and others give their support in any specified ways.

Now to give you as much information as I can about an attorney's advice and his proclaimed knowledge as to procedure, and the result to be attained in making Black Springs an incorporated town. I cannot speak for him but I believe he would attend a meeting you might call of residents to explain further details of such a plan. I have as you know a copy he gave me made from pages of a law book on the subject entitled "Incorporation by General Law". (Actually it sounds complicated to me as I have little knowledge of legal terminology or procedure). His name is: Roger E. Newton (of Springer & Newton, attorneys), at 333 Flint Street, Reno. Phone 323-2728. If you call him to request his attendance at a meeting at Black Springs, Helen be sure to identify yourself as head of the Out Reach Center at Black Springs.

A CRY FOR HELP

I told you what he told me during an interview I had at his office on May 16th. That if he were to take it upon himself to obtain the incorporation of Black Springs (assuming he could even afford the time), without his services being requested and paid for with legitimate fees, he would face disbarment from the legal profession. He commented that he gives his allotted time (and more) to the Legal Aid Society and that the Society could (if they would) help you out in this matter since they receive Federal Funds under the OEO. But there is no ruling on a comparable situation.

I have a personal thought on the matter: Perhaps there are individual attorneys in the Legal Aid Society who would find a "conflict of interest" with their personal clients who may own surrounding property – and you who are owners of Black Springs' property! But no use denying that "the squeeze" is on to get your property through some means. Condemnation? And afterwards declaring the property "public domain". That "feasible study" of your area, to be obtained by funds available under HUD and advocated by Bob Newquist, was a close one! That so-called "Federal Aid" was stopped by your petition. But the public for the most part, and uninformed person thought it was refusing "aid". For the County Commissioners fostered that idea by the public statement headlined in the newspaper: COMMISSION BACKS PLAN TO REQUEST FEDERAL AID. Also that County Chairman Howard F. McKissick, Sr. is quoted as saying that the commissioners are "100 percent in favor of doing something. This grant is a start ----". He placed the burden of blame on the County for letting Black Springs develop as it has with sanitation problems and poor streets. (I'm quoting from a newspaper article) and he said: "We've felt they'd pull themselves up by their own bootstraps, but that hasn't happened". – Well, to comment on that last quote would take some doing, eh? Going back some twenty years ago, wouldn't it? When J. E. Sweatt first sold land to Negro residents and kept himself in control! – But just how many people, do you think, informed themselves further about this so-called Federal Aid? Or realized that once the people of Black Springs put themselves under the Federal agency of HUD they would no longer have control of their own property regarding the disposition or price placed on it. But, would be moved off as Newquist publicly stated to a "model area" on neighboring (non-existing!), public land held by the BLM, and the houses bulldozed off to make room for an "Industrial Park". No further comment!

THE HISTORY CONTINUES

I suppose I ought to take myself off on a long trip and enjoy an attack of ulcers! But I can't. And you know I'll do anything I can to help.

Fondly yours,

(signed) Ruth Cutten

The residents of Black Springs did not accept the offer.

From January 1968 to November 1968, Black Springs tried to retain legal help from 15 different attorneys. Not one of them said yes. They were able to obtain a little assistance through the Legal Aid Society but much more was needed as pointed out in the following document.

WOODBURN, FORMAN, WEDGE, BLAKEY, FOLSON and HUG
ATTORNEYS AND COUNSELORS AT LAW
Sixteenth Floor
First National Bank Building
One East First Street
RENO, NEVADA
89503

July 11, 1968

J. Mac Arthur Wright
Executive Director
Washoe County Legal Aid Society
527 Lander Street
Reno, Nevada 89502

Dear Mac:

On June 28, 1968, I attended what apparently was a meeting at the Black Springs—Outreach Center. I spent approximately three hours there. I enclose herewith a copy of the questionnaire which you sent to me.

As a result of that meeting, I handled a small traffic matter for Mr. Albert Williams. I believe that has been resolved satisfactorily.

A CRY FOR HELP

However, the problems which seemed most pressing to the people who attended the meeting were problems that I do not believe can be handled by an attorney on a one visit once a year basis. Specifically, the problems raised were:

1. The streets in the Black Springs area are not maintained by anyone. As a result they are at best difficult and at certain times of the year I understand they are nearly impassable. The people present were concerned that neither J. E. Sweat, the apparent owner of the street, nor Washoe County, is willing to do anything to alleviate the problem.

2. The water service in Black Springs is felt to be inadequate. The service is believed to be owned by J. E. Sweat. No one has been able to persuade him to update the water service.

3. The building code in Washoe County is apparently not enforced in Black Springs.

The people who attended the Outreach meeting were genuinely concerned with these problems. They expressed an inability to cope with them and with this point I agree. It would appear to me that someone on their behalf should search the records of Washoe County to learn the status of the streets and of the service and then to determine how best to correct the existing problems.

I was also advised that Washoe County employees will not travel on Mr. Sweat's streets to pick up garbage, but that they are willing to do so to make tax assessments which I understand are relatively substantial in that area. These problems are a source of great concern and require far more time than I can spend on a legal aid basis.

The people in Black Springs are also interested in forming an incorporated township or in being annexed to Reno. I have no experience in either of these areas but know that these problems can not be handled by an attorney working once a year on a volunteer basis.

It appears to me that these problems are of a type that should be handled by a permanent employee of the Washoe County Legal Aid Society. I

THE HISTORY CONTINUES

will be happy to discuss my experiences and conclusions with you at any time.

Yours sincerely,
ROGER W. JEPPSON

A News article, dated *July 26, 1968*, states Washoe County will help with roads. It went on to say, because of the condition of the roads, it has been a barrier to home improvement loans for Black Springs citizens. "Lending institutions are reluctant to make loans to individuals whose homes must be reached by crossing private property," the anti-poverty officials said. You see, J. E. Sweat owned the roads. That made them private property, but if he deeded to Washoe County they would no longer be trespassing. But the roads still had to be brought up to county standards before they would accept the deed. Those standards were—widening the streets, establishing proper drainage along the sides, grading them and filling them with gravel. Once this was accomplished, the streets are dedicated and accepted, the county would maintain them.

On *August 8, 1968*, a playground fence was installed around the ball park. The land for the ballpark was donated by my grandparents, Ollie and Helen Westbrook. The Nevada Relief Society donated the fence.

In *October 1968*, Eugene Water Company tried to raise the water rates. A letter of protest was submitted to the Public Service Commissioners from the Westbrooks stating, "We the undersign, is offering protest because the water system is insufficient because of the size of water lines". Eugene Street Water Company sent a letter to all water customers on October 16, 1968 stating, "Pending further negotiations with the Public Service Commission of Nevada a rate increase will not become effective November 1, 1968".

There was a news article, on *November 25, 1968*, regarding land for a community center. George A. Probasco donated 1.234 acres for a community center and playground.

On *November 26, 1968*, the residents wrote a letter to J. E. Sweatt regarding the water conditions. Their complaint, 1) Polluted water;

A CRY FOR HELP

you have to let the water run for a few minutes at the beginning of each day to get fairly clear water. If water sets for any length of time a rust ring will form and your first sign of water is rust color. 2) Inadequate water pressure. There were approximately 15 residents in Black Springs when the water system was installed. At that time the water pressure was inadequate, now there are about 45 residents in the area and it is impossible to get useable water pressure.

There were news articles, on *November 30th* and *December 2, 1968*, saying contractors aided the Black Springs residents in bringing the roads up to standards so that Washoe County would fulfill there promise and fix the roads, sewage and water system.

After we read up to 1968 and the "letter", it was time to call Carol. If you recall, I spoke about Carol earlier and the experience I had with her and Andy in Arizona. Weeks had gone by since we had talked. I e-mailed her and told her what I was doing and about John and ended with, "I am ready." She knew exactly what I meant. Right away, she responded on 2/8/08 with, "Okay, let's talk. I'm ready too." Remember I told you Carol had this vision 35 years ago.

I contacted Madeline and informed her of our own early findings through what we had done and she too was excited. The process had finally begun. Madeline said, "You have only just begun. Watch all the opportunities and everything that is about to come forth." She is always so encouraging.

Mind you, one of the reasons we decided to do this was the grant. We figured in order to complete the application we had to state the reason for applying. We had to find some history and what better way than through reading about Black Springs from these documents. This would make for accuracy on the application and validate the entitlement for funding.

Now, this is what you have been waiting for, Big Daddy's Letter. Let me get you ready for the letter Ollie Westbrook wrote. My mother, her name is Carrie, was the first to read it and brought it to my attention. She called me one day saying she had found a very powerful letter

THE HISTORY CONTINUES

my grandfather had written in 1968. She said she thought I might like to read it. She said, "You will see just how intelligent your grandfather was." I said I would come get it. My grandfather had already passed and although I was sorting paperwork, I had not run across any speech. Therefore, I went to retrieve the letter.

Now that I had the letter, looking at the design, I recognized the letter. I flashed back on my grandfather trying to get me to read it. He was always trying to get me interested in the business of Black Springs, their struggles and how much more had to be done. I was not interested and would always kind of shrug him off. My grandmother would always come to my defense and say, "Baby, she is not ready yet to take all this on. She doesn't even live here anymore!" You see, I had moved to California in 1973.

I have the letter now and for the first time I am reading it. It brought tears to my eyes. Not only how diligently it was written, but also I could visualize my grandfather standing before that committee reciting this letter. Ollie, grandfather, was 6' 5" or 6' 7" tall and weighing in at a solid 265 lbs not fat. He was a very soft-spoken man. Back then he wore overalls and had a short Afro that was short in the back and got thicker as it came forward. Grandfather did nothing fast, but always got the job done. He even spoke slowly as if to ensure you heard and understood every word. He spoke his mind.

When Madeline read the letter, her silent reaction was exciting to watch. Her facial expressions changed, as she got deeper into the letter. Her conclusion was, 'this is a story that needs to be told.'

You read how John reacted to the letter. He was in total awe and concluded with, 'I'm ready. When and where do we start?' That letter sparked a lot in the four of us. Now you read the letter and see what you think.

CHAPTER 8
BLACK SPRINGS CRY FOR HELP

From the League of Women Voters of Reno-Carson-Sparks, December 5, 1968:

<u>*A BLACK SPRINGS CRY FOR HELP*</u>

In our study of Equality of Opportunity in Housing, we may want thoughtfully to read this personal account given to the County Commissioners and to dwell on the assorted ways we keep our Black Community from sharing in the general well-being and amenities of White Northern Nevada.

....

My name is Westbrook, Ollie Westbrook. I have never appeared before you in person, but I have been instrumental in supporting a representative and various petitions. I have also been instrumental in supporting some of you within my small circle of friends. Some of you have obtained my vote because the contents of your talks have coincided with my own ideas, only later, to find that any compatibility of ideas between us was only momentary. Once your election goals were attained, you refused to hear my representative or to entertain my petitions.

Let me now state a few words, so that you may perhaps better understand why I am here.

Gentlemen, I have traveled a long distance, spending a lot of time in search of something better, a better way of life, a place to live, a place to establish a good home. I have suffered many humiliations before and while living in this State, this County, this City.

A CRY FOR HELP

When I came to this city there were no rooms or apartments available for me to reside in from you. But it was not by choice I came to this particular place; call it whatever you may (chance or perhaps an invisible force), nevertheless, I am here now.

From inquiries, I learned that the fruit of the construction building was ripe, and it was possible for me to join in the gathering; this I did.

After a length of time passed, I met a man who told me he had land for sale. After seeing the land, we agreed on a price and after fulfilling my agreement, I received a piece of paper from this man. The paper stated the location, the description and the dimensions of the land. I then went to some of your money-landing agencies stating I had bought land and I was here to make some sort of reasonable agreement, to use some of their money in order to build a house. My desire was to make a home here for me and mine. He agreed all that was fine and good, but where was this land located? I told him. And with a flash of amusement in his eyes, he told me he could not loan money for building in that area because it was undeveloped and unincorporated. I thanked him and went my way for I have a goal to reach and there must be a way.

I then set up a budget from the profits of working in building construction. And after saving a small amount of money, I went to a building supplier explaining to him the situation that I had explained to the moneylenders. So we made a limited agreement, I could get just so much material to build on and when this was paid for, I could get more. But I could get more, and so it was until the building was up. I also bought some used appliances from him and used furniture from department stores so I could move into my building, utilizing the monies, which I was paying for rent to furnish and finish building my new home.

Now enough time has elapsed since my entry into your State and County in order to allow me to become a registered voter; a voter and support to the local County, State and Federal Governments. And since becoming a voter, there has not been one issue that I have not taken a stand on, providing it was a good proposition that would benefit

BLACK SPRINGS CRY FOR HELP

all of the people. This includes your State Sales Tax, school bonds, hospital expansion, recreational areas, convention centers and many others. I supported these Programs because I feel I have adopted this place as my home and I am obligated to do whatever I can to make it a better place for myself and others like me. For you see, there are many others like me searching for the same things, a better way of life, a better place to live.

My home is not complete. There is no running water. I, like others who had come into this area carried our water in barrels, cans and any container that would hold water, from one of your local businessmen. He allowed all of us to get as much water as we could use, day or night, without charge, customer of his or not. But this became tiring, so some of us petitioned this federal installation located about two and one-half miles from us and the feed line is only about three city blocks distance from my house.

The answer? It is against Government Policy to allow private citizens to tap this water line.'

So we came together in group to pool our resources in trying to dig water well for the whole community. But even together, there was not enough. So, this too failed. But this did not stop us because we know there is a better way to live.

So we petitioned this man who had sold us the property. Although he had reservations about such an undertaking, being inexperienced in the installation of public utilities, nevertheless he said he would check into it further. After this was done, he came to us with his proposal.

Now at that time, not many of us knew much about installing plumbing, nether could we afford a craftsman, so together, we gathered information and material and helped each other. We also hired a man with a power shovel to dig holes for our septic tanks.

You see we are continually trying to build and live within your rules, as close as we possibly can, and on our small incomes, needless for me to say, this is not easy.

A CRY FOR HELP

Now, bear with me a little longer while I cover another part of this community, the obvious eyesore. How do you suppose it developed into this condition? If you have not seen it personally, a short time ago the local news media printed pictures showing the worse part of the whole. The pictures showed old used appliances, used lumber, used furniture, used cars and other old discarded items. Now a lot of these were gifts. They were "guilt gifts," from people who were attempting to ease their own consciences about the living conditions of the people by giving them gifts as substitutions. The gifts came in the form of old cars, used furniture, used appliances, etc. Now in reality, the giver knows he is not paying the worth of the recipient, and in fact, often the gift is older than the person who accepted it. So we accepted these things, used them, repaired them, until it is no longer feasible to do so, and then we retired them—unfortunately on our property. Why? As you know, there is a cost in hauling these things away, also a charge for dumping them.

I am not being harshly critical of these gifts, because they have in the past sometimes been an aid in our struggle for survival.

I say again I am telling you these things so you may better understand why I am petitioning you now.

For some time now, words have come to me from different sources that larger parcels of land owners adjacent to my own, and surrounding area, also wealthy industrialists have looked upon this land, this house, this place that I have suffered so many humiliations for and sweated, and shed so much of my blood, that if it were all put in a big container, it would be enough to float my house. I have to go now the easiest and cheapest way is through you men and your positions. Because you know and have the power to formulate and to initiate, whatever law or ordinance that is necessary for this action to take place.

This is why I come before you now, not as a beggar, or one passing through, but as a citizen who has adopted your State and County as his home.

I seek your aid now in helping me to make this a better place, a more beautiful place, in which you would be proud to look upon, and I am as proud to live within.

BLACK SPRINGS CRY FOR HELP

You may ask how can we help, or why? But, if you will recall how you came to be in this position, you are an elected commissioner or a board of commissioners. A product of the people, in a government for the people, who pooled their resources together by making rules that they can live by and of course, for the good of the whole. That is why.

Now this giant governmental body has a executive head (within your State, County, and City): lawmakers, law interpreters and a practitioner of the latter is also in your midst.

Don't ask me about the ways in which you can help since you have at your disposal all of this knowledge, influence, and power.

I ask you again gentlemen, to listen to my plea because by doing anything less or anything contrary, you would be ignoring all governmental ideals, presently set up in your State, County and City. You would be proving to me and other people like me of every race and creed who even now are struggling for an existence, struggling for a better way of life, that there really is no room in your society for any of us.

Your ignoring of my plea, and the pleas of others like me, is really the fact that finally necessitates and makes it essential to bring out the Armed Forces, instigates men to behave as animals, to lock human beings in iron cages. In the end, finally, after much toil in desperation, we receive the impression that you are using your laws and ordinances as a broom to sweep us out of your society.

I sometimes feel in my desperation, in my struggle for survival, in my struggle for me and mine, in my utter frustration, in my feelings for others like me, that perhaps it would be best after all, if you simply dug a hole and planted me in the Valley.

I thank you for your attention.

Ollie Westbrook

The Skyrocket has been launched, now here is a taste of the afterburning that Big Daddy's oratory ignited. Let me give you an example of the

A CRY FOR HELP

power that hit Black Springs. When Andy Gordon, a VISTA worker, came to town, he came very prepared to work. At the ripe full age of 18, this young white Jewish kid volunteered his time and heart to a predominantly Black community. He was given a shack to live in, a cot to sleep on and he never once complained. He always had a smile and a good positive word. He was always there for everyone. He took us places: picnics in Lake Tahoe, Virginia City, skating, nature events and involved the young people in all the community issues.

When Andy arrived, the community adopted him as one of their own. All the parents took him in and treated him as their child. They made sure he had food to eat and gave him advice. Whenever there was any type of family event he was included. We love and appreciate Andy and we know he felt and feels the same. Things really began to progress when Andy Gordon was assigned to Black Springs. As you'll see, the month of January 1969 was a busy month. Andy asked what direction do you as a community want to go? And when told, he took off showing them how to achieve their needs and goals. Read from Andrew Gordon age 19, excerpts from his Application for Freshman Admission to Wesleyan University dated October 28, 1969.

Academic Interests

List, in order of preference, the occupations or professions you are considering for your life work:

    1. Law and 2. Social Work

Name studies you have liked best:

Math, science, social studies. *Least:* English

Given the studies which you liked best, least, and found most difficult: Why do you regard each of them so? Since I had an enormous extracurricular responsibility, I only did well in the classes that were relative to real life and logic and were presented with a stimulating approach.

In what Department do you plan to major? Sociology

BLACK SPRINGS CRY FOR HELP

Work Experience

If you have had employment during the past two years while going to school, state kind of work and approximate number of hours per week (include summers). I have been a Volunteer in Service to America (VISTA) for the past nine months, and my job description states my hours 1st 24 hours a day and 7 days a week.

Black Springs is a black rural ghetto of 75 families north of Reno, Nevada. The following is and ad hoc list of the kind of work I do: Community organizer; advisor and constant catalyst since the beginning of the non-profit corporation, POWER youth group and neighborhood council; Volunteer Fire Company; training for the teenage suicide prevention line; instrumental in writing the comprehensive HUD grant application for an adequate water system; getting Farmers Home Administration to make loans available for self-help housing and individual home improvement; planning and construction of our park with basketball court, swings, etc.; bus stop shelter to protect children from the wind and snow; fire house; public take over and improvement of roads; natural gas to replace expensive propane for heating; library; tutoring program and much more. The things I do are for the people in Black Springs and not done to suit my personal fancy. You must recognize that almost everything listed has been accomplished by many hours of strategy sessions and working with different levels of government and private agencies. The wheels of the Reno, county, and state government turn very slowly, especially when the people in need are black. Even with all the work that was not mentioned I seriously believe I am getting more out of this experience than I could ever put into Black Springs.

College Plans

List other colleges to which you are applying: Princeton University

Have you participated in any special summer schools or programs? Yes *If you have, please describe.* Anytown Arizona is a camp which exposes people to ideas, people from various races, religions and economic backgrounds. Delegates are chosen by Brotherhood Clubs in high schools and churches throughout Arizona. In 1967 I became a delegate, in 1968

A CRY FOR HELP

a counselor and in 1969 the head male counselor. My three summers at Anytown proved to be a very enlightening and rewarding experience.

Wesleyan Interest

Do you have any particular reason(s) for wishing to attend Wesleyan? Wesleyan is my first choice. I am looking for a relatively small college where I would have the opportunity for dialogue with my professors on a personal basis. It is a school where the instructors are both noted in their fields and concerned with student involvement. I am familiar with the community programs in the Middletown area and I want to get involved in these activities which relate to my studies.

I want to go to the East where I have read and heard of historic places people and communities. This would be a unique opportunity to see and experience the things I have only superficially come in contact. For me, Wesleyan appears to be the place.

Describe briefly your opinion about the proper relationship and responsibilities between the individual and the campus community.

I hope to add diversity to Wesleyan, responding and relating experiences, feelings and personal truths with the campus community. To be honest and candid is a definite attribute. The community should provide as a resource center, a gathering place for exchange of information and materials needed for dialogue and new ideas. The atmosphere I desire is open and comfortable, a place for interaction with the community in a way that is relevant to me. The campus environment should stimulate objectively and not stifle it.

Reading

Describe yourself as a reader: Do you read for pleasure? Do you read frequently? What books not required by your courses have you read in the past six months? What book or author has been most significant to you? Why? Reading has become a dynamic and relevant part of my daily activities. I have set up a black studies reading program for myself involving psychologists, white racists, black racists, non-fiction, fiction,

BLACK SPRINGS CRY FOR HELP

periodicals, and essays. In VISTA the print world has come alive for me. My reading encompasses not only pleasure and study but things that directly relate to my work.

It is one thing to read about community organization and another to organize a community; read about white racism and feel white racism; read about black racism and feel black racism; read about bureaucracy and work with bureaucracy; read about administrative personnel and monetary cuts and feel these cuts.

The books I have read in the past six months are: Afro "6", Lopez; The Invisible Man, Ralph Ellison; The Palm Wine Drunkard, Amos Tutuola; Soul on Ice, Eldridge Cleaver; Autobiography of Malcolm X; Nigger, Dick Gregory; Before the Mayflower; A History of the Negro in America, Leone Bennett Jr.; The Other America, Michael Harrington; The Passover Plot, Hugh J. Schonfield; The Adventures of the Negro Cowboy; The Learning Tree, Gordon Parks; Death at an Early Age, Jonathan Kozol; Black Families in White America, Andrew Billingsly; Black Rage, William Grier and Price M. Cobbs.

It is difficult for me to distinguish between the author, William Bradford Huie, and Three Lives for Mississippi and say which influenced me the most. The introductory chapters set the tenor of the environment by telling how a man of a traditional Southern organization (Ku Klux Klan) shows his leadership and virility by physical and mental castration of a black man. The remainder of the book dealt with the premeditated murder of three civil rights workers, who were registering black voters and other confrontations to Southern tradition, by state police and community participation. To these Mississippians the deaths were for the benefit of the state. At the time this all seemed very horrifying but unreal. Last November I and a teacher from Watts were invited to the Louisiana Education Association convention in Shreveport. The LEA is comprised of only the black teachers in Louisiana. We drove through parts of the South and saw and experienced many things I had once read about. Now that I am experiencing what I have read, many of my vicarious experiences in books have become real emotional confrontation. In VISTA I feel and relate.

A CRY FOR HELP

Performing Arts: Please describe any experience you have had in the performing arts, e.g., music, theater, dance. (Please include in your description the opportunities you have had for performance, the teachers with whom you have studied, and the number of years you have studied.)

One of the first projects the youth in Black Springs got organized around was to teach Andy how to "popcorn". Once I freed myself of my self-consciousness and the omnipresent fear of failure, I picked up the new soul dance quite easily. The whole mental mood involved for this dancing has helped me at times when I need to relax, both physically and mentally. Some people refer to me as Andy Popcorn because they catch me pop'n while I am walk'n.

Extracurricular Interests and Achievement

Student Government: Please describe any positions which you have held either in or out of your school. In doing so, please outline your responsibilities and personal commitments to the position(s).

In high school I held the highest positions in class and club. Being a class officer for four years (three as class president) I received much recognition from faculty, administration, community and family.

The pressures and motivations for most of my activities in a high school of white middle class values and priorities catapulted me into an ultra ego trip. In retrospect I find that all of these activities rewarded and developed no one except myself. One project, a collection of food goods for a needy family, culminated in of means over ends. The family was not important the competition among students was.

Vista has been a totally different and fulfilling experience. Being an "honorary" ADC (Aid to Dependent Children) Mother means more to me now than the positions of "honor" I held in school. It is no longer an ego trip but a total learning experience. In VISTA I act as a catalyst, organizing people around issues, developing new leaders in the community behind the scenes away from the lime light. It is no longer superficial but a deeply felt accomplishment.

BLACK SPRINGS CRY FOR HELP

Please list your extracurricular activities in order of their importance to you: 1. ANYTOWN ARIZONA and 2. CHEER

Please describe your involvement in these activities. In doing so, be sure to include why these activities are personally significant to you and in what ways—if any—they may be reflective of you as a person. Please note that the activities which you list need not necessarily be associated with your school.

I have difficulty relating my extracurricular activities in high school since being a VISTA (since February 1969), twenty-four hours a day, seven days a week, does not leave much time for such reflection. The things I do in VISTA are the things I want and need to do without individual priorities-the idea of achieving "life, liberty and the pursuit of happiness" for everyone concerned. Perhaps this sounds corny but I feel right and truthful to myself. At any rate, all I can do is my own little thing at present. Therefore I shall relate my most important extracurricular activities at the time between school and graduation and VISTA.

Anytown, Arizona is the inter-ethnic camp which I spoke of earlier in the application. Much preparation was necessary prior to camp sessions in dealing with people in a way to attract their interest and keep their interest. These moral questions were the hardest to deal with satisfactorily. If anything, a lot of mental gymnastics was achieved.

CHEER (Conference for Human Equality and Educational Reform) originated and was brought about in the summer of 1969 by myself and a few people from the Anytown staff. During the fifteen year history of Anytown nothing concrete had materialized other than personal development. We wanted to demonstrate how people with common ideals but different backgrounds could organize and articulate the ideals relevant to their communities at a two day conference at Arizona State University. We focused in on our views and came up with resolutions and dialogue with the school district for a particular high school, where students were victims of several inequities. I learned many techniques in preparing the conference for several hundred people and came in direct contact with the big and little things to do in running

A CRY FOR HELP

a convention. Responsibilities varied from getting keynote and guest speakers to making sure the lights were on.

Athletics

If you consider athletics to be one of your major interests, please list any times, records, awards, etc.

Gymnastics (4 yrs. All-round; 1 J.V. Ltr.; 3 Varsity Ltrs.; Varsity Capt. Co-2; all-round) and Polo (not in school)

Please describe your involvement in and commitment to these sports.

Gymnastics is a year round training sport that requires determination, mental discipline, physical strength and stature. I enjoyed instructing new gymnasts in the elementary routines and watching them progress. As a male cheerleader I used my gymnastic abilities for football, basketball and pep assemblies. In 1967 I was chosen in a contest to be a student trainer for the United States Gymnastic Team in Winnipeg at the Pan American Games.

CANDIDATE'S ESSAY

The Committee on Admissions asks that you write a short essay which will enable us to know you better as an individual. Your essay may include anything which you find expressive and representative of you as a person. Thus, your essay may be directed towards any topic from candid self-analysis to a discussion of a personal experience or to more general concerns. In short, we want to know and understand you; thus, we shall welcome any statement which sincerely represents you.

I try to look back and pick out the one thing that has affected me the most concerning basic feelings about different people. My thoughts focus on my brother Sandy, the oldest in the family at 23. Sandy has probably been the single greatest influence on my parents, my sister and my self in bringing out goodness.

How can this be? Sandy was born a hydrocephalic, a congenital malformation which damaged parts of his brain and blew up Sandy's

BLACK SPRINGS CRY FOR HELP

head like filling a balloon on a water spigot. Sandy's head dept expanding and the pressure increased. Something had to be done to relieve the pressure since it caused constant crying, sleepiness and vomiting. Many relatives, friends and doctors urged my parents to put Sandy away until he died a prognosis inevitable at the time. My parents searched for a doctor who would help and encourage. Dr. Putman was the man, and internationally renowned neurosurgeon and the man who was so highly spoken of in <u>Death Be Not Proud</u>, John Gunther's account of his son's brain tumor. I accidentally came across this book the summer before last and was astonished at the similarity in thought of the Gunther family and my own.

In one of the many pioneering operations on Sandy, Dr. Putman cut down the secretions and took melon cuts out of his head to decrease it in size. Sandy's head is still conspicuously large and out of proportion with the rest of his body. Enough in fact to be ridiculed teased and pointed to by young and old. Sandy tries to understand. Sandy today is one of a few if not the only hydrocephalic of his complexity and has completed four years of college and is still going at it. His goal is to become a medical librarian.

I guess the whole thing boils down to this, a person born is a life, and was put on earth for some reason, may it be to help science, prove a point or to develop the environment for goodness. I can say that Sandy has influenced my life in such a way that I know is good. If this was done directly or indirectly through my family experiences, intentionally or unintentionally, I am grateful. I am sure that Sandy has given more than I have ever given to anyone. Values like money, kinship ties and comfort all were secondary when it came to Sandy's life as a living being. I have been raised and exposed to people of abnormal shapes and handicaps and learned, (not in books or from someone telling me), to take people for what they are inside and what they have to offer inside. Exteriors are not important to me. It takes longer to learn about people this way. The point is, I learn. I do not feel a need to explain how this affects my concept of life and my direct involvement with contemporary inequities.

You can imagine the impact this young man had on our community. To experience such compassion and human kindness is rare.

A CRY FOR HELP

These were the officers of the Outreach:

BLACK SPRINGS OUTREACH OFFICER ROSTER
Mr. Ollie Westbrook – Chairman
Mr. Jeff Townsell – Vice Chairman
Mrs. Lena Benson – Secretary/Treasurer
Mrs. Helen Westbrook – Outreach Worker
Mr. Bill Lobster – Representative to EOB
Miss Beverly Carthen – Representative to EOB
Mr. D. C. Benson – Alternate to EOB
Mr. Al Williams – Alternate to EOB
Andy Gordon – VISTA
Kirby Lassiter – VISTA
George Preonas – VISTA Attorney
Mr. Barbet Bufkin – Legal Aid Rep.

These were the leaders of the community in January 1969 and boy were they ready for some fighting. Things, as you will read, were about to start happening. I mean a change was finally coming for the small but mighty community of Black Springs, Nevada.

There was an influx of letters, written beginning *January 4, 1969*, to the Public Service Commission. Every resident wrote a letter regarding the inadequate water system. The Public Service Commission answered each individual's letter on January 10, 1969 stating, "Arrangements have been made for me (Reese H. Taylor, Jr./Chairman), to visit the area sometime toward the end of next week for a first hand look at your water system. We then plan on having a meeting with the Westbrooks and Mr. Sweatt of the Eugene Street Water Company, and we certainly hope this meeting will produce some concrete results." As per the Commission's request the Assistant Chief of the Reno Fire Department and the State Fire Marshal made a site inspection of the Black Springs Water System January 15, 1969.

The State Fire Marshal forwarded his findings to the Public Service Commission on *January 17, 1969*. The findings stated, "A minimum acceptable water system for a residential area of this type would require the residual availability of a minimum of 500 gallons per minute

BLACK SPRINGS CRY FOR HELP

for fire protection. This is based on dwellings greater than 30 feet apart in distance which reduces a conflagration hazard. 500 gallons a minute will provide two 2-1/2 inch fire hoses that will produce 250 gallons per minute each at a pressure of 40 to 50 pounds. Most fires in areas of the type construction we have at this location would be handled with smaller hose lines that require an average of 50 to 100 gallons each. However, large fires may require streams of 400 to 1000 gallons per minute."

The State Fire Marshal went on to say, "With the above facts in mind, the water system can not be considered as adequate for fire protection recognition and should be considered a minimal tank reserve. The major problem in this area is compounded by a combination of all of the factors that exist."

The report ended by saying, "The greatest improvement to the fire protection in this area would be my suggestion that the residents form a volunteer fire department that could make an initial attack on any fire that occurs. This would either extinguish the fires or at least hold the fire in check until the contract fire department can arrive at the scene." This report was also prompted by the Christmas Day fire.

There was another study of the area conducted by Dr. Elmer Rusco of the Bureau of Governmental Research at UNR (University of Nevada Reno). This document doesn't give a date only a year, *1969*. The Rusco study points out the following problems. A) The area lacks paved streets, community water or sewage disposal systems or similar services; many of these people are thus living in <u>Group Poverty regardless of their individual incomes</u>. It's a special case of a more general pattern of urbanization without urban services. B) When asked, "Why do you believe the results can be achieved?" The response was, "Because Black Springs has had handy pioneering people who though often lacking formal education, have already put blood, sweat and remarkable ingenuity and care for some 15 years into their home community."

The report goes on to talk about issues regarding the roads. How the community had continually tried themselves to bring the roads up to the county standards so they could get assistance from the county to pave the roads. Rusco states, "Work needs to continue and be completed and county needs to accept roads."

The report speaks about the church currently being the Community Center, Outreach Center and used for young people's classes. When asked about resident participation the Rusco report says, "All community itself. This group will always be involved. Their determinations will always be the guide."

Things were about to change. On *January 13, 1969*, a letter was sent to Mr. Howard Gloyd the Executive Director of EOB regarding the community taking over the water company as you'll read.

FRY AND FRY
ATTORNEYS AND COUNSELORS AT LAW
105 SIERRA STREET, SUITE 201
POST OFFICE BOX 2756
RENO, NEVADA 89505

January 13, 1969

Mr. Howard Gloyd
Executive Director
Economic Opportunity Board
527 Lander Street
Reno, Nevada 89502

Dear Mr. Gloyd:

Mr. J. E. Sweatt of this community has requested our office to correspond with you regarding the status of the Eugene Street Water Co., which operates in the Black Springs area of the County of Washoe. Specifically, Mr. Sweatt directed me to advise you of his position relative to recent phone conversations between Mr. Sweatt and yourself.

Mr. Sweatt advises me that on or about December 30, 1968, he conversed with you regarding that portion of Black Springs serviced by Eugene Street Water Co., and was told by you that an expert had

BLACK SPRINGS CRY FOR HELP

surveyed, analyzed, and evaluated the entire water system and concluded that an investment of $25,000 was needed to bring the water system up to acceptable standards. It now becomes my responsibility to advise you that Mr. Sweatt is financially unable to raise sufficient funds to cover the costs of improvements to the water system.

In view of this situation, Mr. Sweatt has requested that I discuss your second proposal. With regard to this second alternative, Mr. Sweatt advises me that you suggested he should turn over without charge the Eugene Street Water Co., to those persons residing in the Black Springs area, who are receiving services from said water company. Therefore, Mr. Sweatt requested me to seek to ascertain the name of the entity which would assume the operation of the water company, should same be transferred pursuant to your request. Your prompt reply to this inquiry will be greatly appreciated and I remain,

>Very truly yours,
>FRY AND FRY, ESQS.
>Mack Fry

Petitions surfaced again on *January 16, 1969*, asking for a pedestrian walk and shelter for kids waiting for school buses.

On *January 23, 1969*, petitions and letters to County Commissioners regarding the sewage and water problems in Black Springs went out again. My grandparents never stopped producing petitions and made sure all residents received copies especially those unable to attend the meetings and the petitions became their voice.

There was a news article, *February 2, 1969*, regarding Black Springs' roads (Termed "Unacceptable). Remember now, since 1959 the county continuously said the reason they would not pave the roads was because they weren't up to standards. The community had been working for 10 years to pacify the county standards. The Rusco report in January said to the county, come on people, they've been trying. Can they get some help?

On *February 7, 1969*, my grandmother's Outreach activity report read, "After reading article about County Commissioner not agreeing to accept streets, had a case of hypertension. Had to go see the doctor, blood pressure was up to 210 over 120." I had to read the article also dated the 7th that sent her over the roof. Naturally, my grandparents kept the article. When I read it my blood pressure raised. Knowing my grandparents, what assisted in their hypertension was when C. B. Kinnison (County Manager) said, "We've been leaning over backward for these people; the county bought the culverts and did everything we could. The engineers believe the people who offered the rest of the help on the roads should come through."

What does he mean "these people"? Did he not know or even realize what "these people" had been enduring since 1952 and asking for help since then? Did he not realize the undertone of racism in the statement he made? The county owned the roads, it was their responsibility, one would think.

The county manager received six letters from the residents of Black Springs requesting they take over the roads in that area in order that natural gas, city water and sewer systems could be brought in. The roads were the hold up of progress.

Then, I read on further to find yet another statement on the ***11th of 1969***. I couldn't see the month only the day and year. This was said by Senator Cannon, "You know when I was out looking at the problems at Black Springs I saw those youngsters from VISTA working with those people. It just makes you feel good to see how enthusiastic they are."

I know how things were back then, but it still makes your blood boil to know that with all the work the community was doing to progress, and all the obstacles that continued to come their way, I don't see them as, "those people." I see them as mighty determined and encouraged people fighting to just have what every other community in Reno, Nevada had.

Maya Miller, President of the League of Women's Voters of Nevada, sent a letter to Mr. William Lear on ***February 27, 1969*** requesting his help in the Black Springs area. She was a very, very powerful lady.

BLACK SPRINGS CRY FOR HELP

      I remember her as being an older white woman who was a very dear and close friend of my grandparents. She was a tiny small built lady, short hair, a long skinny nose with thin lips. She lived in Washoe Valley. My grandparents met her at a NAACP meeting and heard her speak at other meetings regarding Civil Rights. They soon met, shared ideas and issues they were fighting for and realized they were more powerful as a voice together than separate. They became great friends, spending lots of time together.

      Mrs. Miller didn't drive because of her age and the distance from her home to Reno. Therefore many times my grandparents would pick her up and take her home so she could attend meetings regarding issues close to their hearts, mainly civil and human rights.

      My mother tells me that Mrs. Miller, being a wealthy lady, wanted to send my grandparents on a trip to Africa but they declined. They said there was so much to do here. She understood and they thanked her for the offer.

      I also remember at age 12 or 13 that Mrs. Maya Richard Miller had a stern tone about whatever her and my grandparents were discussing. Here's her letter to Mr. Lear.

February 27, 1969

Mr. William Lear
Building 1202
Stead, Nevada   89506

Dear Mr. Lear,

      We have been watching over a long period of time, but recently with accelerating frustration, the failures of Black Springs, your neighbor, to secure the kinds of community services which the rest of us enjoy.

      It occurs to me that you might very well be the kind of ally who could break the bureaucratic tangle which keeps this small community of preponderantly black citizens depressed.

A CRY FOR HELP

I should introduce myself. I am currently the president of the League of Women Voters of Nevada, and before this term was the president of the Reno-Sparks-Carson League. Several years ago in our study of equality of opportunity in employment and education I made my first visit into the homes of Black Springs which even then had had considerable publicity, partially because of the 1966 March fire. We have been working since then with the Westbrooks and others on one or another; small projects a park, the streets, a day care center, etc. But they are all ridiculously unproductive. We have gone to the county, to the public service commission, to Sierra Pacific Power Co., to the state senators, to our Congressional delegation, to the governor, to the highway department, to the regional planning commission, to the health officer, to the park department and the park commission, to the equal rights commission, to BLM, to the Farm Loans and to HUD. It is a classic in buck-passing.

Because she is hired by the Economic Opportunity Board under the OEO, Mrs. Westbrook, the outreach worker at Black Springs, has managed to get a remarkable distance in the past several months, at least in clarifying the roadblocks; who they are and what their hang-ups are. We have had some encouraging sessions with the Public Service Commission in Carson.

However, in all their assessments of the situation I find that Lear and your plans seem a potential enemy. Your plans for development seem a threat to their home community. The drawings all show beautiful golf courses and ponds and pools in the white community of Stead; large areas of industry in the county, completely surrounding Black Springs, and leaving, therefore, the kind of pocket of undesirable living with which we all are familiar in our cities, especially Los Angeles, where industry has enjoyed the tax advantages of being in the county, or in a tiny town virtually home-owned, and the natives, often poor or black or both, are left in the industrial shadow without services like adequate streets and sewers, and without amenities like parks and play areas for the young.

For years and years and years they have been seeking adequate water, for instance. Now they see the city of Reno sending ample water

BLACK SPRINGS CRY FOR HELP

to Stead, via the pipeline which the military commanded, a pipeline which passes within yards of their homes and none available for them. For in some curious fashion the city of Reno annexed Stead without being <u>next</u>. The corridor would have included Black Springs, and would have meant, therefore city services.

The county will not accept the roads because they are not up to standard. They will not accept the park (1 ½ acres which Mr. Probasco has said he would give) because they don't have the plans, or don't like the ones they have. They have never enforced the health standards for dwellings or water or fire protection which are their own codes. It is again a classic backwater resulting from white racism.

I was encouraged to notice in the paper that you had received an award from the NCCJ and presume that that means that you are inclined to join the efforts we all must make today to right some of these old injustices.

I think that is probably why I am taking the liberty of writing you today.

Time, it seems to me, is running out for us in America for curing this old ill with substantial inputs of our attention. Our work in the League has led us to connections with the Urban Coalition. We are impressed by their publications, at least. I think I am still hopeful that business <u>will</u> turn its incisive and inventive capacities to the problems. We keep being assured these can and should be done locally. And in northern Nevada, Lear looks to me like modern business.

I am wondering if you would not yourself come to visit the area. (I know that Mr. Taylor of the PSC came away with quite a different notion of needs after his personal visit some weeks ago). It would certainly be a helpful start to talk with Mr. and Mrs. Ollie Westbrook, who have developed their home here over the past 15 years. Their home phone is 972-1241, and Mrs. Westbrook's Outreach office phone is 972-0377.

For background I am enclosing a statement very carefully prepared by Mr. Westbrook and given to the Washoe County Commission at

A CRY FOR HELP

one of the innumerable meetings with them some few years ago. It gives, as I cannot, the quality of desperation that these citizens are feeling.

I live in Washoe Valley, but would be more than pleased to join you in such a visit in the hopes that we might with your considerable power be able to move forward into something productive for this community. (You see, I am a little-old-lady at the end of her tennis-shoe strings! And need help!)

Sincerely,

Cc: Mr. & Mrs. Ollie Westbrook

Mrs. Nancy Gomes, pres. LWV Reno

After reading the history now, I know what they were talking about and why Maya, to put it lightly, was so animated.

March 1, 1969, a news article was out; 'Utility Offers Black Springs Water Help.' Sierra Pacific Power Company offered its help to Black Springs in engineering advice; aid in getting a federal grant and possibly some financing said Neil Plath the Sierra Pacific president at that time. Indeed, they did just as they stated.

March 11, 1969, Maya Miller sent a powerful letter to the Regional Director of HUD which more than likely pushed some buttons as you will read.

MRS. RICHARD G. MILLER, Box 621, RR#1, Carson City, Nevada 89701

March 11, 1969

Mr. Robert B. Pitts, Regional Director
Housing & Urban Development, Federal Building
450 Golden Gate
San Francisco, California 94102

re: BLACK SPRINGS, Nevada

BLACK SPRINGS CRY FOR HELP

Dear Mr. Pitts,

We are sorry not to have had any word from you. Your office assured us you would get in touch regarding Black Springs either at the afternoon meeting at Senator Bible's Reno office the day of your visit here with RENOvation, or by phone or personal visit since.

The deplorable water system at Black Springs appears to the black citizens of that community and to us to have very low priority in the white bureaucratic and business communities of Washoe County and your HUD office. While our news media are full of your assurances of HUD help for RENOvation -- $100,000 to piece out the Blayney planning contract for beautifying downtown Reno and substantial help on the construction phases later – we hear nothing from you about Black Springs.

Truckee water, supplied by Sierra Pacific Power Company, flow amply (certified for 4,000,000 gallons a day) within yards of Black Springs to Lear Industries at Stead. Yet SPPC appears helpless to provide 60,000 gallons to Black Springs.

Some background water information you should understand: <u>The Tahoe-Truckee-Pyramid Lake water drainage is a classic in white racism in natural resource management.</u>

White men took Lake Tahoe from the Washoe Indians – and with it took their summer and autumn camping grounds and their winter food supply – and have turned it into a white luxury playground.

White men used Truckee water to develop the cities of Reno and Sparks with clearly discriminatory housing patterns. (15 years ago black people bought in Black Springs because they were not allowed to buy in Reno.)

White men took the water of the Truckee from the Paiutes of Pyramid Lake and diverted it to white farms in Fallon.

The current Pyramid Lake Indian fight against the California-Nevada Water Compact (now before the California legislature) reflects a

A CRY FOR HELP

deep suspicion that that Compact will solidify these old white patterns. In all the 13 years of Tahoe-Truckee-Pyramid negotiation, no Pyramid Lake Paiute was ever a member of the Commission.

We realize that it is not always easy for you in your office in San Francisco to be fully aware of the racial tension your decision will create in outlying communities like Reno. But it is in the hope that you will want to understand them that we have been so insistent on your personal visit to Black Springs.

The League of Women Voters, of which I am the Nevada president, lobbied for money for HUD on the theory that HUD would help to bring some correction of the housing injustices in this country. I hope we will not find this another false hope, lost in governmental red tape and "business as usual."

Yours very truly,

Now upon reading her letter, would you ignore her plight?

A letter was sent, **March 17, 1969**, from Helen Westbrook the Outreach service worker for Black Springs to Senator Alan Bible in regards to constantly being ignored about upgrading the water system.

On **March 24, 1969**, the Black Springs Civic Improvement Association was formed and on April 8, 1969, was formally known as the Black Springs Civic Improvement Corporation which outlined again what their community was in need of.

CHAPTER 9
AN EFFORT TO REBUILD

You may read the following document in its entirety at the Northern Nevada Historical Society.

The Black Springs Community Water Facility—

An Effort to Rebuild

I. INTRODUCTION

The following material constitutes the formal application submitted by the county of Washoe, Nevada, to the Max C. Fleischmann Foundation requesting of the Foundation to finance, in part, development of the basic water facility planned for construction in the community of Black Springs, Nevada. Although the County of Washoe is the applicant body, inasmuch as the people of Black Springs are the intended beneficiaries of the proposed system, the application was prepared by a representative of the Black Springs community.

Before proceeding with the application, a word concerning its organization and purpose is in order. The application contains a brief description of the recent history of Black Springs including the events which have transpired leading to the submission of this request for funds to finance the construction and installation of the proposed water system. The application was developed in this manner because its significance cannot be properly understood, nor should it be considered separate and apart from its relationship to the community and the people of Black Springs. As the history of Black Springs will illustrate, the proposed water facility is an integral part of a comprehensive effort by the people of Black Springs to rehabilitate the community. As such, the facility is essential to the growth and development of the area and to the success or failure of the effort already initiated to improve living conditions in the community.

Bearing this in mind, it is hoped that when evaluating the merits of this proposal, there will be awareness, that more is involved than a request for funds to develop the proposed facility. Rather, it should be understood that the proposal embraces aspects of community living which are fundamental in nature and that by funding the construction and installation of the system, the Foundation will be providing the key to the future growth and development if not the continued existence of the community.

II. GENERAL INFORMATION

Responding to the voice of progress and notions of community and self-pride, the people of Black Springs, Nevada have initiated a comprehensive program for the purpose of rehabilitating their community. This energetic program touches nearly every facet of community life.

Although it is difficult to single out the exact moment when the commitment to rebuild the community became irreversible, it is fair to state that a significant step in that direction was taken when the Black Springs Civic Improvement Corporation, (hereinafter referred to as the B.S.C.I.C.), was organized as a non-profit organization under the laws of the State of Nevada. Since the date of incorporation, the B.S.C.I.C. has been the catalyst activating the forces which have forged the effort to rebuild the community.

The status of the roads in Black Springs was one of the first among many problems confronting the residents of Black Springs which drew the attention of the community. Until recently, the roads were owned by Mr. J. E. Sweatt, a real estate broker and land developer for the Black Springs area. However, after a period of negotiation involving Mr. Sweatt, representatives of Washoe County, and members of the community of Black Springs, Mr. Sweatt agreed to dedicate the roads in Black Springs to the County.

AN EFFORT TO REBUILD

Fire protection is another of the problem areas in which the community has been involved. Since the B.S.C.I.C. was incorporated, the community organized the Black Springs Volunteer Fire Department. Equipment has been obtained and volunteer members from the community are being trained as firemen. Presently, finishing touches are being added to the new, cement-block fire hall constructed to house the new fire truck. The fire truck is itself, an example of community action. The truck was acquired when the community arranged with the State of Nevada Forestry Department to station one of its trucks in Black Springs to be at the disposal of the volunteer fire fighters from the community. Prior to this arrangement, there was no fire truck stationed in Black Springs.

Adjacent to the fire hall stands the Black Springs Community Center. The building was once a home which the State of Nevada acquired through condemnation proceedings. The community purchased the building and it was removed to Black Springs to house the Center. The structure was quite old and therefore, in order to become suitable for the purposes of the Center, extensive renovation was required in addition to laying the foundation upon which the building now rests. Although the remodeling project is nearing completion, the building has already been used for community gatherings including meetings to discuss the proposed new water facility. The Center has also become a community branch of the Head Start program. Head Start is a preparatory school program for the preschool children of low income families. Equipment has been moved into the building and classes on a regular basis are being conducted.

The Center overlooks the community park and playground, another addition to the community. On what was once a vacant lot, there is to be found a baseball field, an asphalt basketball court, swings, teeter-totters, etc., for the children. The basketball court is lighted for "nightball," and for the family, park benches, picnic tables, and the like can be found.

Also, the new bus stop cannot be overlooked. The cement block structure was erected by members of the community to provide shelter for their children as they await transportation into Reno to attend school.

A CRY FOR HELP

The numerous projects undertaken and the measure of achievement experienced are indicative of the commitment of the residents of Black Springs to the task of raising the standards of living in the community. Yet, as impressive as this list is, the story is unfinished. Further examination of the community reveals that other and perhaps more fundamental problems have not been resolved. In addition, the solution to these problems is to a large extent contingent upon the installation of the proposed water system.

Despite the fact that the roadways in Black Springs are now public streets and as such the responsibility of the County, street conditions remain substandard. The people of Black Springs must travel daily upon dusty, gravel roads which resemble a washboard. The County has indicated it intends to pave the streets in Black Springs. However, the design specifications call for laying the water mains and laterals beneath these same streets and thus it is conceivable that shortly after the streets are paved, they will be torn up due to the excavation work necessary to lay the pipes into the ground. Sound business judgment dictates that it would be unwise to pave the streets where such is the case and consequently, the decision to begin work on the streets has been shelved pending the outcome of the effort to develop the water system. Until that time, the gravel, pock-marked roads will continue to plague the inhabitants of Black Springs.

Substandard housing is another of the evils affecting the lives of the people of the community. Many homes in Black Springs are old and in a state of disrepair. Others never were properly constructed. In general, however, such conditions do not exist by choice but prevail because private lines of credit normally expected to provide funds for home-improvement loans or construction of suitable new dwellings have been foreclosed. Private investors have avoided the area, in part, because their equity would be exposed to a substantial risk of loss due to inadequate fire protection. The Federal Housing Administration refused to insure loans for home construction on these grounds. In an area such as Black Springs, the lack of Federal Housing Administration assistance makes seeking private financial assistance prohibitive. Thus, members of the community, foreclosed from the traditional, private sources of financial assistance, have been compelled to resort to the largesse of the Federal

AN EFFORT TO REBUILD

Government for assistance and, unfortunately, the response has not been satisfactory here, either.

The rationale set forth by the Federal Housing Administration for refusing to act as surety on loans for homes located in the Black Springs area questions the adequacy of the community's fire protection system. The recent history of Black Springs tends to justify the Administration's reluctance to come forward with assistance. On Christmas Day, 1968, the home of Mr. and Mrs. Sam Allen was consumed by fire. Christmas dinner, the children's presents and the family's possessions also were destroyed in the blaze although no one was injured or burned. Since that time, other buildings have been destroyed by fire. Only last month, the Huddleston family lost their home and all of their belongings to fire. Again, thankfully, no one was burned or lost as Mr. and Mrs. Huddleston and their children were unharmed. But, how long can this luck continue? Eventually, someone will be injured or a life will be lost due to a fire and until the present water system is replaced, this constant threat will continue to cast a shadow over the community. The Huddleston's experience is a grim reminder of that fact.

As was already indicated, steps have been taken to attack the problem. A volunteer fire department has been organized and equipped. Yet, despite this significant effort, fire protection will never meet reasonable standards unless and until an adequate water system is installed. In addition, the existing fire hazard will not be reduced to an acceptable level until the "tinder-box" homes standing in Black Springs are raised and/or improved. As indicated, the improvement of housing conditions in Black Springs is contingent upon adequate fire protection and this in turn hinges to a large degree upon an ample supply of water. In a sense, then, it seems that the rehabilitation of the community is caught up in a vicious circle with every turn in some manner involving the proposed new water system. From this, it is clear that the proposed system is affecting the development of new programs and has hampered the implementation of on-going projects.

Finally, consideration must be given to some of the more mundane problems which can be traced directly to present system. Everyone realizes that water is essential for domestic purposes such as washing clothes, cooking, cleaning, etc. Unfortunately, because of the manner in which the system is constructed, pressure in the water line is barely negligible when there is a heavy demand on the system from the faucet in certain sections of the community during these particular times of the day. In addition, it is at times an adventuresome proposition when showering in Black Springs. The possibility always exists that water will simply trickle from the showerhead. Although treated somewhat lightly, serious questions concerning personal hygiene must be raised when considering the operation of the present system. It should also be obvious that an adequate supply of water flowing from the tap at an appropriate pressure level will improve the sewage collection and disposal system. Clearly, an adequate water facility will contribute substantially to the improvement of the health and sanitation conditions in the community.

There are other problems which can be attributed to the operation and efficiency of the present water system. Adding them to the list would simply belabor the obvious. Therefore, in summation, two points are offered. From a survey of the problems existing in Black Springs, most of which can be attributed to the operation of the present water system, it should be apparent that the average community dweller is not forced to contend with living conditions as they exist in Black Springs and which the residents of Black Springs must face on a daily basis. Second, several of the problems which can be blamed to the water system may only be simple annoyances when viewed in isolation. However, when they are lumped together as is the case in Black Springs, their total effect is to create an intolerable existence when judged in accordance with the standards of 20th Century living.

CONCLUSION

Formation of the B.S.C.I.C. signaled the beginning of a comprehensive effort by the residents of Black Springs to eradicate the social and economic conditions of poverty which have been nagging the community since its inception. The numerous projects found throughout the community illustrate the significant effort already invested by the people of Black Springs and form the basis of the commitment evincing the community's firm resolve to extricate itself from these conditions. Of practical importance, the technical skills and knowledge exhibited by

AN EFFORT TO REBUILD

members of the community while working to improve living conditions should dispel any doubt or concern regarding the ability of the community to assume the responsibilities associated with the ownership, operation and maintenance of the proposed facility.

Regarding the system, itself, the description of the community development program illustrates that this system touches nearly every facet of community life. Continued improvement of housing conditions, roads, fire protection, health and sanitation, and the like is contingent upon development of the proposed system. Consequently, it is fair to consider the proposed system as the threshold to future community development and as such, it should be understood that assistance which makes possible construction of the proposed system also provides the key to continued growth and development of the entire community.

Finally, consider the specific projects affected by the proposal to develop the new water facility in the community. Paved streets, a sewer system and fire protection just to mention a few are aspects of community life which are commonplace in the average community. Indeed, they are fundamental facts of life which the common citizenry live with and use but which never raise their concern. Unfortunately, the people of Black Springs are well aware of these things because they must face a life from day to day that is without the basic aspects of community living.

However, the people of Black Springs have ceased dreaming and waiting for a better life. They have gathered together in an effort to build with outside assistance where needed a new and better community and life. Aware of the intentions of the community underlying this request for financial assistance, the application to the Fleischmann Foundation for the funds necessary to complete construction of the water system is transformed into a request by the people of Black Springs for an opportunity – an opportunity to build a community in which the basic necessities of life are found. By responding to the community's request, the Fleischmann Foundation will to a large extent be providing the people and community with this chance.

News article, ***April 1969,*** 'The Challenge of Black Springs,' quoted by Assemblyman Woodrow Wilson, R-Las Vegas, was one of the

A CRY FOR HELP

legislators who spoke out about the problems. "I think it can be corrected", he cited a similarly "deplorable situation" in the Indian Colony within the city limits of Las Vegas, in which the senators in Washington managed to get help for the people. Wilson explored several possible solutions to the Black Springs problem. "State and health officers should start condemnation proceedings but the county doesn't want to provide housing elsewhere for them", he said. "When you see a situation like this where there are Negroes involved, that's what laws are for to change the situation".

Once again, on *April 11, 1969*, Maya Miller wrote to Senator Cannon regarding Black Springs.

April 11, 1969

Senator Howard Cannon
Senate Office Building
Washington, D. C. 20515

Dear Senator Cannon,

Thank you for coming to Black Springs this past Tuesday.

Your press release said that you were trying to understand the situation there, and I want to commend that effort, - because to understand Black Springs is to understand a number of aspects of the black dilemma in America. You and I, of course, Senator, will never understand really the deadening despair that has come from the losing rounds of Black Springs people with white bureaucracy.

That was clear when you left the other day. I had been heartened by your visit. But no hope was kindled for them. You were just another of those politicians who keep coming when they run for office but leave them in their backwater afterward. You may get a sense of this hopelessness from the speech I'll enclose of Mr. Ollie Westbrook's to the County Commission.

These are old injustices you're dealing with at Black Springs. "These people" as they are so often referred to by the bureaucrats, came out to

AN EFFORT TO REBUILD

this country like most of our forefathers in the tradition of the "great American dream." They wanted to find a place to live that was better for their children than the old country left behind (i.e. Louisiana, Mississippi, and Arkansas).

But Reno would not let them live in our city. So some of the most resourceful of them in pioneer fashion bought raw land at Black Springs (paying 15 years ago what prime Genoa acreage is selling for today). On this land they have worked and built homes. But on every side they have been preyed upon by white small-time business-men – loan-sharks, land-sharks – who have moved in when the good solid citizens of the Reno banks declined to lend to "these people" in these places.

So, in orderly fashion they have gone – for years they have gone – to local government and state government and now to the federal government, and the buck-passing of these white bureaucracies have been slow, endless, and circular, like a vulture wheeling in the hot summer air. Everywhere there are white business friends who need to be protected, and so the government officer suggests another way of another solution which does not involve his own effort or commitment.

This really is the story of the black man in white America.

To cure the Black Springs problem (which is not just water, but a mesh of inter-related failures of the county to provide just services) will not be to cure the black problem in Nevada. But it would teach us much we need to learn, that no number of reports will ever teach us.

The resentments we are building up among "these people" by our delay and indifference, and among the best of our young people who appreciate the facts, simply will not permit a stable American society, - no matter how many guns we put in the hands of the army or the police.

It is absolutely idle it seems to me, to build up defenses against a foreign enemy while we allow our country to rot away inside.

All the same despairs apply to the Job Corps withdrawal. Carson City has always resented the black part of the Corps, and I guess it should have been obvious to us that no matter how fine and effective a job they would do, they would be thrown out at first chance. I will be interested to see if the Democrats of this state will fight for its continuance.

The excuse of replacing the Job Corps with a local state welfare institution of some kind is a farce. We really do not want as a state to be self-contained. We beat the bushes of the east and south for "outsiders" to come to Nevada to invest (in Caesar's Palaces and Kings Castles). Then, shouldn't we invest some small part of our own forest land to help rehabilitate our nation's prime sickness?

Either we are a whole nation – and responsible for all the people in that nation or we must forget "Americanism". I think it is despair among many young people, and many black people and increasingly among some of us who have tried to pursue the middle way – despair that we will not as a nation responds fast enough, that is our greatest national weakness.

How do you fore see our dealing with Black Springs?

Sincerely,
Mrs. Richard G. Miller

George Preonas, a VISTA Attorney, wrote to Senator Cannon on **April 21, 1969**, in regards to the residents of Black Springs taking over the water system and improving it.

April 21, 1969

The Honorable Howard W. Cannon
United States Senate
259 Old Senate Office Building
Washington, D. C.

Dear Senator Cannon:

As you know, the residents of Black Springs are currently exploring the possibility of taking over the present water system and improving it. Two

AN EFFORT TO REBUILD

federal agencies, the Farmers Home Administration of the Department of Agriculture and the Department of Housing and Urban Development, have monies available for this kind of community development project.

At the present time there seems to be a question of which agency has jurisdiction in Black Springs, and we would very much appreciate your assistance in clarifying the situation. For two fundamental reasons we would prefer to have jurisdiction taken by Farmers Home Administration. First, the FHA has already classified Black Springs as a rural area. This will enable the residents of Black Springs to receive FHA loans to rehabilitate existing homes or to construct new homes. But these loans to improve the substandard housing cannot be approved until the problems of water, sewerage and streets are solved. If FHA were to also handle the problems of community services, the people of Black Springs would not have to deal with two agencies. Second, the bureaucratic "red tape" is far less of a problem with the FHA because it is not necessary to involve to as great a degree the various state and local governmental bodies as must take part in HUD programs. As you know, the county commissioners have not been particularly eager to solve the problems in Black Springs. Moreover, the San Francisco office of HUD has heretofore taken an attitude of complete disinterest.

The county supervisor for FHA, Mr. Wrenn, has been helpful, but indicated that he was unable to make a determination as to his own jurisdiction. Accordingly, he advised us to make an application for assistance (Form 101 – 102), and that the standard review procedure of FHA would determine whether FHA money is available to improve the water system. We are doing so and will send you a copy of that application by the end of the week.

By next month Sierra Pacific Power Company will have completed its detailed engineering proposal for improving the water system. FHA will at that time be able to act on our proposal and make the actual grant/loan. With your invaluable assistance we hope that at that time FHA will be ready, willing and able to proceed with acting on our proposal.

We should also add that since our meeting in Black Springs we met with Mr. Reese Taylor, Jr., Chairman of the Public Service

A CRY FOR HELP

Commission of Nevada. He indicated that the Commission had investigated the problems of inadequate water in Black Springs and said that the Commission was prepared to hold hearings on the matter. He also indicated that the Commission would give its support to our efforts to take over the system from Mr. Sweatt. So it looks like the pieces of our puzzle are beginning to fit together.

On behalf of the residents of Black Springs, we would like to say that we all appreciated and enjoyed meeting with you last week. We greatly appreciate your interest and are looking forward to your assistance.

Yours very truly,

―――――――――――
George Preonas
VISTA Volunteer

―――――――――――
Helen Westbrook
Outreach Worker

April 25, 1969, Sierra Pacific Power Company agreed to help with upgrading the water system.

Senator Cannon responded by letter, on **May 13, 1969**, to Mr. Preonas' letter sent on April 21, 1969. He said, "In summation, how Black Springs chooses to handle its request is up to the community and the available funds in each agency. Jurisdictional disputes should not enter into this decision and the San Francisco office has no authority to shrug off a request for assistance. If the community decides to request HUD assistance, a letter should be sent to San Francisco to have a regional representative come to the community to help draw up the request." He ended by saying, "You may be assured that I will attempt

AN EFFORT TO REBUILD

to assist the residents of Black Springs in this very serious problem, in any way that I can."

On *May 16, 1969*, a Last Will and Testament was sign by J. E. Sweatt bequeathing the water company over to the B.S.C.I.C. As verbatim the will, "FIRST: I hereby direct that all my just debts and memorial service expenses be paid out of my estate as soon as practicable after the time of my death. SECOND: I hereby give and bequeath all of my interest in and to the company known as J. E. SWEATT doing business as EUGENE STREET WATER CO. to the BLACK SPRINGS CIVIC IMPROVEMENT CORPORATION."

I want you to realize this small but mighty community owned their own water rights. And to this day they maintain those rights. Now you may read the entire will at the Nevada Historical Society.

A letter, on *May 21, 1969*, was sent to the State Highway Department from Helen Westbrook, Outreach Worker regarding the conditions of the roads in Black Springs asking for immediate help. This same letter was broadcasted on channel 4 News in 2008. Can you imagine, that 38 years later, they're still trying to complete the roads?

Mr. J. E. Sweatt wrote a letter, *May 26, 1969*, to Howard Gloyd, Director of the EOB informing him that he had drawn up a new will leaving his interest in the Eugene Street Water Company to the B.S.C.I.C. Charles Zeh a VISTA volunteer attorney said, "This was how they were able to secure a grant from U.S. Dept. of Housing and Urban Development a grant of $90,000 for the $150,000 project."

CHAPTER 10
THE P.O.W.E.R. OF YOUTH

Not knowing the exact date P.O.W.E.R. (People Organized to Work for Equal Recognition), came into existence, but knowing it was in *May of 1969*, the Black Springs' youth had formalized. Our officers were: Thurman Carthen Jr., President; Keith Carthen, Vice President and Secretary/Treasurer, Helen Townsell. The Advisory Council was: Larry Westbrook, Chairman; Anthony Townsell and Debra Lobster who were members.

P.O.W.E.R. also drafted a constitution with 9 articles; our name, membership, officers, officers' qualifications, election process, amendment procedures, impeachment process, making of laws and ratification processes all with explicit definitions also each officers' duties and expectations. Six laws were also incorporated. It makes me a little sentimental recalling all of this. You must realize we were youth ranging from ages 5 to 19 in responsible positions, facing civic situations. Our purpose was to create a change, a difference in our community. To have what every other neighborhood had from the start. You'll hear more about P.O.W.E.R.'s involvement.

Just a little side trip, I've found plenty of documents where there's only a month, year and no dates at all. It's amazing how not only Black Springs' residents but high end officials writing important correspondences failed to date them.

Also in May a committee of 30 board members received letters from Howard Gloyd. His purpose as he declared was, "A program to get Washoe County Economic Opportunity members away from behind the meeting tables and out into the poor areas." Some board members requested to serve were the Washoe County District Attorneys office,

A CRY FOR HELP

County Commissioner, League of Women Voters, UNR, Washoe County School District, State Highway Department and the City of Reno.

A news article from the Nevada State Journal dated *June 1, 1969* acknowledged that the Reno Kiwanis Club voted a $7,500 gift to be given to Black Springs' residents intended for their new park and recreational facilities. They said, "We did it for those kids out there. There are about 75 or 80 youngsters and they have nothing at all."

The B.S.C.I.C. mailed out a letter on *June 2, 1969* to the media; KBET, KBUB, KCBN, KNEV, KOH, KOLO, KONE, GAZETTE and THE JOURNAL. The letter read as follows, "The under privileged people of Black Springs, Nevada challenge you the broad casting and news media to a softball game in Black Springs. The prize is one thousand dollars per station in cash or services, when Black Springs wins. If by some miracle you win, we will give you a choice of a sage brush from our park sight or all the well water you can drink from the Eugene Street Water Company or both. The prize that we will win will go toward the park and recreation facilities in Black Springs. We are most sincere about this challenge. If you except, please contact: Mr. Westbrook at 972-1241 or Mr. Lobster at 972-0191. Sincerely, Mr. Westbrook, Chairman." I don't recall if anyone accepted.

June 2, 1969, the Black Springs Adult Education Committee's Chairman Jeff Townsell purposed to provide adult education, tutoring, Black Culture and training programs to the residents. This program consisted of a student questionnaire, goals of tutoring, the relationship between student and tutor and the role of a tutor. There was always big emphasis on education.

Helen Westbrook, now President of B.S.C.I.A., received a letter dated *June 6, 1969* from the Reno Kiwanis Club affirming the donation of $7,500 to the B.S.C.I.A. towards the community center and park.

On *June 11, 1969* George Probasco donates 5.974 acres of land for the park and community center. Even at that time residents were still meeting in each others homes as they had no where else to convene as recorded by Johnnie Mae Lobster then the secretary of the B.S.C.I.A.

THE P.O.W.E.R. OF YOUTH

June 27, 1969, the community sent a request to the Washoe County Planning Board, City Hall to change the street names; Main Street to Kennedy Drive, North Street to Huey Lane, Eugene Street to Medgar Avenue, Mary Street to Coretta Way and East Street to Malcolm Avenue. Note the significance in the name changes.

The community never sat idle as you'll see. Mrs. J. M. Lobster recorded the following minutes. "A special Outreach meeting was called *June 30, 1969* to elect representatives for the E.O.B. Board. Mr. Bufkin was acting Chairman. Mrs. Westbrook said that she had William Lobster, alternate Albert Williams, Beverly Carthen, and alternate D. C Benson. Out of the four only Mr. Lobster have attended the meeting regularly. Without representation on the Board we will loose all the benefits. Mr. Westbrook explained the duties of the representatives and that they meet every third Thursday in the month. Mrs. Butler was elected to represent for Black Springs on the E.O.B. Board. Mr. Bufkin was elected as her alternate. Mrs. J. M. Lobster was elected as Mr. Lobster's alternate.

The Outreach Advisory Council meetings are to be held the 2nd Thursday of every month at 7:30 p.m. The meeting is to be held at the home of the residents in Black Springs." The minutes ended, "We had a very nice meeting. Meeting was adjourned by Mr. O. Westbrook, Chairman. J. M Lobster, Acting Sec."

On *July 2, 1969* a news article regarding the Parks Commission approving the project for a community center came out. Now the original plans included a 7,000 sq. ft. building of concrete block and wood construction, an inside basketball court, an indoor tennis court as well as offices and restrooms as opposed to a house. Yes, our dreams were sizable.

P.O.W.E.R. was very active in this project. They canvassed the county for funds, materials and professional assistance to work with the volunteer labor, the volunteer labor being the residents of Black Springs. After all we had amazing talent within the community.

The County Clerk and the Clerk of the Board of County Commissioners of Washoe County did approve the Black Springs park plans on *July 9, 1969*.

A CRY FOR HELP

Then P.O.W.E.R. took it upon their selves to ask the Washoe County Public Works Director on *July 11, 1969* if they would donate the asphalt material needed (50 tons) for the completion of an outside basketball court that could be used for other activities such as roller skating, tennis, etc.

An empowering news article, on *July 26, 1969* praising the youths' (P.O.W.E.R.) involvement in the community's growth was very uplifting. It basically said, 'Youth, 15 yrs old and younger were concerned and fighting for a better place to live in Black Springs.' As I've stated many times before, what every community already had. We were very serious about our involvement and contributions to the area. We enjoyed being a part.

On *July 30, 1969*, P.O.W.E.R., requested $3,500 from a grant to be used in the building of the community center. They were approved for $1,500 by the EOB.

B.S.C.I.A., on *August 13, 1969* received a letter from George Miller a general contractor, stating that the contract to actually start working on the recreation building and basketball court was completed.

And once again, on *August 14, 1969*, the League of Women Voters gave their support for federal funds for improvements and upgrades to the Black Springs Water System. The League of Women Voters were something else and were consistent with getting an issue resolved once they became part of it, especially when Maya Miller was the president of the organization and you've read some of her very powerful letters regarding the conditions in Black Springs. I really like this quote I read in a Nevada State Journal article on August 14. It sounds like something Maya Miller would have voiced but in fact it was Mrs. Earl Nicholson who at that time was president. "If public bodies cannot act promptly to facilitate legitimate and proper action for our disadvantaged and minority groups we should not be surprised when they resort to illegitimate and improper action."

P.O.W.E.R., on *August 16, 1969* in Reno's evening Gazette news paper, reports to Washoe County Commissioners that more the $11,000

THE P.O.W.E.R. OF YOUTH

in donations had been received for the construction of a 6.4 acre park in the community and along with the $7,500 donation from the Reno Kiwanis Club we had raised about $18,500 total. This is where I interject. You know we almost lost the $7,500.

When the Kiwanis Club first donated the money there was a stipulation that we had 90 days from receipt to start construction. Everything had been completed for some time except the building permit which required an inspector to ok it. The deadline was growing close as the residents of Black Springs frantically continued requesting an inspection for the permit. Mind you, they, the residents, didn't need the County's money anymore which they had been denied over and over again. All they needed was a building inspector to get off their lazy uninterested behinds and go do the work he was being paid to do. Stop dragging the fat. The residents had completed all that was required, sign the darn building permits. My God people, you know I feel those frustrations as well as reliving those same feelings now. I was apart of this history, this aggravation, this life's experiences. September 4, 1969 was the deadline to start construction, after nearly losing the donation the county building inspectors signed the ok September 8, 1969.

My grandfather, on *August 16, 1969* at a Black Springs Outreach meeting commented on all the behind-the-scene work that was done by P.O.W.E.R. He went on to say, "When most of the other youth groups were applying for money for field trips, P.O.W.E.R. applied for a more permanent investment as in helping in construction of the multi-purpose building at the park."

On *September 10, 196,* Howard Cannon, a Nevada Senator at that time, wrote to my grandparents saying he would support "HUD" financial assistance in a better water and sewage system. Even though we had running water it still was inadequate.

Now a little humor, Black Springs' water has always tasted very good. As for sewage, we had what was called cesspools. It was basically a hole dug in the backyard with a cement door with an iron handle attached. I was always afraid that I would be playing or walking to a neighbors house and tumble in. You see, from my house to the

A CRY FOR HELP

Carthen's old house on Medgar there was a pathway to cut through to each others houses. I always thought that within the route there was an uncovered cesspool and close to dark, while walking envisioned falling in and drowning in a pool full of excrement. I know weird dream but that's my memory of cesspools, feces killers!

Previously you read how the residents of Black Springs applied for street name changes. Well, on *September 17, 1969*, the office of the Washoe County Clerk notified the Westbrooks that on July 17, 1969 the street naming committee met with the Washoe County Commissioners for the purpose of changing the street names. They informed them that their street North Street was to be renamed, Westbrook Lane and that their new address would be 241 Westbrook Lane as well as the other changes.

Support letters from both Senators Alan Bible and Howard Cannon were written *September 18, 1969*, in support of HUD assisting in a new water and sewage system for Black Springs.

A *September 28th 1969*, letter to Andy Gordon from Joe Coppa, Commissioner of Sparks was encouraging. It read, "My dear Mr. Gordon". Now the tone in how he addressed Andy shows that Andy had quite an impact upon him. Joe Coppa went on to say, "I am more than pleased to substantiate your application for a supportive 90% grant from HUD for the improvement of the water system for Black Springs." It is evident that Mr. Coppa had great compassion for the community. He went on to say, "This community has a high growth potential, and inasmuch as the present antiquated water system does not nearly answer the needs of the present population, it is imperative that something be done immediately. We can only hope that there will be no more disastrous fires that have occurred there in the past. There could be loss of life the next time." Mr. Coppa's vision seems to embrace Black Springs' vision. "As a member of the Washoe County Commission, I am interested in converting Black Springs into a model community such as occurred in Sun Valley, which has made great progress in that direction the last nine months. This can hardly be accomplished with the present water system. An adequate improved water system is essential for landscaping, gardens, as well as human consumption", Mr. Coppa said. He closed

THE P.O.W.E.R. OF YOUTH

saying, "I wish to commend you personally for your efforts, and with all good wishes for your success in this undertaking, I am, very truly yours," signed Joe Coppa, Washoe County Commission, Sparks District.

Andy Gordon, an astonishing VISTA worker, receives a letter **October 1, 1969**, vowing help will be there from HUD and Washoe County once they had an acceptable water system plan. As previously stated, no one could get loans on their homes or secure home mortgage insurance, at a reasonable rate, mainly because of the antiquated water and sewage system. Although no one wanted to fund a new water and sewage system, these agencies continued to make that a condition before they would assist in anything, especially home upgrades.

The same day, **October 1, 1969**, the City-County District Health Department released their assessment of the area, "Black Springs is a minority community. All of the difficulties of Black Springs are not of the making of the inhabitants. The area on which Black Springs was laid out has a very, very tight subsoil which makes the construction of adequate private sewage disposal systems difficult and expensive. One of this community's great needs is to be sewered and have some sort of a disposal system provided. There is a water system of sorts out there. There frequently are leaks in the lines. A primary need of this community is for a good properly engineered water system. Mention has previously been made of substandard housing. Houses in Black Springs would not meet any building code. The writer cannot say that much of the housing that is out there now is fit for human habitation."

That's pretty heavy. I keep reading these negative reports from County Officials and as I've stated from 1956 to 1969 all the officials seem to be doing is agreeing and stating that it's bad.

P.O.W.E.R. along with Andy Gordon requested a house from the Nevada State Highway Engineer on **October 10, 1969** for the purpose of providing a community center for the neighborhood. P.O.W.E.R.'s meetings were held at Andy's house. In fact we did everything at Andy's. He was more like a big brother than a VISTA worker. We would have study groups, plan improvement strategies, write letters to county officials and have parties. Andy always had time for us. His house wasn't very big.

A CRY FOR HELP

I believe it was a one bedroom. Mr. Bufkin had donated the house. And Andy had only a cot to sleep on, I believe a desk and a couch. We also helped him decorate the place by cutting and collecting old carpet, cutting it into squares and tapping it on the wall. We also collected highway signs and glued them on the wall. We were very proud of our design. We then began planning how we would decorate the community center once we had one. You know, P.O.W.E.R.'S journey and tenacity stemmed from several main families within the community: the Westbrooks, Townsell's, Lobsters, Carthens, Williams, Reynolds, Vernon's and the Stevens. There were more but these were the most involved families of the youth.

We finally received swings for the playground. News article dated *November 15, 1969* there's a picture of my brothers, Maurice and Duane Townsell along with Tomis Crunk, utilizing the swings while Dana Lobster is standing there on her bike watching them. The swings, baseball fields fencing and bases were donated by Mrs. James Eastwood, president of the Nevada Relief Shop.

December 31, 1969, it was yet the end of another year. The year ended with Andy and my grandparents continuing to write letters supporting the drastic need of governmental supported funding to enhance our community to what one might classify as normal. Normal water, housing, streets, sewage, community center, playground all was in the making and the people all very, very, very patiently waiting. Never getting so discouraged that they would give up as I'm sure many officials hoped they could wait them out. I'm sure some officials thought sooner or later they would get tired of waiting or being told no. Or could not or would not perform the tasks placed in front of them. Little did they know, they had just the opposite; they were after all considered by some as uneducated people, yet they were very determined, prosperous and eager to learn and change the community where they had their homes and their families.

CHAPTER 11
CHRONOLOGY OF THE 1970'S

Before resuming the Black Springs' evolvement a little historical excursion is in order. The maturing of our nation had advanced by leaps and bounds materially but the conscience was something different in regards to equality. Since President Lincoln's Emancipation Proclamation in 1863, to Dr. Martin Luther King's, "I Have a Dream" speech in 1963, 100 years had elapsed; technology and industry has evolved but society's moral consciousness staggers. During the 1960's, there were Civil Rights movements surging across the nation.

The **African-American Civil Rights Movement** (1955–1968) refers to the reform movements in the United States aimed at outlawing racial discrimination against African Americans and restoring Suffrage in Southern states, particularly in the South. By 1966, the emergence of the Black Power Movement, which lasted roughly from 1966 to 1975, enlarged the aims of the Civil Rights Movement to include racial dignity, economic and political self-sufficiency and freedom from oppression by whites. Many of those who were active in the Civil Rights Movement, with organizations such as NAACP, SNCC, CORE and SCLC, prefer the term "Southern Freedom Movement" because the struggle was about far more than just civil rights under law; it was also about fundamental issues of freedom, respect, dignity, and economic and social equality.

During the period 1955–1968, acts of nonviolent protest and civil disobedience produced crisis situations between activists and government authorities. Federal, state, and local governments, businesses, educational institutions, and communities often had to respond immediately to crisis situations which highlighted the inequities faced by African Americans. Forms of protest and/or civil disobedience included boycotts such as the successful Montgomery Bus Boycott (1955–1956)

A CRY FOR HELP

in Alabama; "sit-ins" such as the influential Greensboro sit-in (1960) in North Carolina; marches, such as the Selma to Montgomery marches (1965) in Alabama; and a wide range of other nonviolent activities.

Noted legislative achievements during this phase of the Civil Rights Movement were passage of Civil Rights Act of 1964, that banned discrimination in employment practices and public accommodations; the Voting Rights Act of 1965, that restored and protected voting rights; the Immigration and Nationality Services Act of 1965, that dramatically opened entry to the U.S. to immigrants other than traditional European groups; and the Civil Rights Act of 1968, that banned discrimination in the sale or rental of housing. African Americans re-entered politics in the South, and across the country young people were inspired to action.

The Westbrooks recognized the national plight and continued to advance the moral fiber of their community. In *January 1970,* Black Springs was placed on the bookmobiles schedule to arrive every Monday from 1:30 p.m. to 2:00 p.m. Interesting, seeing that most youth were in school and their parents at work. Once again here's bureaucracy undermining civil rights.

The Black Springs Outreach held a general meeting with the community *February 14, 1970* to review the previous year's progress and projects. As stated from the minutes:

"Most of the meeting we discussed and evaluated what we did in 1969. From January to April we tried to get the County to accept streets. Mrs. Maya Miller sent a letter to U.S. Senator Cannon – very dynamic and to the point about pacification and vote-getting during an election year. On April 8, Black Springs Civic Improvement Corporation was formed. We got land for a park from George Probasco, and more was finally donated when the County was trying to think of reasons for not accepting the parcel.

The Kiwanis donated $7,500 with a three-month limitation; we exceeded this limitation when we got tied up in red tape, but got an extension of another three months. Finally, after we showed adequate assurance of completion by having the County take title to the community center and agree to pay the cost of the insurance and utilities, the

CHRONOLOGY OF THE 1970'S

Kiwanis kept the money, asking us to submit another letter. We abandoned the extravagant building ($200,000), and Lloyd drew up plans for a smaller building while we looked around for a structure already built. The County leased the land for a fire truck shelter with permission of Mr. Probasco. The State Highway Department sold us a house and garage to be moved out here for the community center and fire truck shelter. We temporarily lost the fire truck because of lack of heat to keep the pump from freezing and cracking.

We fought for an adequate water system. On May 16, J. E. Sweatt willed the Water Company to the Black Springs Civic Improvement Corporation (BSCIC). The Public Service Commission, which had jurisdiction over the Eugene Water System previously, had relinquished the power to the County. Reverend Hill mentioned that someone may be getting the system from Sweatt, because Sweatt didn't keep up with the tariff by supplying sufficient water pressure, etc. Sierra Pacific Power Company said they would install a 5 hp pump in one well, and will do all the feasibility studies prior and during the application to Housing and Urban Development for an 80% water system grant ($80,000).

On May 23, the EOB Board was invited out to Black Springs to get involved in our area.

The State Highway Department hired an Equal Opportunity Coordinator, who had been instrumental in getting jobs for adults and for youth during the summer.

We got natural gas installed to replace the expensive propane.

Roosevelt Johnson donated land to Sweatt by Huddleston's. The men got together after Mrs. Crunk said that she would buy the block for a bus stop shelter and complete the shelter for the children. The land in front of the grocery store was given to us by the State Highway Department. After much deliberation, the State Highway Department paved in front of the post office.

People Organized to Work for Equal Recognition (POWER) was formed, and was instrumental in several activities for youth and for Black Springs as a whole.

A CRY FOR HELP

The streets were renamed after the County took title to them: Kennedy Drive, Coretta Way, Westbrook Lane, Malcom Lane, and Medgar Lane. We had a verbal agreement with the County that when the water system is installed they would pave the roads without assessment. Everyone was encouraged to call C. B. Kinnison, County Manager, if the roads get bad; he would have someone come out and grade the streets.

The Farmers Home Administration was involved in home improvement in Black Springs, or the building of a new house; this is in effect at present.

The tutoring program was moving along nicely; we now had about 25 tutors from the University and the high schools tutoring on a one-to-one basis in homes in Black Springs.

Mr. Benson said he would head a Clean-Up Committee if a petition were passed around. "In regard to clean-up, we need to get down to business. Unfortunately, people will be cited, but they all have been warned before. We cannot move into a white neighborhood, but that doesn't give us the right to mess this one up. Anyone can move here. The District Attorney's office will not fine people out here because they don't have the money, -- does a policeman ask you if you have the money when he gives you a ticket?

There are many inadequacies out here in Black Springs, and it is the obligation of each citizen to become involved. We are grateful for the things we have received, but realize that progress is needed, and we will not be satisfied by the "great white father's bone he has thrown us."

Let's make it a better year in 1970 . . . "Amen, right on . . ."

We are all appreciative of all the work Helen has done as Outreach worker—the children's thing, the park, etc.—Andy, too. We are disturbed that Helen was pulled out of Black Springs.

Mrs. Dorothy Pearson and Reverend Hill are the Democratic Representatives from out here. We all need to go to the polls—voting power." The meeting was adjourned.

CHRONOLOGY OF THE 1970'S

From the notes of Andy Gordon (VISTA) dated **March 1970**, several adults within the community approached him and Helen Westbrook in mid October 1969 "expressing their concern in their children's studies." By the 6th of November 1969 an informal Black Springs Tutoring Orientation was held at Black Springs First Baptist Church. Andy was able to get 41 interested volunteer tutors from UNR. And an informal meeting was hosted at Jot Travis Student Union at UNR on 24th November 1969 for the tutors.

Helen Westbrook sent a letter **March 5, 1970**, to Senator Howard S. Cannon asking for support in a connecting frontage road. She said, "John Bowden, Nevada State Highway Department, stated that there is enough State Land joining the highway and Black Springs to have a Frontage Road. It was suggested that the Improvement Club get help from the Federal Government."

A correspondence dated **March 11, 1970** from Senator Cannon read, "I am concerned that your discussion with John Bawden may have misled you regarding the Federal Governments activities in this area. Actually, the State of Nevada is the proper contact for this request. In an effort to clarify this matter, I am contacting Mr. Bawden to see what he had in mind when he spoke to you." He concluded with, "I am hopeful we can straighten this matter out so that the citizens of Black Springs will get their frontage road."

The community continued to maintain compliance to the bureaucratic processes while remaining uncompromised in achieving their goals. Also, dated **March 11, 1970** correspondence from H. K. Brown, Clerk of the Board of County Commissioners stated, "Upon motion by Commissioner Sauer, seconded by Commissioner McKenzie, which motion duly carried, it was ordered that the Black Springs Civic Improvement Corporation be assisted in the development of their water system according to the County Manager's memo and that the agency status of the County be reduced in writing in the form of an agreement."

On **March 16, 1970** Helen Westbrook (Outreach Worker), and Ollie Westbrook (Pres. B.S.C.I.C.) documented and distributed the community's accomplishments but went on to say, "It has been a long, hard,

A CRY FOR HELP

frustrating struggle, and although we have come a long way, we have much further to go." He concluded with, "Alone, we cannot accomplish all of this. But with your help and that of the total community, we can reach our goals. We appeal to you to join us in our effort to build a better community."

Andy (VISTA) sent a follow-up letter to the Symons Mfg. Company ***March 23, 1970***. He and Mr. Lobster (Black Springs Fire Chief) spoke with them on March 13th about the possibility of the manufacturing company loaning them concrete forming material for stem walls.

The letter informed them that, "At present we have been given a house and garage by the Nevada State Highway Department, to be converted to a community center and fire truck shelter (we've been given a fire truck by the Nevada State Forestry Division with the stipulation of providing adequate housing for the truck). Both structures will be situated on park land that was dedicated to Washoe County. The County will have title of the Community Center and has agreed to pay insurance and utility expenses. The multipurpose Community Center will be used for a library (we already have over 300 books), tutoring center (where supplies and reference material will be kept), athletic and recreation equipment storage for the adjacent park, meeting hall, etc."

He went on requesting, "Therefore we, Black Springs Civic Improvement Corporation, a non-profit corporation filed in the State of Nevada, are asking if you could loan to us enough forms for the stem walls of the Community Center and the fire truck shelter so we may complete the foundations prior to the lowering of the buildings."

This of course, was spearheaded by the youth group P.O.W.E.R. They received their Bill of Sale for one frame residence and one frame garage from the State of Nevada on ***April 3, 1970***.

By ***April 10, 1970*** the plumbing and electrical were done and the foundation was almost completed. Upon completion the County Parks Dept. would install trees, shrubs and turf; they also donated a BBQ grill. Sierra Pacific Power Company would install lights and the Bureau of Land Management would donate trees. Neighbors, such as

CHRONOLOGY OF THE 1970'S

Philip Osbourne, donated bricks from his yard towards constructing the foundation to the Center as well as the fire house that the residents were planning to build themselves.

On the evening of *April 10, 1970* Mr. Benson, Chairman of Community Beautification said, "People up town say their hands are tied, and in other words they don't care about you." The minutes went on to say, "Mr. Benson will try something else next week, something up his sleeves. Commissioners said that Black Springs' people are satisfied and if we don't stand up and express our feelings and our needs, they will not, know nothing else. That we are people and have feelings and want things better they will know nothing else. If we could start circulating people power in Raleigh Heights, Lemmon Valley, Golden Valley, Horizon Hills, etc. Northern Nevada. If you have the backing of the people you can get action—organized support. TV only takes pictures of the bad places not the good places."

In a letter to Mrs. Westbrook dated *April 25, 1970* from J. E. Sweatt owner of Eugene St. Water Co., he stated, "...I am agreeable to furnish water, without charge for beautification of the Recreation Park....

Furthermore, disregarding my subsequent letter as to contributing water for the community building which is in the process of completing, in light of the splendid work which you and other members of your Black Springs Improvement Association are doing for the children of Black Springs, for recreation; and also of course adults particularly as to the community building, in the way of recreation and advancement of the community, I also will contribute water for said community without charge. I am sure that facilities of the Park and building will provide welcome to all providing of course such privileges are not abused; to all, regardless of race color or creed. I will appreciate invitations to special events that may be held in the Park, and attending community building, that may occur from time to time."

The same evening there was a news article in the Reno Gazette regarding the residents deciding to build their own fire house. A church, Faith Temple had burnt down and this was the 10th building, 9 of those

A CRY FOR HELP

being homes, because there was no fire department within or close to the community. All the residents had were their water hoses from their yards with very low water pressure. This is how the news article depicted the Black Springs situation. "In 10 years they've watched 10 homes burn in their depressed low-income area."

There's that reactive description of our neighborhood. We weren't depressed, we were determined. We were tired of "no" and couldn't just sit by and watch any longer. Every fire building the county or anyone else offered was never up to county and city standards. They wanted to give us "depressed" buildings to go with our so called "depressed" neighborhood.

As the article states, the Nevada Highway Department has since given several houses to Black Springs, but Westbrook says none of them were suitable for a fire house. He said, "They're small and made of wood. We just had to build one that would do the job. Black Springs could eventually be a ghetto, but right now it's a pioneer area. People have a pioneer spirit. They're trying to take the raw land and develop it."

The Black Springs residents formed a special committee for Fire Prevention. They made arrangements to lease land from Washoe County for a new firehouse. The residents collected bricks, boards, and steel and money donations. They already had the talent, they just needed materials.

"We just can't sit by and watch our houses burn. Last year a family was left only with the clothes on their backs. We have to do something," Westbrook said.

Yvonne Micheli, a university coed also helped in getting donations. She was quoted saying, "The people themselves are involved in this, and that's what's important. People always say 'why don't they do it themselves?' Well, they are." She said Black Springs has already received contributions from Helms Construction, contractors Capriotti—Lemon, and Walker Boudwin construction. "The problem in Black Springs is that many of the homes have no foundation. If they have a fire, the entire house goes up quickly," Miss Micheli said.

CHRONOLOGY OF THE 1970'S

Senator Howard Cannon, not letting the Black Springs frontage road concerns rest on his desk, responded to Helen Westbrook on *April 17, 1970*. He said, "The first step must come from the State Highway Department in drawing up and submitting plans for the access road. The plan must then be approved by the Federal Bureau of Public Roads for design and funding. Until the State takes the first step in this matter, the Federal Government cannot act."

Well, I guess we know the procedure. To date, no one takes responsibility for this well outdated problem.

Portals of opportunity began opening for Black Springs. Helen Westbrook was now employed by the Economic Opportunity Board of Washoe County (EOB). This eliminated any suspicion of nepotism concerning the B.S.C.I.C. With a completion date of 1st June 1970 for the multiple purpose center a letter dated *May 19, 1970* was received by Ollie Westbrook from Mike Alcamo, Director of EOB.

Headstart, for the past five months had been looking for a facility in the region to serve Black Springs, Lemmon Valley, and Stead. Mike Alcamo was asking if the community was interested in allowing Headstart to use the facility which would be operated under federal and county guide lines. No need to elaborate, it was done.

J. E. Sweatt, owner of Eugene Street Water Company, sent a letter to all water customers in Black Springs on *May 26, 1970*. The letter stated "that effective June 1, 1970, there would be an increase in their water bill." He broke down the operating expenses and it was quite evident that the expenses exceeded the income. After all, each resident had only been paying $5.00 per month since 1955 and the Water Company was carrying delinquent accounts. The residents didn't complain but complied. The new monthly fee was $6.50.

At a training session Helen Westbrook must have presented a challenge to Dr. Elmer Rusco which prompted a correspondence from the Commission on Equal Rights of Citizens dated *June 2, 1970*.

A CRY FOR HELP

In brief it stated, "I understand that at a recent training session, Elmer R. Rusco of the University of Nevada was asked to spend one month, August, living in Black Springs exactly as the disadvantaged community does, and subsisting on the same income and Commodity Food allocation to be paid by the County. As an interested black, I feel that before such a project gets going, certain questions should be asked and answered..."

Victor A. Morton, Assistant Secretary of Commission on Equal Rights of Citizens went on to say, "We, as black people, have been surveyed and researched to no end. There are already many documents, figures, tabulations, etc., relative to the problems of the poor and disadvantaged, hard core, ethnic communities. However, those who make such researches and surveys have yet to come up with a positive solution to the many problems confronting the nation's impoverished individuals."

In conclusion he said, "Therefore, I state that if Rusco feels that by living in Black Springs for one month, he can come up with immediate solutions, then I will certainly wholeheartedly support such a project with no reservations. Until I am convinced of that result, however, I will continue to object to this project in every way I can." Mr. Morton had very valid questions which more than likely curtailed the project.

A very encouraging letter was sent **June 3, 1970** to George Oshima, Washoe County Public Works Director from the Regional Planning Commission of Reno, Sparks and Washoe County. Richard J. Allen the Director of Planning, in regards to the water system for Black Springs, wrote, "The Planning Commission has found that this proposal is not in conflict with any plans, and encourages expeditious approval of the project."

Charles R. Zeh, VISTA Volunteer Attorney on **June 23, 1970** sent a letter to Mr. John R. Barber, Chief, Rulings Section Exempt Organizations Branch Internal Revenue, submitting further reference to the application of the Black Springs Civic Improvement Corporation pursuant to I.R.S. 501 (c) (3). He stated, "While traveling through Black Springs, one also learns of the substandard housing situation in the

CHRONOLOGY OF THE 1970'S

Community. Many houses are old and in a state of disrepair. Others never were properly constructed. In general, however, such conditions do not exist by choice. Rather, it is fair to assert that these conditions prevail because private lines of credit normally expected to provide funds for home improvement loans or construction of suitable new dwellings have been foreclosed. Private investors have avoided the area, in part, because their equity would be exposed to a substantial risk of loss due to inadequate fire protection. The Federal Housing Administration refused to insure loans for home construction on these grounds. In an area such as Black Springs, the absence of Federal Housing Administration assistance obviously is a damaging factor when seeking private financial assistance. Thus, members of the community, foreclosed from the traditional, private sources of financial assistance, have been compelled to resort to the largesse of the Federal Government for assistance. Even here the response has not been satisfactory."

Mr. Zeh went on to say, "Finally, it must be noted that the community of Black Springs was predominantly settled by Blacks. These people established their community because they were unable to find housing in the major metropolitan center in the area in which Black Springs is located due to overt racial discrimination. The living conditions in Black Springs are a manifestation of this prejudice and discrimination. It is these substandard living conditions which the people through the Corporation intend to eliminate. Consequently, in this manner the Corporation is also dedicated to the elimination of the conditions of poverty, of prejudice and of discrimination."

A letter compiled *June 30, 1970* by Jeff Townsell, Secretary of B.S.C.I.C on behalf of Ollie Westbrook, Chairman of B.S.C.I.C. to Mr. Harry K. Brown, County Clerk Washoe County Courthouse it read, "Due to the agreement from the County Commissioner last year to pave the streets in Black Springs and install the lights in the park, we would like to be on the July 6th agenda to discuss this. There is a request to repair the lower end of the Basketball Court where water stands on the south side."

And regarding the Community's name the letter said, "Due to the near completion of the Community House and the Fire House, we

A CRY FOR HELP

have taken time to discuss the name of the park. Originally, this particular area was called the Grand View Terrace, and if it meets with your approval we think Grand View Park would be the right name for it."

Ollie Westbrook, President of B.S.C.I.C. sent a letter to Mr. Howard Gloyd, Director of E.O.B. *July 8, 1970* requesting additional funding. "The community of Black Springs is making a commendable effort toward finishing a building in this area. This building will house a multi-purpose use for our many young people and their activities, Example: a Head Start School for the pre-school age children, tutorial program for the slow learners that are in school and many other constructive activities for all of Copperfield. However, in our request to complete this building we are asking your help in the amount of three hundred dollars to purchase additional material."

Now, it appears bureaucracy is designed to oppress. Charles Zeh's (VISTA Attorney), earlier correspondence must have ruffled feathers at the IRS. On *July 10, 1970* he wrote to Mr. John R. Barber, Chief, and Rulings Section Exempt Organization Branch IRS.

"Dear Mr. Barber: This is in further reference to my letter to your office of June 23, 1970, answering the questions set forth in a letter from the service dated December 5, 1969. Specifically, this letter is addressed to questions one and two of that letter. As the enclosed material from the Washoe County Assessor's Office indicates, it is an error to attach any legal significance to the fact that certain portions of the community of Black Springs, Nevada are also known as the J. E. Sweatt subdivision. This expression is simply a colloquialism referring to parcels of land located within Black Springs which were previously owned by Mr. J. E. Sweatt of Reno, Nevada. However, this land is presently owned by purchasers from Mr. Sweatt or his successors in interest so that today, Mr. Sweatt no longer holds title to any of the parcels of land comprising the portion of Black Springs locally referred to as the J. E. Sweatt subdivision. In other words, the J. E. Sweatt subdivision is simply the name of a neighborhood in Black Springs."

This particular document seems to depict a systematic process of oppression. Charles Zeh went on to say, "In addition, previous

CHRONOLOGY OF THE 1970'S

correspondence with your office has indicated that pursuant to 42 U.S.C. 3101 et. seq., the people of Black Springs is seeking federal assistance from the Department of Housing and Urban Development to develop a basic water facility. H.U.D. will supply ninety per cent (90%) of the developmental costs of such a project if the community meets certain criteria. One of these is that the …rate of unemployment [in the community] is, and has been continuously for the preceding calendar year, one hundred per cent (100%) above the national average. H.U.D. has indicated that Black Springs is a poverty area as defined by the terms of the statute thereby qualifying for a ninety per cent (90%) H.U.D. grant in this respect. Thus, it can be said that two separate evaluations of the community have arrived at the conclusion that Black Springs is a low-income or poverty area."

Even though justification and clarifications were previously submitted, the I.R.S. still wanted more. Charles Zeh continued, "Finally, an additional comment by way of clarification or qualification relating to material supplied to the service in my letter and memo of June 23, 1970, must be made. Specifically, this is in reference to the Black springs Community Center building, the land on which it is located, the Black Springs Community Park and the land were the volunteer fire department fire hall is located."

He went on to say, "Although the Black Springs Civic Improvement Corporation was directly responsible for the organization and development of each of these enterprises, title to the land sites for these activities is in Washoe County. Also, the County owns the building in which the Black Springs Community Center is housed. The Community has the use of the land and building without charge and the title to the land is contingent upon its continued use for playground, park and community center purposes."

He ended saying, "Unless your office desires further information regarding the Black Springs Civic Improvement Corporation, and its activities, this completes the Corporation's request for an exemption from the payment of Federal Income Taxes."

According to a document titled "BLACK SPRINGS PROPOSAL" dated *July 23, 1970* B.S.C.I.C.'s primary goal was, "…to equip

A CRY FOR HELP

the Community Center and the Work Shop. The Community Center will serve as a meeting place, library, tutoring room, Head Start Day Care, recreation, food and clothing distribution, and information center. The workshop will serve as a training facility to train those persons who are interested in developing different types of skills of their choice."

The document also stated, "We are now preparing a proposal to submit to HUD for $126,000 for improvement of water system. Future plans include individual FHA loans for home improvement, improved street lighting, and this week we intend to approach the County Commissioners again for street pavement and park lights."

The same day, *July 23rd*, Charles Zeh (VISTA Volunteer Attorney) wrote to Paul A. Bible, Esq. He noted, "Since time is of the essence in this matter, I decided to enclose a copy of the rough draft of the brochure which will be used to solicit the private funds necessary to complete construction of the Black Springs water facility. I trust that it is readable and adequate for your purposes. Of course, if either you or the Senator desires a copy of the final draft, copies will be forwarded to you when completed. As I related to you in our conversation yesterday, the Black Springs project has been pending for nearly two years. Now, just when plans are nearing completion another road block threatens the development of the project."

Charles Zeh met the road block by saying, "The water system is a program being developed pursuant to the Housing and Urban Development Act of 1965, 42. U.S.C. Sections 3101 – ET. Esq. The authorizing statute specifies that the applicant body be a governmental entity such as a County Board or a City Council. However, after discussions with legal council for the Department of Housing and Urban Development (hereinafter referred to as H.U.D.) in San Francisco, they agree that the Act says nothing regarding the continued ownership of the system by an applicant body once construction of the facility is completed. In other words, the consensus of opinion is that the Act does not prohibit the applicant body from transferring its interest in the facility to a nongovernmental body has the capability of maintaining and operating a facility. This, in fact, is the approach upon which development of the Black Springs facility has been preceding. Washoe County has agreed to become the applicant body for the facility and to oversee construction of the project. The County has also been extremely cooperative and helpful in providing technical assistance throughout the planning stages of development. However, for reasons of their own, the County is unwilling to actively engage in the business of owning and operating the water system. Whether or not the County should be in the water system business is an open question. However, the upshot of the County's position is an insistence at the present time that it be allowed to divest itself of any ownership interest in the facility once construction is completed. It is only upon this basis that the County will precede with the application. Unfortunately, during discussions with legal council from H.U.D., I was informed that present H.U.D. policies preclude any transfer of the applicant body's ownership interest to a non-governmental body. Because of the respective positions taken by the County and H.U.D., development of the water facility is at an impasse. Consequently, the community of Black Springs must continue to contend with an inadequate water facility and the living conditions associated with such a system."

He stressed the argument further saying, "However, as previously indicated, discussions with council for H.U.D. brought out the point that the authorizing statutes does not deal specifically with the instant situation. It was the consensus of the meeting, therefore, that the present H.U.D. policy in this regard is an administrative ruling rather than a policy dictated by the Statute. It follows, then, that since we are dealing with an administrative ruling rather than with a requirement of the Statute, conceivably this administrative policy might be waived in the present case. Thus, there is this ray of hope if the H.U.D. administration can be convinced of the desirability of the project."

Now, Charles Zeh was not oblivious to Black Springs' plight and the documents show how he championed for basic needs and human rights. He went on saying, "We are presently channeling our efforts in this direction. In this regard our office has requested the assistance of Senator Cannon. His staff expressed a strong interest in this project and informed us that they would attempt to deal with the problem through Mr. George Romney, Secretary of the Department of Housing and Urban Development. Our office was informed by the people from H.U.D. that Mr. Samuel Jackson, Assistant Secretary for Metropolitan Planning and

Development is directly responsible for projects of this nature. Thus, it seems that any information placed before Mr. Jackson regarding the Black Springs project would also be helpful in our efforts to convince H.U.D. to waive its present policy with respect to the Black Springs water facility."

In conclusion Charles Zeh wrote, "There is no question that an adequate water system is needed in the Black Springs community. Therefore, we wish to inform the Senator of this need and of the proposed system. In this regard, we respectfully request of him any assistance he might wish to provide which would enhance the development of the facility. If either you or the Senator desires any further information, or if there are any questions concerning the information already provided, please contact our office. In fact, if arrangements can be made, a meeting or phone conversation with the Senator would be most useful. Speaking for the people of Black Springs, I express appreciation for your assistance in this regard."

The Reno Evening Gazette *July 27, 1970* reported, 'More law enforcement asked for Black Springs.' Due to the lack of enforcement, several Black Springs residents asked the Washoe County Commission to enforce the law. They cited several instances of violation of county ordinances. Leo Sauer, Commission Vice-Chair said, the commission would refer the complaints to "the proper agency."

In the same article Thurman Carthen Jr., President of POWER (People Organized to Work for Equal Recognition), asked the commission to name the park in Black Springs "after a Black leader." The three names suggested were Hiram Huey, the Martin Luther King Memorial Park, and Eldridge Cleaver. The commission said it would consider the names at a later date. Carthen then asked the commission why the Black Springs' park was not included in the general parks budget. Les Russell, Parks Director, said there was a capital outlay this year for Black Springs and Lemmon Valley. "We expect to be in Black Springs shortly, to provide landscaping for the park," Russell said. "We can't do too much until a water system is available," he said. That seems to be the excuse for all improvements 'the water.'

CHRONOLOGY OF THE 1970'S

From the following document dated *August 1, 1970* it shows the community was diverse but inequality was being recognized. In bold print it said, "TO THE COUNTY COMMISSIONERS, and to WHOM EVER ELSE IT MAY CONCERN: WE THE RESIDENTS OF BLACK SPRINGS, DO STRONGLY OBJECT TO HOUSE TRAILERS BEING MOVED INTO OUR RESIDENTAL AREA. SOME OF US HAVE PUT IN FOR LOANS FROM F.H.A. (FARMERS HOME ADMINISTRATION) TO BUILD NEW HOMES, AND WE DON'T WANT HOUSE TRAILERS SITTING IN THE CENTER OF OUR NEW HOMES. A FEW YEARS AGO THE COUNTY PASSED A LAW TO DESIGNATE CERTAIN AREAS FOR TRAILERS. MOST OF THE PEOPLE IN BLACK SPRINGS LIVING IN TRAILERS HAD TO MOVE THEM OUT, AND WE DON'T WANT ANY MORE TRAILERS IN OUR AREA."

The letter continued by asking the County Commissioners some challenging questions. "IS IT BECAUSE THE MAN IN QUESTION IS WHITE? AND THE OTHER PEOPLE WAS BLACK? ARE THE LAWS DIFFERENT FOR WHITES THAN THEY ARE FOR BLACKS? IF SO PLEASE SEND US A COPY OF THE ONE FOR THE WHITES, AND THE ONE FOR THE BLACKS. ALSO WE HAVE NOT SEEN WHERE ANY CITATIONS HAVE BEEN ISSUED ON OUR CLEAN UP CAMPAIGN. AND YOU MUST KNOW THAT SOME SHOULD BE ISSUED, OR HAVE YOU BOTHERED TO LOOK? AND PLEASE, IF THERE BE ANY ZONE CHANGES IN BLACK SPRINGS IN THE FUTURE WE DEMAND THAT EACH RESIDENT KNOW ABOUT IT. OR ARE THE BLACKS ALLOWED TO KNOW WHAT GOES ON IN THE AREA? WE HOPE WE ARE NOT EXPECTING TOO MUCH TO EXPECT TO HEAR FROM YOU IN THE NEAR FUTURE. THANKING YOU IN ADVANCE, AND WE DO HOPE WE HAVE SOME THING IN THE FUTURE TO THANK YOU FOR." It was submitted by the "B.S.C.I.C.; CHAIRMAN OLLIE WESTBROOK, SEC. JEFF TOWNSELL, FIRE CHIEF WILLIAM LOBSTER, ASSITANT FIRE CHIEF AL WILLIAMS; TRUSTEE BOARD; AL WILLIAMS, HONEY WILLIAMS, HELEN WESTBROOK, CARRIE TOWNSELL, JOHNNIE LOBSTER, DOROTHY PEARSON, and A. D. PEARSON". They also sent a copy to the County Manager and the County Bldg. & Health Insp. Att. General.

A CRY FOR HELP

It's evident the sixties had empowered the citizens of Black Springs. Their letter prompted immediate action from the Board of County Commissioners and Washoe County Manager.

On *August 4, 1970* a memo from Gene Clock, RPHS, Acting Division Director (City-County District Health Department Division of Environmental Health) to Mr. C. B. Kinnison, Washoe County Manager regarding his inquiry about Mr. Albert Williams. "I have not first hand knowledge of the problem." Gene Clock, Acting Division Director was referring to an incident four years prior. He went on to say, "About three months ago, Mr. Williams requested a permit for a repair of an existing septic system. He was shown every courtesy and the repairs were approved by this division."

It's amazing how nothing slowed the community down. The B.S.C.I.C. as well as the youth P.O.W.E.R. was constantly active building and enhancing the quality of life within their community. P.O.W.E.R. sent to Gene Sullivan, Director of Parks and Recreation, on *August 4, 1970* a list of items needed for the Little League Baseball Team in Black Springs. Thurman Carthen Jr., President of P.O.W.E.R. and support from community leaders like Fire Chief William Lobster kept the youth active and vibrant.

A letter dated *August 6, 1970* sent to the Board of County Commissioners of Washoe County from William J. Raggio, District Attorney Washoe County signed by: Gene Barbagelata Chief Civil Deputy, "As requested to do, I have reviewed the work assignments regarding alleged zoning violations in the Black Springs area and I enclose copies of letters received from the Regional Planning Commission indicating that the listed alleged violations were all corrected." He went on to inform them the official files could be reviewed at his office. These letters proved all violations were corrected by June 16, 1970. A copy of the letter and supporting documents was forwarded to H. K. Brown, Washoe County Clerk and C. B. Kinnison, County Manager."

The same day, *August 6th*, the Reno Evening Gazette reported, "Black Springs' owners obey county orders to clean up." The article said, "Black Springs' residents, ordered by the Washoe County Commission to

CHRONOLOGY OF THE 1970'S

clean up their property, have done so, Gene Barbagelata, Deputy District Attorney, said today. In June, approximately 20 residents were given two weeks to remove accumulated debris. But there is still a problem elsewhere in the settlement, Commissioner Joe Coppa said Wednesday. He and Commissioner J. C. McKenzie toured Black Springs June 27 and said they found junk autos and refrigerators – some with doors attached – on some properties. Residents with further debris complaints should call the Regional Planning Commission, Barbagelata said. The Planning commission investigates and if the property is determined to be in violation of anti-debris laws, the complaint is referred to the county commission, which can either issue a citation or give the property owner two weeks to clean it. If the owner does not comply, the district attorney's office automatically issues a citation, Barbagelata said."

In the same evening paper under 'Park recommendations' it read, "The commission approved recommendations of the Washoe County Fair and Recreation Board to name a Black Springs park Martin Luther King Memorial Park and the purchase of a bulldozer and equipment storage van."

In a letter from the Office of the Washoe County Clerk, dated **August 7, 1970** H. K. Brown, County Clerk certified that the following order was made at a regular meeting of the Board.

"On recommendation by the Park Commission, on motion by Commissioner Coppa, seconded by Commissioner Sauer, which motion duly carried, it was ordered that the newly constructed park in Black Springs (see Item 70-835) be named Martin Luther King Memorial Park."

This was quite an astounding accomplishment. Martin Luther King Memorial Park located in Black Springs on Coretta Way. Yes, Black Springs was dreaming of equality.

According to a news article on **August 17, 1970** the residents of Black Springs addressed the Washoe County commissioners again. D. C. Benson of Black Springs asked, "Is it against the law for people to have open septic tanks in the county?"

A CRY FOR HELP

"Yes, it is," replied Jack Cunningham, commission chairman.

Benson responded, "Then if it is, I have four of them around the house."

Benson, along with eight other Black Springs residents, asked the county to take action to improve their neighborhood. Benson went on to say, he had been trying to improve the neighborhood for five years. He stated further, "Whenever I try to get the county to do something, they tell me their hands are tied."

The County Manager C. B Kinnison said, "You are going to get a lot of help from us. Some people have suggested we handle the problem a little easy, but if it takes enforcement of the law we are very willing to handle it."

William Lobster, another Black Springs resident, asked the commission to pave the roads in Black Springs before installing a water system.

"To build a street then tear it up for a water system is not good business," Kinnison said. Lobster said he would be willing to pay the road assessment to install the water system if the road could be paved as soon as possible. "We have been going through channels and have come up with nothing," Lobster said. Then he invited county commissioners "to spend a week in Black Springs and drink some of our terrible sandy water and see what you think about it."

On *August 18, 1970* a news article reported again that sanitation laws were being broken by some residents. "You are getting bored with Black Springs' people and we are getting bored coming here," Ollie Westbrook of the Black Springs Civic Improvement Corporation told the Washoe County Commissioners. The residents told commissioners about open septic tanks and the lack of an inadequate water system and asking for more law enforcement regarding this. Westbrook stated and asked, "The law enforcement doesn't allow other people to get away with it, so why do you let us get away with it?"

CHRONOLOGY OF THE 1970'S

D. C. Benson, another Black Springs resident, told the commission there were four open septic tanks in his neighborhood. When a health officer, who acknowledged being employed by the county for "only" three months, visited Black Springs, he said his hands were tied and could do nothing.

Jack Cunningham, Commission Chairman said, "My hands are not tied" promised an investigation and "strict" enforcement of district sanitation laws.

Now, on a proposed water system for Black Springs, residents have asked the county to apply to the U.S. Department of Housing and Urban Development (HUD) for a loan.

Gene Barbagelata, Deputy District Attorney, said the county could take two approaches to getting money for the water system. The first is to apply for funds, then hold the title to the water company and lease it to Black Springs' residents. The second is to apply for funds and develop the area as a general improvement district for water only. HUD policy is to loan money to projects sponsored by governments only and not private projects."

Everything again was contingent upon an adequate water system. No one wanted to nor would they help to improve the conditions of Black Springs because of the inadequate water system. Keep in mind this is 1970 and the residents are still seeking assistance in obtaining an adequate water system. Yet it seems that helping in acquiring a basic necessity for human existence is not the local government's concern.

"Black Springs advised of water district merit", was the headline of a Gazette Journal article on *August 25, 1970*. "Good water for Black Springs?" is how the article started. The answer, "It's possible", County Manager C. B. Kinnison told the Washoe County Commission.

Kinnison suggested that the commission apply to the federal government to designate Black Springs a "general improvement district" for water development. He recommended Black Springs residents petition the commission to set up the water district.

A CRY FOR HELP

On *August 27, 1970* a certified letter was released in regards to the August 25th regular meeting of the Board. "A communication was received from the Department of Housing and Urban Development (H.U.D.) regarding financing of a water system for Black Springs, advising that the proposal to turn over the project after completion of construction to the Black Springs Civic Improvement Corporation is not acceptable; that this procedure would violate the Federal Legislation which provides that grants are to be made only to 'public bodies'", the correspondence read.

Now the B.S.C.I.C. might have been a little disgruntled by the part "not acceptable." But the letter went on to say, "After considerable discussion, on motion by Commissioner Sauer, seconded by Commission McKenzie, it was ordered that Washoe County proceed to make application to H.U.D. for the water system for Black Springs and, if approved, Washoe County actually install the water system only after the property owners in Black Springs have legally petitioned the Board of County Commissioners requesting that a water district be created and that they are willing to assume responsibility for the district; that an election then be held in Black Springs to determine whether or not the property owners are desirous of the proposed water system. It was further ordered that the District Attorney's office prepare the necessary petition forms to be circulated in Black Springs, for the formation of such District."

Charles Zeh, VISTA Attorney, decide to expedite matters by sending a copy of a resolution of the Washoe County Commissioners on *September 4, 1970* to H.U.D., responding to the notice from H.U.D. advising the County that the proposal to transfer the Black Springs water facility, to a non-governmental body, fails to comply with HUD legislative restrictions. As the resolution indicates, the Commissioner's have reacted favorably, as well noted above.

This particular letter dated *October 7, 1970* to Mr. Calvin Lew, Director Program Field Services Division H.U.D., was noting good news:

"The letter from your office of September 18, 1970 was most encouraging. For the first time since the commencement of the project,

CHRONOLOGY OF THE 1970'S

all of the parties seem in agreement regarding the method of proceeding with the development of the proposed system. Perhaps our efforts have begun to show results." Charles Zeh went on to say, "With regard to the realignment of H.U.D., Mr. Harriman Thatcher was in Reno, yesterday, and we conversed on the phone regarding the Black Springs water system. Also, I have sent to Mr. James Price, Director of the H.U.D. Area Office, a letter introducing myself and informing him of the most recent developments concerning the system."

Charles' letter concluded with, "Finally, please be assured that the news that you will no longer be directly involved with the project was extremely disappointing. I am most appreciative of the efforts you have extended in our behalf. You have been most helpful to me, personally, and I extend sincere thanks for your assistance."

The Black Springs Outreach Council held a special meeting **October 8, 1970**. Ollie Westbrook, Chairman called the meeting to order at 7:50pm. And the purpose was explained. Mr. Lobster had asked their legal aid attorney Chuck Zeh, a few questions on what the Legal Aid could do. And why they couldn't handle criminal cases. His answers, Charles Zeh's, were more or less based on present rules and regulations. Mr. Lobster's main question was, 'What does Black Springs need? Water, Sewer, Streets; how can EOB help?' "These three items were bugging the people of Black Springs more than anything else," Lobster said.

Chuck Zeh stated, "That without a proper water system, we could not acquire F.H.A. loans." He went on explaining the progression of the water system stating, "That there is a possibility of getting a $150,000 water system free. We would have to organize the community and be able to take over the system after obtaining it. The matching funds will be solicited from the Fleishman Foundation." Mr. Westbrook said, "No boundaries had been set at this present time. This would be up to the entire community."

Mr. Zeh went on to advise them that Black Springs' whole future more or less depends on a proper water system. "We would have to form a General Improvement District with five officers elected by the people of Black Springs. These people could be elected on a year to year basis or what ever the community wanted. This G.I.D. could also obtain Federal money for our present community center."

Mr. Westbrook stated, "Zoning should be changed." He asked the people present to give this proposal some serious thought.

Mr. Lobster pointed out, "Our present zoning code is A-1." He explained that, "someone could have the zone changed to industrial without our knowledge. And if this should happen and your house would burn 50%, you could not rebuild." He ended supporting Mr. Westbrook saying, "This is why our present zoning should be looked into."

That evening there were multiple proposals, which you can research, and the meeting was adjourned two hours later at 9:50pm. Mr. Jeff Townsell, being the acting secretary, recorded very detailed notes.

A letter from Charles Zeh, to the Director of Area Office H.U.D, J. Price, dated **October 12, 1970** basically stated that the residents of Black Springs were ready to proceed with ownership and responsibility for the operation and maintenance of the proposed water system. Where the residents were lacking in governing a water district, they were more than willing to learn which resulted in great accomplishments.

On **October 26, 1970** Charles Zeh sent a correspondence to H.U.D. regarding the application. He explained, "The application submitted by Washoe County to the Department of Housing and Urban Development requesting funds to develop the proposed Black Springs water facility is based upon a construction cost analysis completed last March of this year. A recent conversation with Brien Walters, the engineer who designed the proposed facility, confirmed my suspicions that due to the length of time that has transpired since the study were completed, the ravages of inflation have taken their toll. Because of the substantial increase in prices, the application is no longer an accurate reflection of the total cost of construction and requires revision upwards. Consequently, the application submitted by Washoe County must be considered as tentative rather than the final request for assistance." Mr. Zeh did ask, "…will we be required to submit a new application?"

CHRONOLOGY OF THE 1970'S

He went on to say, "Since the relationship of the various figures in the application will remain the same, all that will be required to remedy the problem will be to revise these figures upward by a percentage increase. Hopefully, for the purposes of the application, simply supplementing the present application so that it will conform to the construction cost increase will be all that is required. In this regard, please advise." Mr. Zeh was always mindful in covering all areas which might hinder further the need for an adequate water system.

On *November 1, 1970* a meeting was called to order at 5:30 p.m. by Mr. Westbrook, Chairman of the Outreach Council. Mary Ross, the new VISTA worker, was presented to the members and she introduced the speaker of the day, Mr. Chuck Zeh, VISTA Attorney. Andy's time was up. He had moved on to further his education. But he never lost touch of his new family. To date, we are very much in touch.

Mr. Zeh's first question was, "Do we need a new water system in Black springs? Yes." He went on to explain how this could be done. He said, "The people of this area (J.E. SWEATT SUB-DIVISION) will have to form a Water District by a majority vote."

A question was asked, "Where will the money come from to install this water system ($150,000)?"

Mr. Zeh replied, "The Washoe County government has applied to H.U.D. a Federal Government Agency for a 90% grant. The other 10% will come from private donations. The Fleishman Foundation has expressed a great interest in this project. Now this Water District will consist of people living in Black Springs. The first five board members will be appointed by Washoe County. 51% of the people in Black Springs must be in favor of the Improvement District before it can be set up."

A follow up question was then asked. "Where will the water come from?"

Mr. Zeh informed them, "A new well will be drilled, all new pipe and a large storage tank." The meeting was adjourned at 6:30pm.

A CRY FOR HELP

A 2nd meeting of the Outreach Council was held *November 15, 1970*. Their subject was on the Water District. Susan Davis, a visitor from the E.O.B., announced a special meeting on Thursday, Nov. 19th, 6:00 pm at the center. The purpose of this meeting was to explain the E.O.B. program to the people.

Chuck Zeh, our VISTA Attorney suggested that we should do some door to door campaigning to promote this new water system. A special committee to do this campaigning would consist of the following people. Mr. Westbrook, Mrs. Francis Williams, Bill Lobster, Chuck Zeh, Mary Ross, Thurman Carthen, Jeff Townsell and Hosea Stevens, these people would be assigned to certain areas and given a list of names of people to contact. There would be an election held in Black Springs on Dec. 3, 1970. Time from 7:00 a.m. to 7:00 p.m.; place Black Springs Community Center. We would have a voting machine set up in the center. This election was to try and get 51% of people in Black Springs in favor of the new water system. A few other issues were consulted upon and the meeting was adjourned by Chairman Ollie Westbrook and Jeff Townsell was the acting secretary. After the community's perseverance, what resident would dare not to vote or not show up?

In the Reno Evening Gazette *December 2, 1970* it stated:

"Several Black Springs residents hope to build a community water system and they are soliciting community support." Ollie Westbrook of the Black Springs Improvement Association stated, "Registered voters in the settlement are asked to voice their preference about a proposed water system at a special 'Straw vote,' Dec. 10th. There is a great need for water out here. The wells are still flowing but there is a problem of distribution." Westbrook said the water supply in the settlement is now sandy and nearly unfit for consumption.

The article also said if the general improvement district is approved, the association hopes for a federal grant from H.U.D. The grant would be coupled with private donations for the $150,000 water system.

H. K. Brown, county clerk said the county would transport a voting machine to the Black Springs polling place and take care of printing

CHRONOLOGY OF THE 1970'S

the ballots at no cost to Black Springs' residents. He estimated the cost of such a service would be about $100, including three election workers.

On **December 10, 1970** the voting commenced. The entire community participated and the vote was unanimous. This was the ballot question on which a "straw vote" would be taken by the citizens in Black Springs: "Shall a general improvement district be established in the community of Black Springs?" The ballot explained that, "A 'YES' vote means that you favor the creation of a general improvement district in Black Springs. The primary purpose for organizing the district is to own and operate the proposed Black Springs Community Water System. It will cost around $150,000.00 to build the water system and it is expected that the cost of construction will be financed by the Federal government and private investors. In other words, the system will be built and NO COST at all to the PEOPLE OF BLACK SPRINGS. If the water system is built, average monthly water rates will be set at around $7.50 per household.

A 'NO' vote means that you oppose creating the district. If the district is not created, it will be almost impossible to build the new water system because the Federal money will most likely be unavailable."

The results ended with 60 property owners voting "YES" and one "NO"; in regards to non-property owners, 17 voted "YES" and none opposed. The combined total of ballots were 79 and number of votes tallied 78. According to documents apparently one person went into the booth but did not vote which shows a 1 vote discrepancy. The discrepancy really didn't matter, the community had achieved their goal.

What is puzzling, what resident would dare vote 'No' or show up and not vote at all. After all, this was regarding a basic necessity of "LIFE".

Charles Zeh, VISTA Attorney sent a letter to H. K. Brown, Member of the Board of County Commissioners informing the Board of Commissioners of the results of the election. "The election was a 'straw vote' on the issue in that holding such an election is not a step in the formal procedure required to be followed to organize and establish a

A CRY FOR HELP

general improvement district under Chapter 318. The election was held to apprise the commissioners of the sentiments of the community on the issue because it was felt that inasmuch as a general improvement district constitutes a form of self-government, the Commissioners would be ill-advised to organize the district unless and until the community and residents comprising the district favored its creation."

Mr. Zeh also in the same letter said, "Although a quasi-legal proceeding, the election was conducted under the auspices of Washoe County. The election booth and the election workers were provided by the County through the Washoe County Clerk's Office. Most important, the election result has been certified by the Clerk's Office as in any other formal election process."

It's amazing to see how those directly involved with developing this community kept in constant contact with one another, utilizing each others documents and correspondences.

"For a period of about four to six weeks prior to Election Day, an attempt was made to contact each eligible voter residing in Black Springs on the question of the improvement district. The effort was conducted under the guidance of the Black Springs Outreach Council", as Mr. Zeh continued. "The community was sectioned into precincts and Mr. Ollie Westbrook, Mr. Thurman Carthen, Mrs. Dale Reynolds, Mr. Jeff Townsell, Mr. Hosea Stevens, Mrs. Frances Williams and Mrs. Betsy Overfield volunteered to become precinct workers. Each was given the responsibility of personally contacting every eligible voter in the area comprising the precinct to which the worker was assigned. The workers responded enthusiastically and it was only with extreme difficulty that a resident of the area could have avoided hearing of the proposed development. Written material was used to inform the community of the proposed development. Several "flyers" (*which may be seen at Northern Nevada Historical Society*) detailing the improvement district's concept and all that the idea engenders were distributed to the residents of Black Springs. This effort was extended to all those who or whose spouse owned real property in Black Springs but resided elsewhere in the area. They, too, were afforded the opportunity of voting and being informed of the development of Black Springs. The traditional,

CHRONOLOGY OF THE 1970'S

'New England' town meeting was also utilized as a forum for discussion in the community concerning the improvement district concept. Clearly, every effort was made to insure that an informed electorate voted on the issue."

When the Reno Evening Gazette came out **December 16, 1970** there was an article 'County seeks solution to housing problem' Dutch Cook's name appeared. The article was regarding substandard housing and whether or not Washoe County has a responsibility to house people who are removed from substandard housing. The County cited four residents. The fourth was served on Dutch Cook "for an alleged accumulation of debris" on his property in Black Springs. "The commission gave Cook 30 days to clean up his property", the article said.

At a regular meeting of the Board of County Commissioners, Washoe County, Nevada **December 15, 1970** the following order was made: "A communication was received from Charles R. Zeh, Vista Volunteer Attorney, advising that an election was held in Black Springs to determine whether or not the residents of Black Springs are in favor of creating a water district; that of the 78 tax-pay electors who voted 77 voted in favor and 1 person voted against the proposition; election results have been filed with the County Clerk; that they are now requesting the Board to reaffirm and endorse a previous order of the Board (see Item 70-946) and commence formal action to organize and establish the general improvement district in Black Springs no later than January 15, 1971. Mr. Ollie Westbrook was present in support of the request."

Mr. H. K. Brown, County Clerk who certified the document sent to Charles Zeh **December 17, 1970** concluded with the following. "After some discussion, Mr. Westbrook was advised to have their Attorney, Mr. Charles R. Zeh, contact the District Attorney's office to determine the best procedure to follow for the creation of the district." The County Clerk also forwarded a copy to Mr. Westbrook.

Nine letters were sent out from Charles Zeh, VISTA Volunteer Attorney on **January 7, 1971**. This particular one to Mr. Thomas Little, Max C. Fleischmann Foundation read, "Dear Mr. Little: In reviewing the correspondence transmitted between your office and mine, I noticed

A CRY FOR HELP

that at one time, I foolishly indicated to you that the request for financial assistance from the Foundation to promote the development of the proposed Black Springs Community Water Facility would be on your desk sometime in June of 1970. Well, here it is a new year and nearly seven months later and the plans for the development of the facility are only now becoming finalized. The fact that it has taken this long to complete the plans to develop the system should not, it is hoped, detract from the urgency with which this request is submitted. Everyday the community and the people of Black Springs must live without an adequate basic community water facility, this request for assistance grows in importance." The letter concluded with, "Enclosed is the erstwhile prematurely promised request of the Foundation for financial assistance. I am certain that the proposal will receive the prompt and earnest consideration merited by the concepts it represents. If anything remains unclear or if additional information is desired, please advise."

The following letter was sent to Mr. Brien Walter, Walters, Ball, Hibdon & Shaw it said, "Enclosed is your copy of the application being submitted to the Fleischmann Foundation requesting the financial assistance necessary to complete development of the proposed Black Springs Community Water Facility. It took a while but the "basics" have finally been agreed upon making it possible to complete the application.

Of course, you have undoubtedly heard of my fantastic physical condition which explains why you astutely avoided me on the tennis courts this fall. But remember, a spring must follow and my tennis racket will be poised and ready.

Season's greetings and my best for the new year. Let's hope it will see the proposed development of the water system transformed into reality."

Now, this letter to James Price, Director of San Francisco Area Office Department of H.U.D. reads as followed, "Enclosed is the copy for your office of the application being submitted to the Fleishmann Foundation of Reno, Nevada, for the financial assistance necessary to complete development of the proposed Black Springs Community Water Facility. This request is being submitted to the Fleischmann Foundation

CHRONOLOGY OF THE 1970'S

to secure the capital necessary to insure compliance with the "matching fund" requirement of the Department of Housing and Urban Development Act of 1965, 42 U.S.C. §§3101 et. seq., the Community Basic Sewer and Water Facility Program.

Season's greeting and my best for the coming new year. Let's hope that the new year will see the proposed development transformed into a reality with H.U.D. assistance."

The preceding is three of the nine letters sent by Charles Zeh. None were copied to anyone. The Westbrooks were able to obtain the nine letters for their files. When the letters are read in their entirety they almost appear somewhat cryptic in nature.

Charles Zeh sent another letter to Mr. James Price, San Francisco Area Officer Department of HUD stating, "Since forwarding to the Max C. Fleischmann Foundation the request for the private financial assistance constituting the "matching fund" for the proposed Black Springs Community Water Facility, other correspondence with the Foundation through its representative and member of the Foundation's Board of Trustees, Mr. Thomas Little, has followed. Mr. Little informed me that the Trustees meet on a monthly basis to consider requests for assistance. The trustees met last Friday, January 15, 1971. Because of the length of the Black Springs request, Mr. Little surmised that the request would only be given a preliminary consideration at the Friday meeting with a final determination table until the next monthly meeting. I have not been informed that this was not the case. If substantive action on the merits was in fact taken, however, you will be notified immediately."

This letter ending with, "If anything else remains unattended to, please advise. Also, I have not received an acknowledgment from your office noting receipt of the Fleischmann Proposal. I am most interested to learn whether or not it ever reached your desk." This letter was copied to Ollie and Helen Westbrook, BSCIC also to George Oshima, County Public Works Commissioner. What's interesting is that Charles Zeh is asking Mr. James Price and Mr. Thomas Little for advice?

A CRY FOR HELP

A letter was sent to Senator Alan Bible from Charles Zeh on January 28, 1971, and a reply was sent to him on **February 5, 1971**. There is no document so the contents are unknown. Senator Bible wrote, "This will acknowledge your letter of January 28 received by me February 1, along with the proposal submitted to the Max C. Fleischmann Foundation requesting the private matching funds necessary to construct and install the proposed Black Springs Community Water Facility."

Building codes were being enforced which the community has always supported. According to Reno Gazette news article **February 19, 1971** a suit was filed by the Washoe County seeking a court order to demolish a building in Black Springs, claiming it a nuisance.

On **Jan. 15, 1971** the Washoe County Commission ordered the plaintiff to abate the nuisance, and a copy of the order was posted on the building, the article says. The building would be demolished and 'charge the defendant for costs.'

Reno Gazette reports **February 25, 1971** that the Washoe County Commission today created the Black Springs General Improvement District for improving the community's water system. The Commission February 16th, agreed to provide $15,000 for engineering test and well drilling in connection with the project. The Max C. Fleischmann Foundation of Nevada had approved a grant for $65,000.

By now the applications to the Department of Housing and Urban Development (H.U.D.) had been submitted and the community sat anxious. Several important steps had been taken in the effort to develop the proposed water facility in the last few weeks.

On **March 9, 1971** a fire inflamed Black Springs First Baptist Church and damaged a portion of the edifice. Smoke damage was extensive except a tapestry depicting Jesus. Although there was no article stating it, the Black Springs Volunteer Fire Department was more than likely instrumental in assisting to extinguish the fire.

Charles Zeh was quite elated with anticipation. He drafted letters of appreciation to Senator Alan Bible and the Honorable Walter

CHRONOLOGY OF THE 1970'S

S. Baring *March 15, 1971* and to Senator Howard W. Cannon *March 18, 1971* respectively. Mr. Zeh stated, "At the present time, as you are probably aware, the community of Black Springs is simply a conglomeration of homes without any official status, not even as an unincorporated area. We are extremely proud of the fact that, if the general improvement district is created, it will become the first truly local governing body established in the community."

Because of their expression of interest, Mr. Zeh's letters' said, "Transforming into a reality the idea to develop a community water facility in Black Springs has been a most elusive endeavor. Each time the goal seemed within reach, it has eluded our grasp in a sea of revisions, new suggestions and further considerations. However, the community and people of Black Springs have persevered. Their efforts have resulted, with the generous help and good will of many individuals and groups along the way, in the events of the past few weeks. These successes have brought the community to the most difficult stage of all in the attempt to install the proposed facility, that of waiting for H.U.D. to render a decision on the application for the Federal contribution essential to the completion of the project. All that remains to initiate actual construction on the system is for H.U.D. to take this crucial step. It is hoped that the accomplishments of the past weeks have cleared away the debris of unattended matters so that at long last it will be possible for H.U.D. to consider this project on its merits."

A letter dated *March 22, 1971* on United States Senate letterhead, seemed personal and showed an overwhelming support. The letter was from Senator Alan Bible; it read, "Dear Mr. and Mrs. Westbrook: This will acknowledge your letter of March 15 received by me March 18." No copy was found of the letter the Senator received; this causes history to become elusive at times.

The Senator went on to say, "I shall be happy to inquire of the Department of Housing and Urban Development in connection with Washoe County's request for a grant commitment for the Black Springs area." So what was the inquiry concerning? He ended with, "When I have additional information I will be in touch with you. Cordially", and signed Alan Bible. You see Senator Bible and the Westbrooks were friends.

A CRY FOR HELP

According to the minutes of the B.S.C.I.C (Black Springs Civic Improvement Corporation) of *April 6, 1971* a meeting was called to order on April 2nd to discuss a coalition called the Neighborhood Corporations. This coalition was designed to make sure that all "dollars" could address themselves to special interest groups with special interest grants.

The meeting was opened by Mr. Westbrook chairman of the B.S.C.I.C. He introduced Mr. Cloyd Phillips, Assistant Director of the E.O.B. Mr. Howard Gloyd, Director of the E.O.B. was also present and would be the speaker. He asked for the names of the groups that were represented. The groups present were P.O.W.E.R (People Organized to Work for Equal Recognition), Black Springs Volunteer Fire Department, Black Springs Civic Improvement Corp., Lemon Valley Senior Citizens, Stead Community Council, Parent Advisory Council, Black Springs First Baptist Church and Mount Hope Baptist Church. Mr. Gloyd informed them that the Black Springs group would be the nucleus of Neighborhood Corporation. Also, it was stated, there was $32,500 in grant funds to get some action started.

Black Springs must have had an impact on HUD procedures. In the evening Reno Gazette *April 21, 1971* it read:

"A "council of government" will be necessary in the future to obtain Department of Housing and Urban Development funds for sewer and water projects, Urban Renewal Director Bruce Arkell told the Reno City council Monday.

A letter from the department said the funds will not be available unless the area is "certified," he said. "Substantially that requires a council of governments or similar organization."

Arkell said, "The council would be a volunteer association of the governmental units in Washoe County. It would set priorities on projects, apply for funds, and coordinate the work.

Some organizations of this type have been successful, while others have not. The most successful were those formed because there was an "almost mandatory" need."

CHRONOLOGY OF THE 1970'S

He said he was approaching Reno first because if it didn't want to pursue the matter, there would be no sense in talking to Washoe County and Sparks officials.

But, he said, "If the city does plan to pursue any HUD projects, now is the time to consider forming the council, rather than waiting until the federal government says the council must be formed to get funds.

The certification requirement would not hold for such low-income areas as Black Springs, but would hold for programs in Reno, such as a Mary Street storm drain."

Councilman Claude Hunter said Washoe county and Sparks indicated at a recent meeting they were not opposed to the council of governments. But, he added, they did not appear likely to provide leadership in forming the council.

July 6, 1971 at 2:00 p.m. was the time set for Dutch Cook, 225 Kennedy Drive, Black Springs, Nevada, cited to appear before the Board to show cause why a criminal and/or civil action should not be commenced against him for the violation of Ordinance No. 57, for having one skip loader, one mobile crane, two dump trucks, one oil distributor truck, one water truck, one concrete pipe, miscellaneous trucking and heavy equipment, two caterpillars, one flat bed truck, and one portable mixer on property located at Medgar Avenue, Black Springs, zoned A-1. Proof was made that citation was served on June 28, 1971, on Dutch Cook, in care of Georgia Schultz, 225 Kennedy Drive, to appear at this meeting.

Larry Struve, Deputy District Attorney, appeared and stated that on April 20th, Mr. Cook was given 10 days to abate the violation, and the matter was referred to the District Attorney's office on June 22, 1971.

H. S. Bronneke, Zoning Administrator, appeared and stated that he inspected the property this morning; that all the equipment listed were still in evidence with the addition of two more wrecked cars; that no attempt had been made to remove any of the equipment.

A CRY FOR HELP

Since Dutch Cook did not appear, on motion by Commissioner Coppa, seconded by Commissioner Rusk, which motion duly carried, it was ordered that Mr. Cook be given ten days to remove all the equipment from his property, at which time the District Attorney's office would be authorized to prosecute.

As of **October 16, 1971** no actual work had started on the Black Springs' water and sewage project. Monies had been approved and bidding for the jobs was to be sent out. Reported by the County Manager Russ McDonald in the evening Reno Gazette, there are "problems in completing arrangements to receive federal funds for development of the proposed Black Springs water system." McDonald said a test well must first be drilled to prove portability of the water before federal money will be sent, but the state engineer's office has refused to grant a well permit, because of a ban against community well-drilling in the Lemon Valley area. So here was yet another delay.

Another news article **October 28, 1971** did state that "Public Works Director George Oshima, County Manager Russ McDonald and an attorney for the Office of Economic Opportunity will be meeting to decide how to obtain a test well permit for the area."

In related action, "the commission authorized execution of an audit contract with Kafoury, Armstrong, Bernard and Bergstrom, covering financial arrangements for the proposed Black Springs water project.

Federal authorities require the audit before they approve distribution of funding. There are constantly hurdles to clear in order to receive the basic necessities of life."

Charles Zeh, who was now Executive Director of Washoe County Legal Aid Society, sent a letter to the Westbrooks on **December 7, 1971**. He said, "George Oshima telephoned to inform me that the County has begun advertisement for bids to drill and test the well supplying the source of water for the new water system. At the Commissioner's meeting on December 15, the bids will be opened and if within reasonable limits, the contract will be approved. As I relayed over the phone, the actual drilling and testing of the well could begin almost immediately

CHRONOLOGY OF THE 1970'S

thereafter and we should have the answer not too long afterwards to the ultimate question of whether or not there is water of sufficient quality and quantity to meet the H.U.D. requirements."

Mr. Zeh's letter went on to say, "Mr. Oshima also advised that the County is moving forward with plans to develop a new sewer system in Black Springs with H.U.D. monies. Thursday, December 9, 1971 there will be a meeting at the County Manager's Office at 9:30 p.m. to consider the proposed project." Now, what is interesting is that this meeting was to be held at night.

The letter continued, "Discussion will focus largely upon the economic feasibility of the sewer line with specific reference to hook-up fees and use-rates. Subject to the issues that might be raised at the State Welfare Board Meeting, I will attend the meeting in Mr. McDonald's office. It is also important that someone from the community be present. I trust that both of you will be able to attend and I would hope that Lobster could make the meeting as well. Mr. John Meacham, City Engineer, will represent the City of Reno at the meeting. The City is necessarily involved as it owns the sewage treatment plant into which the new sewer line will feed."

He went on to stress, "Unlike the water system, the new sewage line will serve the people on the other side of old Highway 395. It would be useful if those people were also represented at the meeting. If you have the time, would you please attempt to arrange for someone living in that area to attend the meeting? Also, if there are any problems with this format, please advise."

The Nevada State Journal *December 22, 1971* reported:

"Several Washoe County officials have requested assistance from Reno councilmen on a proposed sewage system for Black Springs. But the entire discussion between Washoe County Manager Russell McDonald, county Public Works Director George Oshima and Reno officials indicated that the Black Springs area and the surrounding communities are a problem, especially because of the possible lack of water."

A CRY FOR HELP

In March of 1970 Reno agreed to co-sponsor an application to the Department of Housing and Urban Development (HUD) for funds to provide sewer lines from Black Springs and the neighboring communities of Horizon Hills and Panther Valley. The county agreed to go along with Reno making the application, which was for the Federal Government to provide 90 per cent of the estimated $830,000 cost of the sewer lines. Also, the 90 per cent matching funds would cover only construction, leaving local entities, whether special districts or government units, to pay a larger portion.

HUD later answered that only Black Springs qualified for "impacted" funds. This left the matter in a confused state, and because Black Springs was not annexed the hookup fee and user charges were doubled. But the main problem was the water situation. In July 1970, the state engineer declared the area a "designated ground water basin." This put the state in charge of determining use priorities of water, and anyone wishing to drill wells had to obtain state permission. Also, area governments split the cost for an updated water study to see just how much water was in the area. Officials had recently said the study report was not expected for another year.

The county-Reno discussion was left in the air, as McDonald said: "I just wanted to advise you" and see if Reno might be able to assist. He offered another suggestion: "You could annex the area (Black Springs)." But that suggestion was quickly dismissed by Reno councilmen.

On Thursday, **December 23, 1971** the Reno Gazette reported:

"The residents of Black Springs were without water since Tuesday near midnight. The community said Wednesday night that sometime the previous night the main water pump developed electrical problems. Men worked on the problem Wednesday, but to no avail.

During an informal County Commission session on Thursday, Chairman Roy Pagni said he had just been informed by J. E. Sweatt, owner of the Black Springs water system that the system's pump motor is broken and new parts will arrive from Fresno Friday morning. In the meantime Washoe County will provide a tank truck to help supply

CHRONOLOGY OF THE 1970'S

water to Black Springs' residents, County Manager Russ McDonald said. County commissioners said they had received telephone calls from some of the system's 45 customers, complaining they had been out of water since Wednesday morning. This was a re-occurring problem. Residents were without water for about three days in early November during a breakdown of a pump at the same well."

A new pump motor arrived Friday, **December 24, 1971** from Fresno. County road equipment helped clear snow to allow passage of repairmen to the well site for installation of the motor and the water service was to have been in operation by noon. This meant there would be water on Christmas Day.

Snow plows were not seen in Black Springs. Normally the residents had to do their own plowing out of the neighborhood. The community would band together to keep the unpaved streets passable.

That evening, the Reno Evening Gazette reported, "the city of Reno might reduce its sewage line hookup fees to Black Springs to enable residents to better afford service, allowing replacement of septic tanks, Washoe County Manager Russ McDonald has suggested to the Reno City Council.

The move would help remove potential pollution threats, and the situation was discussed at a council meeting this week on proposed plans for a sewage system in Black Springs. To date, no progress has been made by the city in assistance requested from the federal department HUD for funds to provide sewer lines from Black Springs and neighboring communities of Horizon Hills and Panther Valley.

McDonald suggested the city could reduce its outside city limits sewage hookup fees for Black Springs' residents. The city's laws currently say the hookup fee in the city is $300, with a double fee of $600 charged outside limits. User charge in the city is $45, while outside limits the charge is again double, $90."

A total bid of $11,129 from Reno Pump & Supply was accepted for construction of a test well for the Black Springs Water System, to establish

A CRY FOR HELP

water quality, according to a news article on **December 28, 1971,** "The purpose was to establish water quality. The entire cost of the system, once completed, will be about $160,000 with about 90 per cent of construction or $97,000 to be financed by a grant from HUD and the remaining cost to be covered by a grant from the Max C. Fleischmann Foundation."

In another article the same evening, "The council denies Black Springs a break in fees. Mayor John Chism stood alone as the city council on a 6-1 vote said it will adhere to its present hookup and user fee rates, which are twice as high for persons outside the city, such as those in Black Springs.

Councilman Carl Bogart questioned whether the city could enter into a special agreement with one area and not leave itself open to following the same procedure for other areas such as Rewana Farms.

City Atty. Robert Van Wagoner said city law permits the city manager and the sewage service commission to create special rates when existing rates are inequitable or unfair either to the city or the user, or when the character of sewage is such that its burden on certain residents is greater than on the average resident.

Mayor Chism said Black Springs is a hardship case. Septic tanks won't work there, he said, and "if you took the Black Springs annual income and compared it with other areas here, it is probably as low as you can get."

But Bogart said the request came from the county, which is not in a hardship situation. He said the city would be setting "a very dangerous precedent if we do what the county wants us to do." The council was taking "the easy way out," Chism said. No one wants to admit to prejudice or racism and discrimination, but what else can you call it when reviewing the history."

Reno Evening Gazette editorial, on the **December 29, 1971** read:

"Black Springs' residents have been having their troubles with sewage disposal in their small community to the north of the Reno city limits.

CHRONOLOGY OF THE 1970'S

Ground conditions are such there that septic tanks won't work properly, and the settlement is casting about for some kind of relief in its plight.

Making matters much worse is the fact that the city charges double for sewer systems in the non-incorporated area. That would mean it would cost Black Springs' residents $600 per home just to come into the system, plus something in the neighborhood of $8.00 per month in services charges.

The city has consistently refused to grant waivers to its own hardship cases, and it can't reasonably be expected to hold to that course while granting favors to out-of-town residents.

The higher fees, as we see it, are part of the price anyone must pay for choosing to live outside the incorporated area. It's one of the city's few means of compensating for the other, free services it renders to most residents who live close by and use municipal facilities but escape paying city taxes. It's also one means of encouraging "bedroom" communities to opt for annexation to the city. You must take into account that the residents of Black Springs were force to purchase land in the area due to discrimination."

Still, a person must sympathize with the Black Springs community in its genuine dilemma and hope that some sort of compromise might yet be arranged. But that would take more than urging from county officials. It was prevalent that the Civil Rights Act of 1964 and the Civil Rights Act of 1968 still needed to be adhered to. "Jim Crow" was still alive and operating in its elusive fashion.

Another article in the Gazette the same evening said, "Sewer service would not be extended to Black Springs now, but several properties north of this low-income area would get the service soon under an interim plan proposed Tuesday."

The Black Springs Community Association sent a letter to Mr. Ollie Westbrook, Chairman of the B.S.C.I.C. on **February 4, 1972**. The letter was in reference to Day-care facility. During a meeting held

A CRY FOR HELP

on 28th January 1972, the members of the Black Springs Community Association agreed to request permission from the B.S.C.I.C., to use the Community Center as a day-care center. Cleo Hammond, Chairman of the B.S.C.A., requested a response by February 10th when their next meeting would convene. The B.S.C.I.C. did not respond right away due to up coming changes in the Washoe County department of parks and recreation.

Helen Westbrook of the Economic Opportunity Board had a plan to ensure every elderly person in Reno-Sparks, Nevada received a free meal. She applied for a grant under Title III of the Older Americans Act to support a program called "Meals on Wheels." She received the grant and the program was to begin 1st March 1972 and ending 28th February 1973. She recognized the goals of the Meals on Wheels program would only touch the surface of the needs in Washoe County. Only 100 Senior Citizens would receive meals each day, out of the vast number of Senior Citizens who needed such meals is a monumental task. However, to be able to provide a hot, nutritious meal to 100-plus needy Senior Citizens each day was a start in the right direction. The Meals on Wheels program is still active to this day.

'Black Springs' sewer system plan stalled', was reported in the Reno Gazette on *April 7, 1972.*

"Black Springs will probably have the community water system soon, and preliminary street paving will begin but sewer system plans will have to wait.

County Manager Russ McDonald said this week federal officials told him and Public Works Director George Oshima Tuesday in San Francisco no sewer grant funds would be available before July 1st. McDonald said the county has applied for a grant from the Department of Housing and Urban Development for the sewer system, but may not be able to get as much money as it wants.

In the meantime, plans can proceed for the water system and paving can start. Paving would not be damaged should later street cuts be made for sewer lines, he said."

CHRONOLOGY OF THE 1970'S

On docket 72-1407 from a Commissioners Board meeting a Planning – Change of Land Use District Case No. C-9-73W was heard. The document states, 'As no appeals were filed, on motion by Commissioner Rusk, seconded by Commissioner Coppa, which motion duly carried, it was ordered that the recommendation of the Board of Adjustment denying Change of Land Use District Case No. C-9-73W to Dutch Cook, P.O. Box 143, Black Springs, Nevada, to change from A-1 (First Agricultural with TR (Trailer) overlay to E-1 (First Estates) With TR (Trailer) overlay on property located approximately 2.9 acres situated east of Medgar Avenue, adjacent to U.S. 395 North, Black Springs, Washoe County, Nevada, be upheld.'

A letter **September 18, 1972** to the Westbrooks from Charles R. Zeh, Executive Director, of Washoe County Legal Aid Society said, "As you are probably already aware, HUD has approved the plans for the construction of the water system in Black Springs. Also, George Oshima advised me that the County has already begun to advertise for bids to construct the system. Consequently, the project has begun to move again and once construction begins, I am certain it will progress rapidly."

Upon completion of the water system the Improvement District would take on the administration, maintenance and operation of the facility. Mr. Zeh said in his letter, "I have made inquires at the University in the hopes of interesting the business and economics departments in providing training and technical systems to the members of the improvement District Board of Trustees in the field of management, accounting, and general business practice. Also we will need help in establishing and maintaining an accounting system. As always, you will be advised as matters develop."

On **October 6, 1972** a news article stated a bid had been made for the construction of the new water system in Black Springs. The goal was to have it completed before winter. The estimated time for work was 60 days.

On the same page under Washoe County Commission roundup commissioners denied a request from Dutch Cook for a zoning change

A CRY FOR HELP

to allow "increased trailer density on 2.9 acres of property in Black Springs. Commissioner went along with a recommended denial from the Regional Planning Commission which felt availability of water in the area was questionable."

In the Washoe County Commission roundup *November 16, 1972* the news article stated:

"An ordinance creating the Black Springs General Improvement District and appointing a board of trustees was approved. McDonald said the trustees would be given training by county employees and Sierra Pacific Power Company in operation of a water system which is being constructed in the community..."

A meeting of the Board of Trustees of the Black Springs General Improvement Council was held **February 24, 1973**. The meeting was called to order by Chairman Westbrook. After roll call, the meeting was turned over to Mr. Earl Doty, Consultant, E.H. White & Co. The meeting was basically stating that now that Black Springs had its own water district they had certain responsibilities to uphold.

"... He further explained that he had worked up two budgets; one was presented to the Public Utilities Commission, and one copy to the Tax Commission. Both budgets were signed off and approved, and both offices indicated that the budgets looked fine to them...

The County Manager also received a copy of the budgets, and indicated that he was pleased with the way things are shaping up. He stated, "The next step is that the County will have a public hearing on the 4th Thursday in March, however, this is only a formality, and there is nothing to worry about..."

It had been 21 years since the Westbrooks, my grandparents, moved to Black Springs and 17 years for my family. We'd persevered through hardships and struggles of the inequalities of society. Now married in July of 1973 and living in California, the progress of Black Springs was relayed to me through family and friends. The majority of the news was good, but as in any growing community there were negatives. When I would come home for visits though, it was apparent that improvements were taking place.

Although bureaucracy was oppressive at times, Black Springs residents were a very determined and overall a united community. In the areas where more knowledge was needed in building a community they became educated. They accomplished their goals through non-violence and adherence and compliance to what was legislated.

This had been some journey. In April 1970 they applied for help for a decent water system; August 1970 were informed they would need to form a government entity within the community to receive HUD assistance; October 1970 residents began learning all aspects of governing a water district; February 1971 the Black Springs General Improvement District was formed.

This had been an adventure for the Westbrooks, my grandparents. They had witnessed and been so involved and instrumental in so much. It brings tears and sighs to me reflecting on the past while writing. But they were well on their way to a beautiful home and community. Hard work does pay off.

Nevada State Journal, Sunday, *July 29, 1973* reports:

"Trucks Take Water to Black Springs.' The U.S. Army Reserve is trucking water to the Black Springs area as a result of a recent well cave-in that caused a loss of water pressure in the area, the article said.

Under normal conditions, county trucks would be used to temporarily supply the water, but the county units are all being employed on the numerous fires in this area.

Public Health Environmentalist Dave Minedew said Saturday, "We couldn't find a tanker anywhere. We really had to scrape around."

He said he called the Army Reserve's 979th Engineer Company in Reno, and they responded by providing two large tankers to help haul the water to the Black Springs holding tanks."

A CRY FOR HELP

Black Springs has always been a resilient and resourceful community. Interest groups within the community such as the youth group P.O.W.E.R., B.S.C.I.C., the Volunteer Fire Department, and churches would organize fundraisers for improvements to the area.

On *October 13, 1973* the Black Springs Volunteer Fire Department hosted a dinner dance. Mr. Westbrook, who enjoyed being behind the grill, did the majority of barbecuing, although the community in whole participated. The fundraisers were always festive, full of fun, raffles, music and of course great food. And all events were designed to address specific community needs.

A letter which the Black Springs community had patiently waited for was sent *April 30, 1974* to Ollie and Helen Westbrook. The letter from Charles Zeh Executive Director of the Legal Aid Society said, "The time has come to finalize arrangements on the Black Springs Water System. Please call my office and arrange a time for a meeting when we can put all the relevant materials together and review the current status of the system."

The meeting for the Board of Trustees of the Black Springs General Improvement District held *November 5, 1974* was quite interesting. Those present at the meeting were Board Members Ollie Westbrook, Thurman Carthen, Sr., Jeff Townsell, Barbet Bufkin; Counsel for the District, Charles Zeh; Area residents, Stan Cook, Dutch Cook and Reverend Eddie Hill. "There being a quorum present, business was conducted for the District. The first matter brought before the attention of the Board was the matter of the two positions on the Board which expire on December 31, 1974. Counsel for the District, Mr. Zeh explain to the Board members that under the appropriate provisions of the Nevada Revised Statutes, nominations for those Board positions must be closed thirty days prior to the election. Mr. Zeh also advised that the elections be conducted sometime during the month of December, preferably late in December, in order to fill those two position prior to the time they become vacant, but nevertheless at a sufficiently late date that notice can be given to all qualified electors of the District who desire to run for the vacant positions. Fittingly, Mr. Zeh suggested that nominations be accepted until November 21, 1974, at 3:30 PM, that the nominations then

CHRONOLOGY OF THE 1970'S

be communicated to Dave Howard of Washoe County By November 22, 1974. . . and that the election, with the approval of Mr. Howard, will be set for December 23, 1974." This now became a task for the General Improvement District to inform the community in little over a month and a half. . .

The Board was also advised that Walters Engineering had offered to handle the bookkeeping for the system and do the system's billing. The final arrangements have not been made, however, and that those arrangements were to be finalized at a meeting on November 7th, at 4:00 PM at Walters Engineering firm offices. . ."

Mr. Zeh also recommended, "...that the notice prepared by the Legal Aid Office advising of the transfer of the system, method of payment, and amount of payment be adopted by the District and distributed by the Board members to District water system users that legal counsel for the District be given authority to enter into any agreement with Walters Engineering to handle the books and billings for the system pending the training of a community member to assume this responsibility...." All Board members voted in favor of the recommendation.

For the months of **December 1974 and January 1975** there are no documents of the Board's minutes to review. But it was evident Stanley Cook was then seated on the Board, and the balance of the civic-mindedness of the community and the Board would tip. With the community now being diverse, this was the first white resident on the Board, and factions began to arise.

Dutch Cook who is Stanley Cook's son, the same Dutch Cook who was called before the Washoe County Commissioners for county code violations in the early 70's, started attending the Black Springs Improvement District board meetings regularly.

Mr. George Oshima, Washoe County Public Works, was sent a corrected statement **December 30, 1974** from Walters Engineering for the professional engineering services they had rendered. Mr. Oshima was sent another corrected statement the **January 13, 1975** on the same file. Then on **January 16, 1975**, another breakdown of the cost of engineering services was sent. These letters were regarding billing in the amount of $1,121.16.

Mr. Oshima sent a letter to Mr. Zeh, on **February 12, 1975** regarding the "receipt of a bill from Walters Engineering in the amount of $1,121.16.

I have been delaying any action by the County since the Commissioner have approved an estimated expenditure of $4,000.00 to redevelop the well, called Well No.4.

Due to the unanticipated cost that the County Commissioners had agreed to absorb, he was requesting that the Black Springs GID consider accepting the bill as an operating responsibility of the District. Mr. Oshima was more than happy to discuss the details of the bill with Mr. Zeh and the District Trustees. . ."

Mr. Zeh sent a reply **February 18th** informing Mr. Oshima that the next regular meeting of the Board of Trustees would be held March 3rd and he would bring to their attention the bill from Walters Engineering in the amount of $1,121.16. He would also be meeting with Ollie Westbrook, Jan Fanning, the District Bookkeeper, and Thurman Carthen, District Treasurer, on February 27th to review the District bookkeeping system and the revenue collection experiences.

Chuck Zeh continued the letter to Mr. Ohsima stating, "My initial reaction to your request is somewhat negative in light of the information I currently have at my disposal regarding the financial condition of the district. It seems our initial collection experience is worse than even that which was experienced by the County. It does not seem expedient for the County to saddle the District with such a large expenditure. On the other hand, the Walters firm should be compensated for their work. Perhaps some kind of accommodation between the County and the District can be negotiated."

According to a correspondence to Chuck Zeh on **February 28, 1975** from George Oshima, "As of 5th November 1974, the operations of

CHRONOLOGY OF THE 1970'S

the Black Springs Water System was relinquished to the Black Springs General Improvement District, by Washoe County."

Mr. Oshima stated, "One of the 'loose ends' is the transfer of the power charges. Will you kindly notify the Sierra Pacific Power Company immediately that the account Folio 9980.1, Route 1918, is to be billed to the improvement district. By copy of this letter, the power company is being notified to cancel the service in the name of Washoe County..."

Based upon the minutes of the special meeting, on *April 7, 1975* of the Black Springs General Improvement District Board of Trustees was called to order by Chairman Ollie Westbrook. The minutes had such a tone of professionalism and matter-of-factness. There were 4 issues on the table, all regarding the transfer of the water system. They were addressed in order with resolutions on some. The first was the matter of the filing fee for filing of the Order of Inclusion of Additional Real Property. It was moved a check be drawn on the District account payable to the Washoe County Legal Aid Society. Second was the matter of overpayment by Washoe County to Sierra Pacific Power. A check would be drawn on the District account, payable to Washoe County to reimburse the County. Third, the matter of reconciling the District books with County accounts arising out of the transfer. Any remittance to the County of the balance was tabled until the District bookkeeper and the County bookkeeper could reconcile their books. The fourth was the Walters Engineering bill for approximately $1212.

The minutes stated, "During the discussion by the Board, it was pointed out that the County had agreed to transfer the water system to the District without any defects and that the bill for engineering services actually arose out of a problem with the system that had occurred prior to the transfer. It was also pointed out, however, that the County had already contributed time and funds well in excess of that which was originally contemplated when the system was first proposed. The Board was also advised by the counsel for the District that it would perhaps be necessary to seek further considerations from the County in the future. Accordingly, it was moved by Mr. Bufkin and seconded by Mr. Townsell that a check be drawn in the amount of $300 as the

A CRY FOR HELP

District's contribution to the County for payment on the Walter Engineering bill. The motion was unanimously passed."

A petition was circulated on *July 19, 1975*. It stated, "The signatures and addresses below are from the people of Black Springs who have been informed and want to go on record as opposing the Reeder Development Corporation's proposal to build a private sewer plant practically adjacent to the Black Springs area." There were 38 signatures submitted.

The regular monthly meeting was called to order on *October 6, 1975* and all members were present which included, Chairman Ollie Westbrook, Vice-Chairman Jeff Townsell, Secretary-Treasurer Thurman Carthen, and members Barbet Bufkin and Stanley Cook. Guests included were Dutch Cook, along with Jannette Fanning, Accountant for the District, and Chuck Zeh, Legal Advisor for the District.

After the minutes were read from the last meeting, Mr. Cook made reference to the part in the minutes about, "Mrs. Fanning keeping the office opened on Saturday and suggested that she should be the only one to collect monies.

Mrs. Fanning advised that she had written about that in her financial report which would be addressed later.

Mr. Cook then advised that he was unaware that a meeting with George Oshima had been held. Mr. Westbrook explained regarding the meeting with Georg Oshima, and asked if there were any more corrections to the minutes. Mr. Bufkin moved that the minutes be accepted and Jeff Townsell seconded the motion. . ."

Mr. Westbrook then read the correspondence regarding a change of the boundaries of the district, which was a letter from Chuck Zeh.

"Stan Cook stated that since the district was being restricted due to lack of water, why couldn't something be done with the other well to help the water supply.

CHRONOLOGY OF THE 1970'S

Chuck Zeh stated that he was unable to contact them regarding the equipment that is down there. He stated that they could possibly re-develop the well, but that it would be quite expensive.

Dutch Cook asked if he could make an offer for the well. Mr. Westbrook read the note that Dutch had written, which stated that he would offer $100.00 for the well, and remove the tank and well house, if he could pipe water to his property.

Dutch made the remark that the District had connected water to some places that were not in the original water system, and deleted some houses that were in the original one.

Chuck Zeh informed Dutch Cook that all he had to do was to write a letter asking that he be included in the District. . ." The meeting ended with the regular business.

November 3, 1975, the regular Board of Trustees' meeting was opened by Vice Chairman Jeff Townsell. In attendance were members Thurman Carthen, Stan Cook, and Barbet Bufkin. Chairman Ollie Westbrook was absent. Others present were Chuck Zeh, Jannette Fanning, Dutch Cook, and Brien Walters and Jack Lundigan both with Walter Engineering Company.

"Mr. Townsell explained that it was his understanding that Mr. Zeh had to leave the meeting early due to another commitment, and stated that he would turn the meeting over to Mr. Zeh. . ."

Also, within the minutes, "Mr. Zeh then introduced Brien Walters and Jack Lundigan from Walters Engineering. Mr. Walters stated that he has been involved with the District's Water system for quite a while. He stated that he is very interested in the District and the system, and would like to stay close to it. He stated that he was hopeful that some sort of arrangement could be worked out to everyone's satisfaction, whereby they could work together, to handle any problems that might arise. He stated that he has found that large problems can be prevented, if the smaller ones are taken care of immediately, and not put off. . .

A CRY FOR HELP

Mr. Lundigan stated that another thing he wanted to talk about was how the billing was going, but after listening to Mrs. Fanning, it seems she is doing a good job.

Dutch Cook then stated that he was here concerning some old business. He stated he wanted to know if he is going to be taken into the District or not. Chuck advised Dutch that the Board is considering it, and will have to vote on it. Dutch stated that the reason he is here tonight is that Lee wants to know if he will get in.

A discussion followed regarding wells in the valley, and the water table, and Dutch again stated that Lee is waiting to know if he (Dutch) will be taken into the District, because Lee has two wells in the valley that pumps 1300 gallons per minute.

Chuck Zeh stated that his office would prepare the petition for Dutch at no cost, and then the Board will vote on it. Mr. Zeh stated he didn't know whether the board would reject it or accept it, but all considerations would be taken. . ."

After answering Dutch Cook's question about sewage, "Jack Lundigan stated that since Chuck must leave the meeting soon, the one thing he and Brian Walters wanted the Board to take into consideration is a possible working agreement to retain the Walters Engineering Company at a nominal monthly fee, so that they would be available at any time the District would need them. Mr. Cook asked what a nominal fee would be. Brian Walters stated that $50.00 would be a figure to work with. Mr. Lundigan stated that in the meantime, he would leave his night number, so that if anything came up, the Board would be able to reach him." It was then "suggested that Mr. Walters put his proposal regarding the retainer fee in writing, so that the Board could review it at their next meeting.

Mr. Zeh excused himself from the meeting, and Mr. Walters and Mr. Lundigan left with Mr. Zeh." The meeting resumed as usual.

It is now *January 1976*, the Board of Trustees of Black Springs Improvement District's members remained the same. There are no documents in regards to a regular Board meeting for *December 1975*.

CHRONOLOGY OF THE 1970'S

One of the biggest concerns in Black Springs among the adults was the well being of the youth. Mrs. Westbrook, Mama Helen as the children knew her in the community, wrote a letter to Commissioner Dwight Nelson on *January 9, 1976* regarding improvements in the park. The requests were for fast growing shade trees for the park; resurfacing the basketball court; repairing the swings, and other equipment. "These requests were submitted early in 1975," and Mrs. Westbrook was asking the County for their "undivided attention" to these matters.

Mrs. Westbrook was relentless in her endeavors in improving the conditions in Black Springs. She wrote to Russ McDonald the Washoe County Manager on *January 11, 1976*. She stated that the community was "now experiencing a rapid growth in population, also an increase in water" usage. Therefore the "septic tank systems in use are becoming inadequate. . ."

She stated we have discussed this problem with others adjacent to our area in efforts to find a solution. "Studies have been made before, during and after the installation of this new water system in Black Springs. The results of these studies, shows that no one community or settlement can bear the cost of installing its own sewage disposal unit."

Mrs. Westbrook's letter was another cry for aid. She was calling upon the City, County, State, and Federal governments to aid Black Springs before a health hazardous situation developed that could endanger not only the immediate area, but the lives within Reno.

She went on to inform Mr. McDonald that the danger is real. The children that live in Black Springs were bused "to the most populated schools in Washoe County. . . We do not want to become blight on this beautiful state. This is why we're attempting to reduce the possibilities to a minimum." She was asking if there was "any aid that will reduce or alleviate this problem that would contribute greatly to the health and safety of untold numbers of people concerned."

Helen Westbrook was quite an activist, but most of all she was a humanitarian at heart. She was extremely active within the church. Being the Educational Scholarship Coordinator for Black Springs First

A CRY FOR HELP

Baptist Church, several youth throughout the Washoe County were able to benefit from the scholarship fund and went on to further their education.

The regularly scheduled meeting of the Black Springs GID was held *March 2, 1976* and was called to order by Vice-Chairperson, Jeff Townsell. All Board members were present except Chairman Ollie Westbrook. Others present was Dutch Cook an area resident, and Charles Zeh, Esq., Counsel to the District.

"Stan Cook read the minutes for the meeting conducted in January. It was noted that the minutes should be corrected to reflect that the recommendations by the District Counsel to reject an offer to purchase the old District well should expressively indicate that the offer was made by Mr. Dutch Cook. Upon the reading and correction of the minutes, Mr. Bufkin moved and Mr. Stan Cook seconded that the minutes be approved as corrected. The motion was adopted.

Next, Counsel for the District pointed out that the District had received notice from the County that tax liens existed on the property transferred to the District by Washoe County. The liens were for any taxation that had arisen since the County and then the District assumed ownership of the property. Counsel for the District indicated the District had until April 22, 1976 to pay the liens amounting to approximately $90.00 or suffer forfeiture of the property to the County. Counsel for the District then advised that he would confer with the Treasurer and other relevant County officials regarding the situation. It was explained, further, that possibly both the County and the District had failed to check the tax rolls upon the transfer of the property from the County to the District and that therefore, both entities were unaware of back taxes on the property. The board was also reminded that the County was to transfer ownership and operation of the Water System to the District free and clear of prior existing problems. The matter of the back taxes, therefore, would be discussed with the County officials in that light, the fact that the property was transferred to the District by virtue of quit claim deed, notwithstanding.

Then, the matter of bond insurance for the District was discussed. Counsel for the District pointed out that the premium renewal date was March 19, 1976. The insurance company has requested that a questionnaire be completed by the District so that rates can be computed. Counsel for the District will attempt to resolve this matter with the company..."

Next, "Given factual situations, regarding Petition for Inclusion for the Benson property, it was moved by Thurman Carthen and seconded by Barbet Bufkin that the District no longer awaits their petition for inclusion. The District proceeded forthwith according the statutory guidelines to commence the procedures for consideration of the petitions for inclusion within the District which the District has or is about to receive, that the appropriate notice be given of the statutorily required hearing be submitted for the next regularly held Board meeting of the District which is to be held on April 5, 1976. Because Stan Cook has property which may be involved, he abstained from the motion. The motion was adopted. Voting in favor were Thurman Carthen, Barbet Bufkin and Jeff Townsell. Stan Cook abstained and Ollie Westbrook was not present to vote on the motion.

Then, District business concerning payment of operating bills was considered..." The bills had been paid. "It was therefore moved by Stan Cook and seconded by Thurman Carthen that the payment of these bills be ratified. The motion was adopted.

Finally, the two matters tabled from the January meeting, the offer of Dutch Cook to purchase the old District well and the format for the standard, District water service user contract, were again tabled for consideration at the next regularly held board meeting. Meeting was adjourned."

The regular monthly meeting was called to order by Chairman Ollie Westbrook on *April 5, 1976*. All Board members were present. Others in attendance were Jan Fanning, Bookkeeper; Roy Hibdon, District Engineer, and Charles Zeh, District Counsel. Dutch Cook was not present.

"Upon dispensing with the reading of the March 1976 minutes, Chairman Westbrook convened the public hearing on the petitions for

A CRY FOR HELP

inclusion of real property within the District submitted respectively by Mr. and Mrs. Robert Powell, Dorothy and Frank Higgins, S. F. Cook, and Stanley and Alva Cook. Chairman Westbrook then relinquished the floor to Charles Zeh. Counsel proceeded to explain that the public hearing on the four, respective petitions was being conducted pursuant to requirements . . ." which require "a public hearing on any petitions for the inclusion of additional real property within the District Boundaries. . .

Counsel reviewed for the Board the circumstances giving rise to the hearing and the filing of the respective petitions with the Board. Counsel pointed out that the need for the hearing and filing of the petitions arose primarily because the parcels represented by the petitions had been omitted from the original District boundaries while having previously been a part of the old Sweatt Water System. The original intent of the new system was to serve the original customers of the Sweatt System and that therefore the filing of the petitions are necessary to conform the District to the original purpose for which it was largely created. With that in mind, Counsel pointed out that on behalf of the District, Counsel had prepared, without cost to the respective petitioners, the petitions for inclusion of real property within the District; one each for Mr. and Mrs. Powell, D. C. and Lena Benson, Frank and Dorothy Higgins, S. F. Cook, and Stan and Alva Cook. With the exception of the petition prepared for the Bensons, all other petitions had been properly filed with the District.

Counsel advised that correspondence had been received from the Bensons requesting that he answer certain questions. Those questions were in turn, answered by Counsel for the District. In addition, Counsel requested that the Bensons act immediately and reminded them further that if they did not proceed now, they would be required to proceed for inclusion at their own expense. To date, no further reply has been received by the Bensons. Given the fact that Washoe County had agreed to underwrite any expenses associated with revisions and District and Water Services Area boundaries caused by the inclusion of various parcels represented by the respective petitions on file, it was asserted that the county could not be expected to wait much longer while the District attempted to finalize its business. Therefore, in light of the fact that the Benson's had been given well over two months to respond,

CHRONOLOGY OF THE 1970'S

it was determined at the previous Board meeting to proceed forthwith and not wait any further for the Benson's to return their petition.

Counsel then explained the standard by which the Board should deliberate on the respective petitions presented before it. The Board was advised that the standard was that of public necessity and convenience and that this was the only factor determining their decision. Explaining further, the standard translated into a decision as to what was best for the District and constituents therein. Chapter 318 gave the Board the option of accepting any, none, or a portion of any petition before it, and that moreover, the Board was advised that the question of public necessity and convenience concerning these petitions evolved into whether or not the District water supply was sufficient to permit the inclusion of the various parcels or portions thereof." On that question, Counsel had requested the presence of Roy Hibdon, of Walters Engineering; the engineering firm retained by the District and introduced him at this time.

"Mr. Hibdon then explained that originally, the District had been operating upon the premise that under the old water service area, the District was obligated to serve a usable land size of 90 acres and the potential demand for water which that land size represented. At the request of Counsel for the District, however, Mr. Hibdon explained that he and Counsel had recomputed the developable land size represented by the District boundaries, as constituted and with the addition of the respective Cook properties, the Powell property, and the Higgins property. The result was that the District boundaries, as proposed to be amended would represent a land size and potential demand reflected by a total of 63 acres.

. . . Mr. Hibdon's calculations based upon the available water supply, the District could serve a land size represented by 78 acres, assuming residential use, 1/3 acre plots, an average of 4.0 people per residence, and assuming an average daily use of 150 gallons per person. Based upon these assumptions and calculations, it was the opinion of Mr. Hibdon that the District could annex and join in the District all properties currently before the District. Further, it was recommended that the parcels be included in that they also represent an additional source of revenue to the District. . ."

A CRY FOR HELP

After all properties had been consulted upon and accepted, it was moved and seconded that the Water Service Area boundaries be amended to conform identically with the boundaries of the Improvement District as currently amended. The motion was unanimously adopted.

Mr. Zeh, Executive Director of Washoe County Legal Aid Society sent a letter to Ollie Westbrook on *June 8, 1976* informing him that ". . . the order of inclusion of the properties annexed to the District at the meeting held on June 7th is ready for his signature and the attestation signature of Thurman Carthen."

In reviewing the documents, with the change on the Board, the communication between the members, was faltering. Mr. Zeh on *June 18, 1976* sent a letter to Mr. Westbrook explaining that beginning with October 1974 Board meeting, a review of their files indicated that they have board minutes for each meeting with the exception of the meetings for the months of *December 1974, January 1975, April 1975, and August 1975*.

Mr. Zeh had no idea whether or not the meetings were actually held, but was requesting copies if there were minutes. He would also supply the Board with any missing minutes he had for their files.

Mr. Zeh went on to remind him that the Order of Inclusion adding the parcel of land owned by the District was ready for signatures. The signatures were needed to properly list the boundaries of the District.

June 30, 1976 a letter to Ollie Westbrook was sent by Mr. Zeh. This letter was to introduce Bob Murphy, a VISTA attorney with their office. Bob Murphy would be attending in Mr. Zeh's stead, the District Board meeting to be held on July 12th 1976. Bob would be reviewing with the Board, the material that Mr. Zeh had prepared and was ready to discuss before the Board for the meeting which was scheduled for June 21st 1976.

Mr. Zeh informed Westbrook that he and Stan Cook were in attendance on that date and time but apparently the other members

CHRONOLOGY OF THE 1970'S

failed to note the meeting, since he and Cook were the only ones present. Mr. Zeh felt this was "unfortunate since the material Bob will be reviewing was of considerable import to the District."

Mr. Zeh stated he would be returning to Nevada by the 26th July, a Monday and strongly suggested and advised that the Board schedule another special meeting to be held on that date at 8:00 P. M. At that time, he could review further with the Board the material that Bob would be presenting. In addition, he would review the regulations governing the election procedures for the District. Would you please confirm this special meeting with my secretary?

The regularly scheduled meeting of the Black Spring GID was called to order on *August 2, 1976* by Jeff Townsell, District Vice-Chairperson, acting in the absence of Chairperson, Ollie Westbrook.

The absence of Chairperson, Ollie Westbrook on numerous occasions was due to his work schedule. Helen Westbrook started attending the Board meetings as a community member. Her presence would undoubtedly be helpful in what would eventually transpire.

"With a quorum being present, the Board first addressed the current bills outstanding of the District. . ."

Next, the matter of the form for the application of service by customers with the District was considered." The Board adopted the application for service as prepared by Counsel for the District ". . . with the exception of providing for a 92.5 cent fee for each one thousand gallons used after the first ten thousand gallons by District customers."

Third, the Board considered rule 6.B. as prepared by the District counsel. The Board adopted ". . . the rule respecting termination of services for non-payment and for failure to observe District rules."

Fourth, the Board adopted "the five and ten day notices, providing for the termination of services for non-payment of utilities or for violation of District rules."

A CRY FOR HELP

On *August 3, 1976* Ollie Westbrook was sent a letter from Mr. Zeh. Zeh's letter stated, "Enclosed please find the Summary of the Black Springs General Improvement District meeting held on July 12, 1976. Note, no quorum was present and thus business could not be transacted.

Also enclosed are the minutes for the regularly scheduled meeting conducted August 2, 1976. A quorum was present for the meeting thus, business was properly transacted as reflected in the minutes.

We have sent sufficient copies of the meeting held on the 12th July and 2nd of August for your distribution to each of the Board members."

A letter sent to the Black Springs GID board members from Charles Zeh on *September 21, 1976* notes a perplexity within the operation of the Board. Mr. Zeh states, "Last Monday evening, *September 13, 1976*, the regularly scheduled meeting of the Board of Trustees for the Black Springs General Improvement District was to be conducted. When I arrived at the offices of the District for the meeting, no one was present. Accordingly, on the next day, I drafted a letter to the District calling for a special meeting to be conducted at the District offices at 10 o'clock a.m. on Saturday morning, September 18, 1976. In my letter, I requested that there be a confirmation of the meeting. Our office received none. Nevertheless, my secretary and I attempted to contact the Board on Friday and then again on Friday evening. We could not make contact and therefore, I assumed that since there was no contact and no confirmation of the meeting that the meeting was not to be held.

For whatever reasons, interest seems to be falling off concerning Board business. This cannot happen. The Board is a legally constituted governmental entity organized under the laws of the State of Nevada. You, as members of the Board, are duly elected public officials with a public responsibility to the community, the State of Nevada, your neighbors, your friends, and your relatives and families.

The water system represents a significant achievement for the community. I am aware that the final organization of the District has been a drawn out process. We have about come to the end of that

CHRONOLOGY OF THE 1970'S

process, however, and thus, now is the time for interest to be rejuvenated, not to fall by the wayside..."

Mr. Zeh went on to inform the Board Members of the District an election of three Board members is to be conducted at the biennial general election to be held on November 2, 1976. He detailed the procedural process the Board should take and then moved to another matter of importance to the District.

Mr. Zeh states, "I have discussed the audit situation with Don Pringle. Upon reviewing the books of the District, he indicated that in no event would the cost for conducting the audit and secondly, of assisting in establishing the District books consistent with the form required by the Tax Commission and the Revised Statutes, cost the District more than $750.00.

He indicated further, that there was a strong possibility that it would cost less than that. I also suggested to him that $750.00 would put a considerable strain on the District budget. He recognized this fact and would do the best he could on the matter.

In addition, I suggested that two bills be submitted for his services, one for the audit itself and a second billing for assisting the District in setting up the books and forms required by the Tax Commission. I don't believe he has done anything on the books, to date, and thus it is not too late for someone else to do this work for the District. I strongly advise, however, that the District avail itself of Mr. Pringle's services."

What follows will be directly from a meeting of the Black Springs GID held the next day after Mr. Zeh mailed his letter to the Board Members.

A special meeting of the Black Springs General Improvement District was held on **September 22, 1976** in the Community Center Located at 301 Kennedy Drive. The meeting opened at 7:45 P.M., with roll call, which indicated a quorum was present. The members present were, Ollie Westbrook, Chairman; Jeff Townsell, Vice Chairman;

A CRY FOR HELP

Thurman Carthen, Secretary/Treasurer; and Stan Cook, Member. Barbet Bufkin the other Member arrived late due to another meeting.

Mr. Zeh, Counsel for the District, was not present but two others were, Jannette Fanning, District Bookkeeper, and Helen Westbrook a community representative.

"The purpose of the special meeting being called was to take care of pressing matters concerning the up-coming election.

Mr. Westbrook, Chairman, informed the Board that if they each worked diligently, the necessary paperwork could be taken care of, and filed with the Registrar of Voters for the County, in proper time. He advised that several of the members had been working that day, contacting people in the community, to enlist possible candidates for the election. He advised that all petitions for membership must be filed with Dave Howard, Registrar, no later than 4:00 p.m. on Friday, September 24, 1976.

Mr. Westbrook further stated that in order to keep the District running, if no candidates were obtained, it may be necessary for the present Board members to re-file, and run for the next term. He stated that since these members have now had the experience, and have knowledge about the District, he felt that if they were re-elected, they could give more input into the District, from their past experience.

Mr. Westbrook also stated that in the future, it is necessary for the Board itself to take care of its own business, and see that things get done. Many, many minor items that should have been taken care of months ago are still hanging fire, and these little items are the ones which, when done, will allow the Board to run smoothly, without much effort on the part of the Board members.

Mr. Westbrook stated that we must first select an election committee. He explained that it would be necessary for one member of the election committee to be present at the center at all times during the opening of the polls on November 2, 1976, from 7:00 a.m. to 7:00 p.m. He also advised that it would be necessary for a Notary Public to be present.

CHRONOLOGY OF THE 1970'S

After consulting, Stan Cook volunteered to act as Chairman of the Election Board, with Barbet Bufkin and Thurman Carthen assisting. It was decided that since the polls were to be opened 12 hours, they would each work a 4 hour shift at the Center.

A discussion was held regarding the fact that Board members do not come to the meetings prepared to take care of business. It was felt that one of the reasons was that the members do not receive a copy of the minutes of the meetings, in order to study the business conducted at the meeting, and to continue with any unfinished business at the next meeting. Upon finalizing this discussion, Thurman Carthen moved that Mrs. Fanning, Bookkeeper, continue to attend the meetings, take minutes and see that a copy is mailed to members of the Board, in ample time for them to study them prior to the next regular meeting. Stan Cook seconded the motion, which carried.

Mr. Westbrook then brought up the fact that he had approached the Community Services Agency of Washoe County for technical assistance in the maintenance and bookkeeping portion of the Board business. He asked Mrs. Fanning to read a letter which was sent to Joe McClelland, Chairman of the CSA Board. That letter is attached hereto and made a part of these minutes."

The letter in short said, "As Chairman (Ollie Westbrook) of the Black Springs General Improvement District, I am asking the Community Services Agency for technical assistance in getting the district operating as it should be. . .

After discussion as to what part CSA would play in the District business, it was agreed that the Board should consider the possibility of entering into an agreement with CSA for this technical assistance. Mr. Westbrook explained that our letter to them would be read at their Board meeting, September 23, and they would reply to our letter, advising us of their decision. At the time we receive their reply, we will then be able to decide if we want to accept or reject their offer.

Mr. Westbrook then stated that at the time we agreed to pay Walters Engineering $50.00 retainer fee, the agreement was to continue for

A CRY FOR HELP

six months, and at that time, we were to decide if we wanted to continue retaining them. That six month period is just about up, and we need to decide if we wish to continue.

Mr. Cook suggested that we table this discussion and decision until we decide what we will do about CSA, and until we are sure that the Public Service Commission had been met with, and accepted the district. All Board members agreed to this.

Discussion turned again to the election at the Center. It was decided that since Mrs. Fanning, Bookkeeper is a Notary Public; she should attempt to make arrangements to work at the center that day (November 2) in order to comply with the rules of the election. Mrs. Fanning is to be paid the sum of $40.00, for her day of work at the center on November 2.

With reference to Pringle & Pollard Accountants, it was decided to postpone a decision to use him, until we have heard from CSA.

Jeff Townsell stated that since Mr. Westbrook will be unable to attend the meetings on Monday nights, because of his work schedule, he hoped that Mr. Westbrook will help him prepare an agenda for the meetings over which he must preside. Mr. Westbrook agreed." There being no further business, the meeting adjourned at 9:20 p.m.

This special meeting was called the day after Mr. Zeh sent his letter to all the Board Members with directives in running the election. November's election would bring unrest within the community of Black Springs. Mr. Westbrook sensed the unrest, and through his years of struggles he gained knowledge to help maneuver through what the community would come up against.

A letter form the Washoe County Manager's office dated *September 27, 1976* sent to Ollie Westbrook confirmed another improvement to Black Springs.

"Washoe County has applied for a federal grant in the amount of $94,000 for three Community Development Projects. The application

CHRONOLOGY OF THE 1970'S

was submitted under the provisions of the Housing and Community Development Act of 1974. The projects are curb, gutter and street improvements in Black Springs for $34,000..."

A letter was sent **September 30, 1976** from Cloyd Phillips, Executive Director of the Community Services Agency of Washoe County, to Ollie Westbrook, Chairman of the Black Springs GID. The letter said:

Dear Ollie:

With reference to your letter, dated September 22, 1976, to the Chairman of the Board of Directors, unfortunately, the Chairman was ill the night of the Board meeting, (September 23, 1976) and your letter, was not brought up before the Board. However, I have talked with the Chairman, and he has directed me to offer your District technical assistance, as you described in your letter.

The first step is to enter into an agreement between the Black Springs General Improvement District and the Community Services Agency of Washoe County. In order to do this, we will need certain documents and information which I assume can be provided by yourself and Mr. Zeh of Legal Aid Society.

As soon as an agreement has been entered into, this agency will assist you toward meeting the deadlines for your election, for appearing before the Public Service Commission, as well as assisting you in the field of bookkeeping, collection, delinquent accounts, etc.

We will need to work closely with Mr. Zeh with regards to the Public Service Commission appearance, as well as the Nevada Tax Report, and by copy of this letter to Mr. Zeh, I am informing each of you to plan on a meeting with me sometime during the week of October 4, 1976, after you have discussed this with your Board of Trustees. Since time is important in many of these matters, and particularly in the up-coming election, in which we will also assist you, you may want to call a special meeting with your Board and Mr. Zeh to get the necessary documents and information together, prior to our meeting to enter into an agreement.

A CRY FOR HELP

Mr. Zeh, Executive Director of Washoe County Legal Aid Society and Counsel for the District sent a letter to the Board Members *October 5, 1976* in response to the action the Board took. He stated:

"I note from a copy of a letter dated September 30, 1976, provided me by the Community Services Agency of Washoe County that you have apparently contacted that Agency in reference to District business with the Public Service Commission and the Nevada Tax Commission. From the copy to the September 30, 1976, letter, it would appear further that you are requesting assistance from the Agency with the audit of the books of the District and setting up the District books in a form consistent with the statutory and tax commission requirements.

This overture towards the Community Service Agency is quite obviously an important step being taken by the District. It also would appear that it runs to matters identical to those which I have been negotiating with Don Pringle on behalf of the Board.

I was never provided with a copy of the letter which the Board sent to the Community Services Agency. Perhaps that was an oversight. I feel, however, that this breakdown in communications, whether or not an oversight, cannot and should not continue. Certainly, you can understand my position on this. Your letter to Community Services Agency basically withdraws, without notice, the authority vested in me by the Board to make arrangements concerning the District books. If you did not like the arrangement that I had negotiated with Mr. Pringle, that's fine. If you want someone else to do the books and the negotiating, that's fine. In the future, however, please let me know so that I am not left out in the cold, contacting people in the community on behalf of the District when the District's intentions are elsewhere.

In the event the Board is able to contract with Community Services Agency, I look forward to working with Cloyd Phillips and his program. Upon completion of the applications with the Public Service Commission and the Nevada Tax Commission, however, I believe it would be time for our office to review its association with the District."

CHRONOLOGY OF THE 1970'S

There was a draft of agreement for delegation of activities "... entered into as of November 1, 1976, including attached conditions governing certain activities of General Community Programming (Program Activity Code SKI) financed under CAP Grant No. 90660 – P.A. No. 05 during the period to which are to be carried out jointly by the BLACK SPRINGS GENERAL IMPROVEMENT DISTRICT, hereinafter referred to as the "Delegate" on behalf of the Community Services Agency of Washoe County, hereinafter referred to as the "Grantee.""

Notices of Election were distributed according to election procedures. As a document states, "An election will be conducted in Black Springs at the Community Center on November 2, 1976, for the three positions on the Board of Trustees of the Black Springs General Improvement District which become vacant when the current terms expire on December 31, 1976. The new terms commence on January 1, 1977, and will run for a period of four years. A plurality of votes is required for election and the polling place will be open from 7:00 AM on the date of election. The polling place will close on the same date at 7:00 PM ...

The Black Springs General Improvement District was created pursuant to N.R.S. Chapter 318 and was chartered to own, operate, and maintain community sewer and water facilities in the District. The Board of Trustees is the governing body of the District."

The November 2, 1976 Election, would create a strain, a possible demise of the community. With the election completed, it resulted in three White residents placed on the Board of Trustees. A superiority complex and greed would manifest immediately and wedge a rift in the community harmony, 25 years of struggle.

The Board of Trustees now consisted of Stanley Cook, Marie Eckart, Frank Higgins, who where white, Thurman Carthen and Barbet Bufkin who were black. Marie Eckart was the mother-in-law to Dutch Cook whose father is Stanley Cook. This in itself was a flag for Mr. Westbrook to remain in close affiliation with the Board of Trustees to protect the community from distinction. He offered to handle the maintenance problems for the Water District.

A CRY FOR HELP

Marie Eckart, now the Chairperson for the Black Springs GID Board of Trustees, sent a letter to Mr. Ollie Westbrook **February 1, 1977** in regards to his offer, Marie Eckart replied:

"During a meeting of the Board of Trustees for the Black Springs General Improvement District, the members of the Board discussed your offer to handle the maintenance problems for the Water District.

It is our understanding that you will be willing to take care of minor maintenance problems and to work closely with Mrs. Fanning regarding delinquent accounts. We further understand that you are willing to be employed at the rate shown in the Rules and Regulations for the Water District, i.e. $12.00 per hour.

Accordingly, a motion was made and seconded that your offer be accepted and upon final vote, the motion carried.

Therefore, if this is agreeable with you, please advise the Board of Trustees, so that we can make arrangements to advise the community of your position with the Water District.

Also, trusting that having been a past member of the Board, you are aware of the set-up concerning employment at this time, we would like to accept your offer in a contract basis, rather than making deductions for taxes, etc. until such time as the Water District might have more employees."

Mr. Westbrook sent his affirmation for the maintenance position on **March 10, 1977.** In the letter he thanked the Board for their vote of confidence to serve the Board and the community as Maintenance Director.

Mr. Westbrook, in his letter, brought to the Boards attention, "...the petition to the Board for expanding the Districts service boundary northwest of the pumping station," he urged the Board not to "entertain any request to enlarge the service area. Reason being that the Nevada State Water Engineer had declared a moratorium in all of Lemon Valley as of five years ago. These rulings meant that no large supplier

CHRONOLOGY OF THE 1970'S

could drill any new wells for water. Mr. Westbrook pressed the Board members to deny any and all requests to expand the service area of the District.

Based upon documentation, a Criminal Complaint had been lodged against the Board of Trustees of the Black Springs General Improvement District. A letter was sent to Ollie Westbrook *April 6, 1977* from Washoe County District Attorney's office stating ". . . no criminal complaint will issue against the Board of Trustees."

Joseph B. Key, Deputy District Attorney, went on to say, "In regard to actions taken by the Board of Trustees of the Black Springs General Improvement District on March 19, 1977, NRS 318.116 deals with the basic powers of general improvement districts and grants power to the Board of Trustees to furnish water in paragraph 14.

NRS 318.0956 and 0957 deal with conflicts of interest of Board members in contracts entered into with a Board member. I see no conflict of interest in the action taken by the Board even though certain members may have been biased or prejudiced in favor of the applicant. . ."

Mr. Westbrook knew that if the Cook family could not be stopped, that what the community had struggled for 25 years to achieve, would end in expulsion of the inhabitants. The residents would lose everything.

The letter continued, "The fact that the Chairperson of the Board is the applicant's relative, as well as was another Board Trustee, does not, in itself, create a conflict of interest although it does necessitate a closer scrutiny of the Board's action. This would be particularly true if other applicants were denied water hookups."

According to the Deputy District Attorney, the special meeting held on March 19, appeared as ". . . an official meeting of the Trustees, attended by a quorum capable of transacting district business."

The Deputy went on to say, "It appears that the Board could have denied the application if there was proof presented to the Board

A CRY FOR HELP

that their granting the applicant's request for water would pose a clear and present threat, endangering the safety of the water supply. There is no evidence presented to indicate this may have been brought to the Board's attention and properly documented prior to the vote, nor is there evidence of contra facts presented, upon which the Board could have based its decision to grant the request.

Assuming there was evidence presented to show a danger to the water system, I believe the Board may be guilty of exercising poor judgment but not of a criminal offense."

Through documentation it appears that on *April 13, 1977* an application and permit was granted from Washoe County Department of Public Works for excavation in public streets and alleys. The purpose was to open water service to 360 Medgar Drive; the Cooks property.

A letter was sent to the attention of Stan Cook and Ollie Westbrook on *April 15, 1977* from Walters Engineering. The letter was informing them that last week the civil engineering consultants had spent some time at Black Springs discussing the operation and maintenance of the distribution system and the more important aspects of the water supply.

". . . The District has a supply which is limited on an annual basis to a maximum of 34 million gallons or to the amount that can be shown as used on or before October 5, 1977, whichever is least. No extensions on the permits are going to be allowed by the State Engineer.

However, the more critical limitation is the amount of water the District's wells would pump over a series of hot days, Walters Engineering stated. Their records indicate that the combined output of the wells is in order of 60 gallons per minute. Without the meter records, Walters Engineering could not tell exactly how much the wells will pump or how much the community would use on a hot day."

Walters Engineering suggested that conservation measures should be preached. Based on use in Sun Valley and past history at

CHRONOLOGY OF THE 1970'S

Black Springs, it appeared "that this 60 gpm will be needed to serve the over 70 customers at Black Springs over a series of hot days..."

Walters Engineering recommended "... that unless such an additional peaking source can be developed immediately, or if the District feels the added revenue of new customers justifies hauling water at certain times this summer, no additional connections in Black Springs be allowed..."

The engineering firm did state that if the District had made previous commitments, one or two connections would not make that much difference if conservation measures were stressed.

Water conservation was an important realization for the Westbrooks. Mrs. Westbrook had contacted the Truckee Meadow Water Conservation Committee. They in-turn sent information regarding their program. In the letter dated *April 18, 1977* TMWCC stated "... the committee is responsible for the water conservation teams that are installing shower restrictors and toilet tank dams in residences in Reno and Sparks..."

TMWCC "... hope that property owners, improvement associations and water companies will join together in promoting water conservation efforts throughout Washoe County. To help get started, the Truckee River Water Conservation Committee offers to provide, at no cost, water conservation kits like the one enclosed, to all residences in the unincorporated area of Washoe County..."

A surmountable challenge hit the community of Black Springs that prompted the Westbrooks to seek legal representation from another attorney other than from the legal counsel for the Board of Trustees, Charles Zeh. The Westbrooks were seeking an injunction against the Black Springs General Improvement District Board of Trustees. On *April 19, 1977* Stanley Cook wrote two letters, one to Thurman Carthen, Secretary/Treasurer and the County Commissioners.

The letter to Thurman Carthen said, "I am resigning my directorate in the Black Springs General Improvement District as of this

A CRY FOR HELP

date (April 19, 1977). The reasons are too obvious to have to discuss. Enclosing my only copy of the combination lock for the file cabinet. The keys and rule book issued to me are in the top drawer. Sincerely Stanley Cook."

The letter to County Commissioners said:

"I am resigning my Directorate in the Black Springs General Improvement District as of this date. A recall petition has been started against Directors Mrs. Eckart (Chairperson), Mr. Higgins (Vice-Chairman), and my self. I can't speak for Mrs. Eckart or Mr. Higgins but I personally want to save the District the trouble of a recall. I also want to try to protect myself personally from possible future lawsuits resulting from the October 5th, 1977 water cut-off date imposed by Mr. Roland Westergard which will probably bar future hook-ups to the Districts water system. The undeveloped property owner's have not been notified nor has the moratorium been legally publicized as yet.

Please be aware of the District's possible problems during this transition period. Sincerely, Stanley Cook."

The Westbrooks, not being members of the Board of Trustees, became the intermediaries on behalf of the community, and retained David Dean, Attorney at Law, for legal representation. The Westbrooks action was to stop Mr. Cook from burdening the water supply and litigating the validity of the Board's exploits.

The cost for seeking Temporary Restraining Order, Preliminary Injunction and final litigation would fall within the range of $1200.00 to $1800.00. This would be payable in monthly installments after the initial $500.00 retainer was paid.

This is all documented in a letter to Ollie Westbrook dated ***April 22, 1977*** from David Dean, Attorney at Law. He also suggested that Mr. Westbrook secure commitments from the interest residents of Black Springs. He went on to recommend that Ollie and Helen Westbrook act as trustees of any funds collected from Black Springs' residents. And finally, that if this matter is to be pursued, that it be done with deliberate speed.

CHRONOLOGY OF THE 1970'S

This was a very intense situation for the community of Black Springs. After 25 years of creating an environment, a community, where Black people could call home and possibly be a viable asset to Washoe County and the City of Reno, their livelihood was on the verge of demise by some White residents and their self interest.

A Notice of Application for change of land use was posted by the Regional Planning Commission on *April 29, 1977.* The change was in reference to Cook families properties. Such a change from A-1 to C-2 would provide for any commercial use. A-1 zoning provides for agricultural uses and limits residential use to one mobile home per one acre.

Mrs. Westbrook through this intensity kept her mind focused upon building up the community. She sent a letter of reminder to the Washoe County Parks Commissioner. There were 4 old issues concerning the Martin Luther King Park: a sprinkling system for the lawn; lawn around the community center and playground; painting on the outside of the community center; and new cabinets in the kitchen.

When it involved the community and youth, Mrs. Westbrook was persistent. She asked for the Parks Commissioner's undivided attention as soon as possible, and to let the community hear from him. She also added on 4 new requests: resurface basketball court; repair play equipment and basketball nets; a flag and flag pole; and a sprint track.

On *May 3, 1977* Mr. Gene Sullivan, Director of Parks and Recreation responded, thanking her for her letter. He indicated to her that their earlier meeting on April 29, they were using all available manpower to complete Sun Valley and Lemon Valley Parks.

These two projects would be completed by June 7, 1977, and immediately after that the Department of Parks & Recreation would begin fulfilling Black Springs' request.

The letter ended with Mr. Sullivan saying, "Please be assured that the County is interested in the Martin Luther King Park and wants to acquire the two parcels of land that would provide a better facility."

A CRY FOR HELP

A Complaint with two Claims was filed *May 13, 1977*, in the Second Judicial District Court of the State of Nevada in and for the County of Washoe. The Plaintiffs were Ollie and Helen Westbrook, Eddie Hill and Barbet Bufkin. The Defendants were Stanley Cook, Marie Eckart, and Dutch Cook, individually, Black Springs General Improvement District Board of Trustees.

The Complaint states, "That Defendant Dutch Cook is a relative of Stanley Cook and Marie Eckart and that certain hereinafter nepotistic, illegal, negligent and fraudulent acts were conspiratorially committed by certain Board Members which exposed the residents of Black Springs to known risks of water shortage, rationing, depletion, and other harmful results."

First Claim number VIII of the Complaint states, "That on April 13, 1977, person or persons unknown obtained permit No. 685 in the name of Black Springs General Improvement District. Said permit does not show the name of the person(s) supposedly acting on behalf of said improvement but Plaintiffs are informed that Trustee Stanley Cook was such person. That the Board of Directors did not authorize the procurement of said permit and said procurement is violation of trusted fiduciary duties."

First Claim number XIV states, "That Stanley Cook and Marie Eckart had a duty to refrain from nepotistic action on behalf of their relative Dutch Cook; had a duty of due care to refrain from exposing Black Springs residents to risks of water shortages; had a duty as Trustees to investigate available water supply; had a duty to refrain from the unauthorized and illegal use of Board powers which permitted Dutch Cook to attach a 2" (two inch) commercial tap to the water main for the express purpose of establishing a multi unit mobile home park and truck stop; had a duty to refrain from self interested actions."

First Claim number XV went on to say, "That despite the duties mentioned above, said Stanley Cook and Marie Eckart called a special meeting – unknown to the general Black Springs population and other Board Members – for the conspiratorial purpose of granting Dutch Cook permission to attach a 2" (two inch) commercial tap on the water system despite the Lemmon Valley moratorium."

CHRONOLOGY OF THE 1970'S

Second Claim number V states, "That the procurement of the permit in the name of Black Springs General Improvement District was based on a misstatement of fact, done with knowledge of falsity and with intent to cause Washoe County officials to rely on the misstatement to the detriment of Plaintiffs as residents of Black Springs."

Second Claim number VI states, "That Stanley Cook, Dutch Cook and Marie Eckart conspired to use trustee position illegally for the purpose of giving Washoe County officials the impression that the Black Springs General Improvement District had legitimately approved the undertaking of commercial ventures and had legitimately approved the 2" (two inch) water tap."

Second Claim number VII states, "That in fact, said conspirators did call a non-official special meeting for the purpose of defeating the Lemmon Valley moratorium and for the nepotistic purpose of benefiting family member through illegal use of Trustee powers. Proper notice was not given to the full board or to the residents of Black Springs. Said conspirators then undertook to convert said non-official meeting into an official meeting."

Second Claim number VIII states, "That the acts committed by Stanley Cook and Marie Eckart were intentional and did proximately cause irreparable injury to Black Springs residents. That the acts complained of caused risks of water shortages, devaluation of property values, incurring of expenses and mental anguish."

On Barbet Bufkin's, member of the Board of Trustees, affidavit he states:

(II) "That a general meeting of the Board of Directors occurred on March 12, 1977. That at said general meeting no action was taken on the application submitted by DUCTH COOK, whereby the request had been made that DUTCH COOK become a water user."

(V) "That on March 19, 1977, a special meeting of the Board of Directors was called without written notice and without notice of the issues planned or issues to be raised or resolved." Mr. Bufkin

A CRY FOR HELP

attended and "... discovered that the question of permitting a relative of STANLEY COOK and MARIE ECKART to attach a two (2) inch tap onto the Black Springs Water Main was under discussion." Mr. Bufkin (VI) "... did not approve of the actions undertaken by STANLEY COOK, MARIE ECKART and FRANK HIGGINS and that he did not take any part whatsoever."

Mr. Bufkin knew (IX) "... that despite the knowledge of the risks of water shortage STANLEY COOK, MARIE ECKART and FRANK HIGGINS preceded to approve DUTCH COOK's application for a two (2) inch commercial water tap." Bufkin being (X) "... a board member knew that permit No. 685 issued by Washoe County was not brought to the attention of the full Board and was obtained without the approval of the full board."

Mr. Bufkin (XI) "... was informed and believed that the interest of the Black Springs Community will be served by the removal of the (2) inch commercial water tap because said two inch tap allows for the consumption of three times more water than would be consumed by a residential ¾ inch tap."

Mr. Thurman Carthen also a member of the Board noted in his affidavit, (II) "... on March 19, 1977, a special meeting of the Board was called by the Chairman but official notice of said meeting was not given to him and was not present at said meeting."

Mr. Carthen (III) "... had cautioned the Board to wait for the moratorium report before granting any permits to anyone or permitting authorizing any additional persons to become water subscribers."

Mr. Carthen knew (IV) "... of his own knowledge that STANLEY COOK attempted to use trustee powers for his own self interest" and knew (V) "... that the two (2) inch tap placed on the Black Springs Water System was done without authorization from the Black Springs General Improvement District Board." Also, (VI) "... that the permit obtained from the Washoe County Department of Public Works by STANLEY COOK, whereby the Black Springs General Improvement District is named as contractor, was done without authorization..."

CHRONOLOGY OF THE 1970'S

Another affiant, Frank Higgins, was also a member of the Board of Trustees. He attended the special meeting on March 17, 1977 and (III) "... was told that MR. STANLEY COOK stated that it was not really an official meeting and it would not become part of the minutes." Higgins believed (IV) "... that the action taken at the meeting was somewhat illegal."

Mr. Higgins (V) "... did not fully understand what STANLEY COOK and MARIE ECKART were attempting to do because, he had no notice of the meeting and this was his first meeting as a director." He (VI) "... did not advance notice of the agenda and didn't know the particulars involved in granting of permit to DUTCH COOK." He (VIII) "... was told that said meeting was a get-together for a discussion period and his vote in favor of granting a permit to DUTCH COOK was given on the belief that the actions were not official." He (IX) "... would not have given his vote for approval of a water hook-up to DUTCH COOK if he had known that STANLEY COOK and MARIE ECKART would attempt to make the meeting appear to be an official meeting."

Mr. Higgins rescinded and withdrew (X) "... his vote in favor of granting a water hook-up to DUTCH COOK." He stated (XI) "... that his vote was procured through confusion, misrepresentation, misunderstanding and misstatements."

Ollie and Helen Westbrook and Rev. Eddie Hill, the last Affiants, being first duly sworn as were all Affiants, collective gave deposes.

All the Affiants were concerned (IX) "... about the building of a truck stop and trailer park in their neighborhood and the use of a two (2) inch water tap to service said commercial ventures."

The Westbrooks had (I) "... been residents of the Black Springs Community for 23 years". Ollie knew through, knowledge of his own, (II) "... that the COOK family had misused trustee powers for their own self interest." He also knew (III) "... the Cook family had obtained 5 water permits and that the family used trustee powers for nepotistic purposes."

Ollie Westbrook knew (IV) "... that DUTCH COOK had obtained a permit for one trailer home to be place in Washoe County" and

A CRY FOR HELP

(V) ". . . that the actions of the Trustees on March 19, 1977, were taken without written notice and without public knowledge of the agenda."

Mr. Westbrook knew (VI) ". . . the Board Members were aware of State and County Moratorium and aware of the potential water shortages prior to March 19th." He (VII) ". . . warned the Board, prior to the granting of the unofficial permit, to attach a two (2) inch water tap, which the engineers' reports advised against adding additional subscribers and warned the Board of potential water shortages. (X) ". . . All other residents have a ¾ inch tap for home use and that the two (2) inch tap recently placed on the water main by DUTCH COOK threatens the community water supply."

Mr. Thurman Carthen, one of the Board of Trustees, on a *May 17, 1977* correspondence, was notified by Washoe County Manager that they had received a letter of resignation from Stanley Cook. According to procedure, ". . . the remaining members of the Board of Trustees should appoint a successor to Mr. Cook who will serve until a successor is elected to this position at the next biennial election."

They had 30 days after receipt of his resignation, and if not filled the Washoe County Commission would have to fill the vacancy.

On *May 18, 1977* the Reno Evening Gazette wrote about: 'Tough new water measures adopted.' ". . . Washoe County commissioners unanimously approved their anti-waste ordinance Tuesday. The first of its kind in Nevada, the ordinance will not become law until the commissioners hear citizen reaction to it at an 11 a.m. public hearing June 7 at the county administration building. . .

The county ordinance would apply only to property owners in unincorporated areas of Washoe County. It is further limited to persons served by community water systems or public water companies. It would not apply to property owners with wells. . ."

A letter from Charles Zeh dated *May 27, 1977* to the Board of Trustees, was a summary of a consultation he had with Brien Walters on the Dutch Cook situation. Charles Zeh met with Brien Walters

CHRONOLOGY OF THE 1970'S

on 19th May 1977 for about two hours discussing several issues, the most important being the Dutch Cook situation. The letter only noted Mr. Walters' observations. One would be "licensing Dutch Cook to operate a commercial enterprise such as a gas station would not necessarily increase the danger of a water shortage on the water system, as stations are not high water users or consumers and thus, would consume water perhaps no more or even less than the average home."

Mr. Walter's most insightful observation was that "a 2-inch water line carries sufficient volume to entirely drain the water system. Dutch Cook, therefore, could drain the system, whatever the use he might put to his tap into the line. At least, the 2-inch line permits 60 gallons of water per minute to pass through it. The two wells, acting in concert, can produce water only at the rate of 60 gallons per minute. Thus, Cook could become the sole user of water in the system, regardless of the purpose (commercial or residential) for using the system."

Brien Walter, according to the letter stated, "The District should not be afraid to allow Cook to construct the gas station on the premises and sell water for commercial purposes for the gas station. As indicated, a gas station is not a high water user and thus, could simply be another source of revenue for the District without threatening the District water supply. A car wash, however, would be another situation and should not be permitted."

The threat was that Cook owned one skip loader, one mobile crane, two dump trucks, one oil distributor truck, one water truck, one concrete pipe, miscellaneous trucking and heavy equipment, two caterpillars, one flat bed truck, and one portable mixer. After all, Cook was cited for violation of Ordinance No. 57 in July 1971. Both Mr. Zeh and Mr. Walters were aware of Cook's commercial assets.

The Regional Planning Commission of Reno, Sparks and Washoe County, posted a notice of application for change of land use Case No. C-25-77W on **May 27, 1977**. The change would reclassify Stanley F. Cook's property from A-1 (First Agricultural) with TR (Trailer) overlay to Land Use District M-1 (Industrial).

A CRY FOR HELP

This meant that if reclassified to M-1; it provides for any commercial use and most industrial uses. It prohibits residential use, churches, schools and similar uses.

The bookkeeper for the Black Springs GID, Jan Fanning, received on *May 31, 1977* a copy of the draft of the proposed by-laws for the District. Charles Zeh Legal Counsel for the GID had sent the draft on the 25th May 1977 asking Mrs. Fanning to reproduce the draft and make them available to the Board members. They can use the draft as basis for discussion.

The Washoe County Board of County Commissioners meeting was called to order on *July 12, 1977*. In regards to Stanley F. Cook's change of land use Case C-25-77W, the Regional Planning Commission recommended denial of reclassifying the property.

The Nevada State Journal reported on *July 13, 1977:*

'Residents Appeal for help.' "A group of Black Springs' residents appealed to the Washoe County Commissioners Tuesday for help in dealing with a man they characterized as a troublesome neighbor.

Ollie Westbrook, past chairman of the Black Springs General Improvement District, accused Stanley Cook of keeping trash, heavy equipment and, at one time, trying to start a wrecking yard illegally on his property in the Lemmon Valley area community.

He made his accusations after commissioners denied Cook's application for a change of land use to allow an 11-acre trailer court south of Highway 395 and West of Heindel Road.

"We're asking you to help us get this man off our back," said Westbrook, who said he was speaking for the residents of the predominately black community.

Westbrook also accused Cook of "trying to take complete control of our local government (the little improvement district) by ignoring its regulations and "Flaunting county ordinances."

CHRONOLOGY OF THE 1970'S

He said Cook is improperly obtaining water from the improvement district. The district has filed a lawsuit against him which is scheduled for a hearing this morning before Washoe District Court Judge John Gabrielli, but the district has been unable to find Cook to serve papers on him.

Cook did not appear at the public hearing on his land use change request. So, Commissioners directed the county staff to investigate possible violation of county ordinances after Westbrook showed them pictures of Cook's heavy equipment storage. . .

Commissioner Dwight Nelson noted that the Washoe-Storey Conservation District found that the site had been greatly disturbed by grading and filling. This might be another zoning violation, said Nelson. . ."

On *July 14th*, there were several articles regarding Black Springs' water woes. Pointing to one in particular in the Reno Gazette reported water has a problem all Washoe County areas share, though each had its own little twists.

"RESIDENT OLLIE WESTBROOK of the Black Springs General Improvement District has charged Stanley "Dutch" Cook of trying to take over Black Springs "with violations of the rules that the district set up concerning connections to the water system."

Westbrook has taken Cook to court over a two inch hook up to the district's water line. Other residents, said Westbrook, have three-quarter inch hook-ups.

Though the hook-up was approved by Black Springs' water board, Westbrook challenges that decision since one of the two favorable votes came from Cook's father.

Stanley B. Cook, the father resigned from the board April 19, saying in a letter to Thurman Carthen, "the reasons are too obvious to discuss…I personally want to save the district the trouble of a recall."

But Westbrook said the Cooks' interests go beyond water.

A CRY FOR HELP

"For the past years, through the years of 1967 up to the present time, he has tried to gain control of this community through various methods, most of them legal up until this time."

If Cook gets the hook-up "people will have to go to him on their hands and knees and beg him for water," Westbrook said, adding that this approximately 60 residential community was not founded for commercial purposes.

"This is a community of brotherhood," he explained.

Because Westbrook wants to keep it that way, we are taking him to court because we feel that he has broken the law and we want to bring him before the bar of justice in order to answer the question."

DUTCH COOK DISAGREES with Westbrook, especially when it comes to accusations that he wants to control the community.

"Just my own property," he specified.

As for his accuser he said, "He is called Big Daddy out there and he likes to control everyone."

Cook refers most questions to his attorney, Wallace Stephens, of Sparks, who was in Court last week for pretrial arguments in the case.

Westbrook and his attorney, David Dean, were seeking an order to dismantle the two inch hook-up.

HOWEVER DISTRICT JUDGE JOHN GABRIELLI said he wanted to maintain "status quo" and rather than unhook the connection, he issued an injunction against "using or drawing water from the tank until further notice from this court."

He also prohibited Cook from building any commercial structure and provided for regular inspection of the hook-up to make sure it is not being used.

CHRONOLOGY OF THE 1970'S

Judge Gabrielli added he is "fully aware of the critical water shortage and the feelings here of the people involved," so his hope was to "preserve the peace."

WHETHER PEACE IS PRESERVED depends on the outcome; the final decision of Cook's trial.

Westbrook said he favors going through the judicial system, but noted that some residents had talked of other means.

"Whether or not this community will flourish depends on the courts," he said.

He is not the only one interested in the outcome of the trial..." Washoe County Manager John MacIntyre said "... he will wait until a decision comes from the Court before he takes any action.

"I think it is in the interest of every body involved to see what kind of interpretation comes out of that court case," he said."

Another article reported:

"The case shaped up Wednesday as an attempt by plaintiff Ollie Westbrook and a majority of water district trustees to portray the defendants as the Grinches Who Stole the Water System..."

The article also stated:

"Board secretary-treasurer Thurman Carthen, who missed the Saturday meeting, testified that he later conferred with the board's attorney Chuck Zeh and then wrote to the younger Cook disapproving the two-inch application and returning his $500 fee. Carthen said the board then met and ratified that action.

He and the other board members who testified were in court Wednesday without Zeh. The board is a defendant in the suit, but at least two trustees have joined in as plaintiffs—in effect, the board is suing itself.

A CRY FOR HELP

Plaintiff-defendants Carthen, Bufkin and Higgins said they came down to testify without counsel because they feel the question needs to be cleared up."

There was a letter sent to Senator Howard W. Cannon sometime after *July 14th*. The letter was drafted in Mrs. Westbrooks handwriting and signed by Thurman Carthen, Secretary/Treasurer of the Board of Trustees.

The letter was again requesting help. The community was "asking and pleading"; since the Senator was instrumental in helping Black Springs get the grant for the water system from HUD. The letter stated:

"The General Improvement District has a Board of 5 people who govern the District and a Legal Aid attorney, who is to advise the Board.

The Legal Aid attorney seems more to be defending the defendant than the Water District. His name is Charles Zeh.

Maybe if you could talk to him and find out what his problem is. We need him now.

Since Legal Aid is a federally funded program, we feel you are the last hope we have of saving our water system. Since November 1976 to April 1977 we have requested by letter and telephone, Mr. Zeh, he would not respond. It seems he no longer has the interest of the Water System anymore."

It is obvious from the response letter from Senator Cannon dated *August 3, 1977* he knew what Helen Westbrook was asking. Before signing his letter his secretary had typed, he crossed out Mr. and Mrs. Westbrook and wrote in Helen & Ollie. After all they were friends.

He thanks them for the recent letter regarding the difficulties with the legal aid attorney for the Black Springs General Improvement District.

He went on to inform them:

CHRONOLOGY OF THE 1970'S

"As you well know, the District is an autonomous entity, separate and distinct from those individuals who make up the District and as such, it has the same legal obligations and rights as do all individuals. Mr. Zeh as the Board's attorney must defend this board, not represent those individuals who might have a grievance against it or who might comprise it.

I certainly sympathize with you in this situation and am sorry that there is nothing I can do to help you. However, since this matter is now being decided by the court, it would not be prudent of me to make any further comment as to the disposition of this case.

If you have any questions or need further explanation, please do not hesitate to call on me again. I will be pleased to offer any clarification I might be able to."

Walters Engineering sent David Dean Attorney at Law a statement on *August 8, 1977* "for Professional Engineering in connection with preparation for and court appearance per subpoena in connection with Cook water service application—Black Springs General Improvement District," the total amount due, $450.00.

The letter from Brien Walters, P. E. Walters Engineering to Black Springs General Improvement District dated *August 8, 1977* was regarding water rights. This letter which he copied Zeh, was based upon consultation between himself and Charles Zeh on 19th May 1977.

"We recently talked with the State Division of Water Resources regarding the District's water rights and the Proof of Beneficial Use recently filed." Mr. Zeh Legal Counsel for the District must have been the representative for the recent talk.

"According to the State Engineer, the water rights originally purchased from the Eugene Sweatt Water Company, applications numbered 21462 and 20853 had two limiting factors. One was for 45 homes and the other not to exceed 34 million gallons per year."

His basic point was "the fact 62 units are and have been served (water pumped) should be a factor in the District's favor. The District

A CRY FOR HELP

should immediately file an application to the State Engineer's office for additional bonified services for the additional water rights."

Russell McDonald, County Manager responded to Ollie Westbrook's request in drafting bylaws through a correspondence dated *August 19, 1977*:

"Attached are a set of suggested bylaws of the Black Springs General Improvement District and the Board of Trustees. In drafting the bylaws, I have had to make certain assumptions of fact which may be incorrect. I have provided you with the original and 4 copies together with 5 copies of the recent publication of the Attorney General relating to the Nevada Open Meeting Law.

The proposed bylaws are based upon authority contained in NRS 318.08, 318.085, 318.090, 318.0956, 318.0957, 318.205 and Chapter 527, Statues of Nevada 1977 (amendments to Nevada Open Meeting Law). I have attempted to incorporate in the bylaws the essential requirements of the Open Meeting Law which the Board of Trustees of the Black Springs General Improvement District is now bound by.

I take no pride of authorship and if, after discussion with the Board, amendments are suggested, please advise me." The letter was signed Russell W. McDonald.

On A*ugust 24, 1977* in the Second Judicial District Court the deposit for a cash bond was paid for Preliminary Injunction in the amount of $2,500.00. The County Clerk filed the receipt on 25th August 1977.

On *August 29, 1977* in the Second Judicial District Court of the State of Nevada, in and for the County of Washoe the Temporary Injunction was made.

"IT IS HEREBY ORDERED, that during the pendency of this action, or until the final determination thereof, or until the court shall otherwise order or as modified by agreement between the parties,

CHRONOLOGY OF THE 1970'S

Defendant, DUTCH COOK, his agents, servants, employees, and attorneys be, and they herby are enjoined and restrained from:

1.) Using or in any way authorizing the use of and/or obtaining water from the two (2")-inch connection which was installed on his property in Black Springs pursuant to permit No. 685 issued on April 13, 1977 by the Washoe County Department of Public Works. 2.) Building any commercial or other property upon the property serviced by the two (2")-inch connection which construction must of necessity be authorized in reliance upon the availability of water. 3.) From in any way extending the subject water line to property outside of the Black Springs General Improvement District.

IT IS FURTHER ORDERED, that inspection of the subject connection shall be permitted by the Defendant for the purpose of insuring that this Injunction is being complied with. Such inspection to be at reasonable times and in such manner as may be agreed to between the parties hereto.

IT IS FURTHER ORDERED that a preliminary injunction be issued a herein set forth, on plaintiff's filing an undertaking in due form, to be approved by the Court in the sum of TWO THOUSAND FIVE HUNDRED (2,500.00) DOLLARS." This injunction was ordered by Judge John E. Gabrielli.

This whole situation damaged the brotherhood in which the predominately Black community had embraced. It would remain irreparable.

Mr. Westbrook received a letter from his attorney, David Dean on **December 19, 1977.**

"It seems that Mr. Walters is holding his office responsible for payment of the $450.00 bill. This was the statement from August 1977. David suggested maybe this could be paid by the Black Springs Plaintiffs and charged to the Defendants when the suit has been finalized."

A CRY FOR HELP

Five months had elapsed and there was no documentation to show that the Black Springs General Improvement District was conducting business.

The City of Reno on *January 13, 1978* from the Office of Community Development posted:

"TO ALL INTERESTED CITIZENS AND ORGANIZATIONS:

The Community Development Department of the City of Reno is preparing an application to HUD under the fourth year funding of the Community Development Block Grant (CDBG) Program. In an attempt to involve as many people and organizations as possible, the attached material is being sent to you. Applications for funding under this Program will be accepted until February 6, 1978...

For the 1978-1979 fiscal years, the City of Reno will receive an estimated $976,000 from HUD. Community Development members will be happy to assist any applicant with the forms. Your participation is encouraged."

There's no documentation to show that the Black Springs General Improvement District acted upon this opportunity.

A somewhat cryptic document dated *February 18, 1978* indicates a meeting of the Black Springs General Improvement District Board. Members present were Frank Higgins, Barbet Bufkin, and Mildred Washington. Thurman Carthen and Marie Eckart were absent. Mildred Washington was occupying the seat vacated by Stanley Cook.

The document states, "Elect officers": Chairman Bufkin, Vice Chair Mrs. Washington and Secretary/Treasurer Carthen.

Black Spring General Improvement District Board of Trustees sent a notice to all District customers on *March 5, 1978*. The notice was informing the community of the new elected officers for the year 1978.

The positions now held by the Board of Trustees were: Barbet Bufkin Chairperson, Mildred Washington Vice Chairperson, Thurman

CHRONOLOGY OF THE 1970'S

Carthen Secretary/Treasurer and members Frank Higgins and Marie Eckart.

On *April 18, 1978* Washoe County sent out letters from the Office of the County Manager, notifying communities of the Community Development Block Grant Small Cities Program:

First, "this letter advises you of Washoe County's wish to receive citizen input on projects under the Community Development Block Grant Small Cities Program. The Department of Housing and Urban Development will accept pre-applications for Community Development Block Grant Small Cities Program from cities under 50,000 population and counties in metropolitan areas such as Reno. The deadline for submitting the pre-applications is May 15, 1978."

Second, "for Fiscal Year 1978, approximately $770,000 will be available for grants to applicants from the Nevada standard metropolitan areas. There are two types of assistance available. These are Comprehensive and Single-Purpose programs. These programs are designed to benefit low and moderate-income persons, members of minority groups and residents of blighted or deteriorated neighborhoods."

An attempt was made by the Black Springs General Improvement District to capitalize on the Community Development Block Grant Small Cities Program. On *April 27, 1978* Thurman Carthen Secretary/Treasurer sent a letter to Mr. John MacIntyre County Manager:

"The Black Springs General Improvement District is pleased to respond to your request for input into the projects under the Community Development Block Grant Small Cities Program.

"However, on such short notice, it will be very difficult for us to present some sound base cost figures on the different projects."

Mr. Carthen went on to list some projects in the order of priority for the Black Springs community. Other than this letter, there is no documentation to show a pre-application was submitted.

A CRY FOR HELP

Chairman of the Board Barbet Bufkin on verbal approval by the Black Springs GID Board during a meeting *April 25, 1978* sent a memorandum, "To all customers of the Black Springs Water Company."

It was written specifically for those having delinquent accounts on the books.

"The Black Springs General Improvement District can no longer carry delinquent accounts and therefore shall start operating as other utility companies operate."

He states further on, "Those customers who have not brought their accounts to a current status will have their water service terminated as of July 1, 1978. If this is the case, the account must be paid in full and a deposit of two months water fee ($18.50) must be paid, prior to the water being turned back on. It is with regret that we must take this action. THERE WILL BE <u>NO EXCEPTIONS</u> TO THIS RULING."

According to a written note at the bottom, the ruling would be ratified at a Special Meeting, May 5, 1978.

A meeting of the Board of Trustees of the Black Springs General Improvement District was held on *August 24, 1978*.

The members present were: Barbet Bufkin, Thurman Carthen and Essie Prien. Marie Eckart and Frank Higgins were absent. Chuck Zeh, Counsel for the District, Jannette Fanning Bookkeeper for the District and various members of the community were also present.

Something must have transpired. There was a change on the Board. Mildred Washington was on the Board now Essie Prien resides on the Board. There is no documentation to show why the change occurred.

After roll call indicated a quorum was present and the minutes from the July meeting were read and approved. The bills were then presented for payment. After discussion, the motion was carried and the bills were set up for payment.

CHRONOLOGY OF THE 1970'S

"The next item on the agenda was discussion of the Cook water line and the removal of same. Mr. Cook was asked if the line has been removed. He replied that he is awaiting the Boards proposal.

Mr. Zeh informed him that the District wants the line out, and what is Mr. Cook's proposal?

Mr. Cook stated that he would like to leave the line in so that he would be first for hook-up when Westergard increases the services.

Mr. Carthen then asked if the water line is being disconnected from the District's line. He stated that since Mr. Cook is the one to hook up the line, even though the rules state that the District will hook-up new lines, we should now take action to remove the line from the District's line. Mr. Zeh then advised that he can negotiate with the Cook's attorney to have the line disconnected.

Thurman Carthen then moved that Mr. Zeh be given until Wednesday, August 30th to negotiate with Mr. Cook's attorney in regards to disconnecting the Cook water line from the District, and Mr. Zeh immediately advised the Board of his findings. The motion was carried.

The Board then gave their attention to the matter of petitioning certain Board members for their resignation so that more active members of the community can take their place on the Board.

Mr. Zeh stated that there is a section in the Nevada Revised Statutes that allows the removal of people from the Board if they hinder business being conducted, and that is through petition to the County Commissioners.

He, Mr. Zeh, suggested that a letter be sent to Mr. Higgins asking for his resignation, since the reason Mr. Higgins is not attending is his work schedule, and that it will not be necessary to notify Mrs. Eckart, since she has been previously notified.

Mr. Carthen moved that a letter be sent to Frank Higgins asking for his resignation and thanking him for past participation, and that

A CRY FOR HELP

Marie Eckart be petitioned to be removed from the Board. The motion was carried.

Mr. Zeh also stated that we must set a definite meeting to discuss the change of rates and the change of rules and regulations, since the last planned meeting could not be held due to lack of quorum. He advised that once again it would be necessary for the Board to advertise in the newspaper, and it was unanimously decided that the meeting would be set for October 7, 1978.

It was also decided that there would be no September meeting held, since members of the Board would be out of town during the month, and that the next regular meeting also be held on October 7, 1978." The meeting was adjourned.

The Board of Trustees did hold a meeting in September but there are no minutes.

The regular meeting of the Black Springs GID District Board was held **October 7, 1978.** All Board members were in attendance. Ollie Westbrook, Maintenance, Jannette Fanning, Bookkeeper and members of the community were also present.

The meeting opened at 10:50 a.m. with reading of the minutes from the September meeting and they were approved.

". . . The guests and Board members were then informed that items 4 and 5 on the agenda, regarding discussion for increase in rate of tariff and change of rules and regulations would have to be delayed since Chuck Zeh had most of the pertinent information on theses matters and Mr. Zeh was not present. Mr. Zeh had stated at the August 24th meeting that these issues were important and a definite meeting be set for discussion which should have been at this time. . .

Mr. Brown, who is in the process of building a home in the community, then asked about the possibility of securing water. Mr. Bufkin advised him that unless the State increased the number of services, the Board's hands were tied, and new services cannot be installed.

CHRONOLOGY OF THE 1970'S

Discussion followed regarding the fact that there doesn't seem to be anything. Mr. Bufkin assured the members of the community that the Board could not just do things on their own. Legalities were involved, and all of this took time. He stated that both the Board and the Community should work together and this has not been done in the past. But by working together and everyone taking an interest in the district, more could be accomplished..."

William Lobster, Chief of the Black Springs Volunteer Fire Dept sent a letter on **October 17, 1978** to the Washoe County Manager & Commissioners on behalf of the Black Springs GID. He stated the community of Black Springs felt that there was a party living at 395 Westbrook Lane who was in violation of both the Health and Building codes of this area. He listed three violations: Living in a trailer with no water; horse, goats on property, and a junkyard with about 12 cars and a truck etc. He asked for their immediate attention and forwarded copies to the Building Inspector and the Health Inspector.

Time for a little personal reflection, I know there are still residents who have horses in Black Springs but I can't say remembering goats. Most residents, including my family, had chickens.

One day, Mr. Jones brought a live pig home to butcher. You heard the pig squealing and squealing as Mr. Jones chased the pig around in his carport. He would block the only exit and eventually the pig would be caught and the squealing stopped. Within the next few days, Mr. Jones would be giving neighbors some part of the pig.

Fresh "chitlins", that was the first time I had ever seen them. For years I couldn't eat them anymore. Prior to that I would always look forward to New Years, because that was the only time of the year we would have chitlins. And I would eat more than everyone but my brother Jeff Jr., he definitely out ate me.

The Washoe County Manager, John MacIntyre sent a letter on **December 11, 1978** to the Department of Housing and Urban Development with the revisions to 'Washoe County's Community Development application B78-DS-32-0004.' The application originated September

A CRY FOR HELP

15th and was amended on December 8th. Black Springs would not be included in this phase at this time.

A meeting of the Black Springs GID Board of Trustees was held on **December 21, 1978**. A quorum was present which were Thurman Carthen, Barbet Bufkin and Essie Prien. Frank Higgins and Marie Eckart were absent. The meeting was called to order with the reading of the November meeting which there are no documents for.

Because of the meeting being held later in the month than it normally are held, and no quorum was present at the regular meeting date, the bills were paid on Saturday, December 16th so late notices would not be received.

"The next item was Board reorganization. Mr. Zeh presented a letter of resignation from Marie Eckart, and advised that the vacancy on the Board must be filled within 30 days from date of letter in order to be legal with the appointment.

Mr. Bufkin asked if anyone would like to make a suggestion for a replacement. Thurman Carthen suggested that we consider some names and see what we come up with.

Mr. Zeh suggested that they appoint someone who will be able to support the new members coming on the Board and is familiar with the Board.

Mr. Williams suggested that the community appoint someone to serve. He stated that we don't need someone who has served on the Board before.

Mr. Lobster pointed out that we needed five active members who will take an interest and show up for the meetings, someone who is interested in the water system and in the community. He advised that if some past Board member was willing to serve and they can't find anyone else, it wouldn't matter to him.

CHRONOLOGY OF THE 1970'S

After discussion, the names submitted were: Johnnie Stevens, Mrs. Dale Reynolds and Dehlno Emde all whom were present and voiced the fact that they would be willing to serve. After further discussion, since no decision could be made, it was decided that a special meeting would be held on December 28, 1978 . . . with a one-item agenda, that of appointing someone to replace Mrs. Eckart on the Board.

During the course of discussion, it was brought out that Mr. Higgins has been a very inactive member, and an attempt should be made to obtain his resignation so that someone could replace Mr. Higgins and this should be done prior to the December 28 meeting, so that both seats could be filled at the same time.

Mr. Williams then asked about the balance due Mr. Westbrook on his last bill submitted. Mr. Bufkin and Mr. Zeh both explained that there was a matter of duplication between the bill Mr. Westbrook presented and the firm that repaired the totalizing meter and it would be taken care of as soon as this was checked out. . .

The next item on the agenda was preparation of the Budget for the next year as well as appointing an auditor for the program year 1977-78. Mr. Zeh advised that he talked to Stan Rahn of Salman, Levoy and Rahn accounting firm, who offered to do the audit for the sum of $950.00. He thought that based on the hours involved in the audit, the price was a fair one. He advised that he also talked to Mr. Rahn about taking over the bookkeeping and handling the district books and mailing of statements. They would not of course, handle the minutes, filing, or working at the community office. Mr. Rahn would keep the district books for the sum of $100.00 per month. Mr. Carthen and Mr. Bufkin voiced their opinion that the new board should have something to say about this situation." The motion was moved and carried to accept Mr. Rahn's offer for audit of the books, then moved that the matter of bookkeeping be tabled until the new board members are seated and could have a voice in this matter.

Mr. Carthen then suggested that the matter of the Dutch Cook Water line be put on the agenda for the January meeting. Mr. Williams

A CRY FOR HELP

stated that yes; he would like to see it on there. There being no further business the meeting adjourned.

On *December 27, 1978*, the Division of Water Resources granted a permit;

"This permit is issued subject to existing rights. It is understood that the amount of water herein granted is only a temporary allowance and that the final water right obtained under this permit will be dependent upon the amount of water actually placed to beneficial use.... The State retains the right to regulate the use of the water herein granted at any and all times.

The total number of units to be served under Permits 30366, 30446 and 34012 is limited to the 63 units now being served and the total combined duty under this Permit and Permits 30366, 30446 and 34012 shall not exceed 23.65 million gallons annually."

Mr. Barbet Bufkin Chairman of the Black Springs GID sent a letter on *January 12, 1979* to the Washoe County Board of commissioners. The letter was a priority list to be considered under the County Block Grant for the Black Springs area – 1979. Their first preference was the rehabilitation of approximately 14 existing homes, and funds for construction of new homes approximately 45. Second was water, seeing that Black Springs was in dire need of an additional well to service the proposed new homes, and to supply a better water system to the homes existing. Third was sewage. Black Springs was on a septic tank system and sewage was needed because of the density and a low to none septic tank percolation. Fourth was completion of curbs and gutters. They needed to be completed throughout the entire area for proper drainage and/or run-off.

On *January 29, 1979* a pre-application was submitted to the Housing and Community Improvements Program. This was a single purpose pre-application containing four projects. The projects consist of housing rehabilitation and water improvements in Black Springs, administration, housing information and referral, flood and drainage facilities and land acquisition for the mentally handicapped. The number of persons benefiting would be approximately 14,500. Black Springs' portion would amount to $448,000.00.

The Cooks' once again submitted an application for change of land use on **February 2, 1979**. This was an attempt to change from A-1 w/TR Overlay – Provides for agricultural uses and limits residential use to one mobile home per one acre to M-1 which provides for any commercial uses and most industrial uses which prohibits residential, church, school and similar uses. The hearing was schedule for Tuesday evening, February 20th.

'Dissolution hearing set for Black Springs improvement district' was the title in the evening Reno Gazette on **February 7, 1979**.

What more could this community possibly endure?

"A hearing to decide if the financially troubled Black Springs General Improvement District should be dissolved was scheduled Tuesday by the Washoe County Commission.

The hearing was set for March 20th, after commissioner received a scathing letter from the Nevada Department of Taxation criticizing the district's accounting procedures.

Prior to the hearing, the commission must mail notices of the session to all voters and property owners within the Black Springs district as specified by law.

The law empowers the district's parent body, the commission, with the options of dissolving, taking over or letting the district's governing body continue.

The letter, signed by Roy Nickson, executive director of the State Taxation Department, said that the district is not being properly managed and that the district's Board of Trustees, have not complied with the state law that governs general improvement districts.

The letter notes that when the district was formed in November 1974, the department appointed auditors to provide fiscal reports for the years 1975, 1976 and 1977.

A CRY FOR HELP

The three audits and two notices from the district were the only documents received by the department since the district's operation, the letter said.

The letter also said that, "Correspondence sent (to) the district on several occasions by certified mail, were returned 'unclaimed.'"

Audits for the year 1975 and 1976 revealed that only memo records were maintained and minutes of meetings were not kept.

The audits for those years concluded that "it is, therefore, impossible to ascertain the all payments are, in fact, properly authorized. The district does not maintain adequate accounting records necessary for maintaining reliable financial information."

Last December, an audit of the district for the fiscal year of 1976-1977 showed that $997 had been "misappropriated" and that another $2,428 was missing.

During that year, gross revenues for the district should have amounted to $6,100. Instead, the recorded cash flow showed that only $3,672 had been recorded as revenue, the audit said.

Nickson's letter goes on to state that Albert Williams, a state Highway Department mechanic and new chairman of the district, had met with him last January.

Williams, who succeeded Barbet Bufkin as chairman in January, had said before, "I don't want to take office until this shortage is corrected."

During that meeting, Williams said he would take "positive action" to correct past deficiencies in the district's operation.

The letter suggests that the commissioners let Williams present his corrective proposals before them.

CHRONOLOGY OF THE 1970'S

"Based on his testimony . . . (the) board may desire to permit the district to operate under stricter supervision," the letter said.

It also states that the commission should also consider giving Williams a "period of time" to evaluate the effectiveness of his proposed measures.

Nickson and Williams were unavailable for comment.

Commissioner Steve Brown, who represents the Black Springs district, was absent during the meeting. . ."

The regular meeting of the Black Springs GID Board of Trustees was held on **February 8, 1979.** Members present were Louis Chacon, William Lobster, Johnnie Stevens, Al Williams and Frank Higgins, who left after submitting his resignation. Others present were Chuck Zeh Counsel for District, Jannette Fanning Recording Secretary and various members of the community.

Minutes from the meeting of January 13th were read. Corrections were made regarding non-property owners serving on the Board. If they didn't own property they should not be on the Board and if they owned property, Mr. Williams had no objections. Also, Mrs. Reynolds, who was nominated to serve on the Board, refused to accept the nomination.

The minutes of January 13, 1979 were read. A correction was noted in the next to last paragraph. Both sets of minutes were accepted.

After the bills were presented and motioned and accepted, the recording secretary read the new permit received from the Department of Water Resources. A discussion followed.

"Ollie Westbrook advised that when it comes to the new well, the plans were when the Board applied for an increase in the water amount; they applied for permit for a new well because the system it now has will not furnish and keep up with the supply demand. The new well should be used for ground storage for a quick recover. At that time there was a

A CRY FOR HELP

question. The State interpreted the permit as 23 million annually, and our engineers and the county interpreted it as 34 million. This has now been settled with the new permit we have. It gives you an annual usage of 34 million gallons and a permit for a third well.

Mr. Williams asked if we should wait before taking any new applications. Mr. Lobster asked that the secretary read the rest of the permit.

Ollie Westbrook then explained that the two wells we now have is for 34 million gallons. We can put in a new well but we still cannot exceed 34 million gallons annually. Mr. Williams suggested that Walters Engineering be contacted to get this straight. Ollie Westbrook agreed.

Mr. Williams stated that we were not going to accept any new hookup at the present time, and Mr. Zeh stated that we are limited to 63 hook-ups which are what we now have. He advised that the original request was for 140 hook-ups but at present we don't have the water capacity, and even if we did, we are still limited to 63 hook-ups. Mr. Lobster asked if another application to the State would be in order. Mr. Zeh responded that they had submitted applications to increase service to 93 under the existing wells in order to be able to honor new applications. Another time they asked for 140 hook-ups, but they still have given us only 63. You may want to submit another application.

Mr. Williams advised that while talking to the Nevada Tax Commission, he complained about the fact that we were limited in expansion, and they mentioned that they would take this into considerations.

William Lobster asked if Walters Engineering designed the other two wells."

They did the entire system for the district, Mr. Zeh advised. "Obviously, it would have been better to have the increase on the old wells and in that way, you wouldn't have to dig a new well. However, it is also nice to have a permit for a third well. It does cost money. I'm talking about $30,000 roughly and I don't know where you can get the

CHRONOLOGY OF THE 1970'S

money. In any event, talk to Walters Engineering, then report back at the next Board meeting. If it is necessary to commence to dig another well and find funds, then you can ask for an extension of time for this permit and ask for permission to correct the same system and increase that.

Mr. Westbrook advised that an application has been filed with Washoe County under the Small Cities grants. It was sent to the County and the Commissioners have taken action on it. It originates from HUD and in order to approve it, they have to check the income of some of the people in the district. I gave them as much information as I could. I advised that we have about 15-18 people on fixed income. They accepted that as a good start. If the people in the neighborhood will give out the information they require when they request it, we have a good chance of being approved for approximately $50,000 to get another well.

Mr. Williams then asked Mr. Zeh if we should hold off taking applications for hook-ups and Mr. Zeh responded that we should absolutely not take any. We are authorized for 63 and that is how many you have. With all three permits we now have, we cannot exceed 63 hook-ups.

Mr. Westbrook also pointed out that with the two wells we now have, if one of them goes out we are in trouble. It would take only about five days to drain the entire system.

Mr. Williams then advised, that with reference to the new well, we should hold up on this until the next meeting.

Mr. Lobster then moved that the Board table the matter of the permit until such time as the Chairman can contact Walters Engineering and get from the engineers their advice as to what we should do and then proceed with the paper work. The motion was carried.

The recording secretary then read letters from the District Attorney's office and from the Tax Commission, concerning a hearing on the dissolution of the District. Mr. Williams then explained to the community that the main reason he wrote the letters concerning past due accounts was to get the people to the meeting. He advised that he must show the County that he and the Board can bring the district out of the

A CRY FOR HELP

red and operate it the way it should be operated, and one way to do it, was to keep the accounts current. Therefore, anyone whose bill was not paid would have their water shut off and it is as simple as that.

Mr. Zeh then pointed out a portion of the letter from Larry Struve and suggested that the Board contract with Stan Rahn to handle the books. He advised that he had suggested this before the Christmas Holidays. You now have a new Board. You might consider contracting with an accounting firm so that the books can be handled in compliance with our reporting requirements.

Mr. Lobster pointed out that if Stan Rahn did the books for $100 per month, the cost would be $1200 per year. We received another figure from $800 to $900 per year, plus he would set up the bookkeeping system and start the books. I don't think we are that stupid. If we are trained in setting up the records, and Mr. Brickley would do that free, it would not cost the district anything and we can keep the books.

Rev. Hill then asked what the Board's criterion was for bringing the water bills up to date. It will state in the By-laws how far a customer can get behind, Mr. Williams replied. We are now in the process of drawing up the By-laws. You will be allowed to get 60 days behind. In the third month if the bill is not paid, the water will be cut off.

Rev. Hill then asked Mr. Zeh if there was not a set of By-laws drawn up during a meeting in Zeh's office.

Mr. Zeh replied that he didn't recall that meeting. He recalls that we did adopt a set of rules and regulations at the time Mr. Westbrook was Chairman.

Rev. Hill advised that he recalls the meeting where a set of By-laws were drawn up.

Mr. Zeh stated that he might have drawn up a rough draft, but did not recall that they were in final form.

Mr. Williams stated that right now we don't have any By-laws."

CHRONOLOGY OF THE 1970'S

Mr. Zeh asked if anyone had been assigned by the Board to draw them up.

"Mr. Williams advised that he had a petition for him to draw up the By-laws, and Mr. Zeh reminded him that according to law, it must be done in open meeting.

The discussion then turned to the next item on the Agenda, a letter from the District Attorney's office regarding the Cook hook-up.

Mr. Williams explained that he contacted the District Attorney's office to get a legal opinion regarding the Cook hook-up. There is no place in the minutes where permission was given to have that hook-up. Mr. Dannan advised me to ask Mr. Zeh if the hook-up is legal and to put it in writing and show the minutes where it was voted on. We should have the Board write a letter to Mr. Zeh, however, since there was not time, Mr. Williams stated to Mr. Zeh that he wanted to hear from Mr. Zeh right now as to whether that is a legal hook-up. If not a legal hook-up then the Board will vote to direct Mr. Zeh to send a letter to Mr. Cook to have the line removed and Mr. Cook will pay for the disconnect and the water he has been using.

Mr. Zeh replied that in his opinion the regulations we have adopted permit only three-fourth inch hook-up. What the Board did, I am not aware, since I was not present at the meeting. I have not seen the minutes. The Board may have done something I am not aware of. Furthermore, it would be helpful, if you want those answers from me, to give me a copy of the agenda well in advance, and let me know in advance what questions you want answered.

Mr. Williams advised that in the minutes, Mr. Zeh was strictly against Mr. Cook getting a hook-up. All of a sudden he got one. Nobody voted yes or no.

Mr. Zeh stated that he thinks it is against regulations as far as the size of the hook-up is concerned.

Mr. Williams then asked if the Cook land was annexed to the District. He advised that the map has never been filed and never been

A CRY FOR HELP

signed. The land has not been annexed into the District. That is what they mean by the Board being in violation. He then again asked Mr. Zeh if the line was legal or not.

Mr. Zeh advised that he would not give an opinion.

Mr. Williams then stated that he would like a motion from the Board that these minutes be sent to the Department of Taxation and to the District Attorney's office.

Mr. Lobster moved that the minutes be sent to the Department of Taxation and the District Attorney's office, and as soon as we receive an answer, we take immediate action on the water line. Mr. Chacon seconded the motion, which carried.

Mr. Williams then pointed out that Mr. Higgins has resigned from the Board. It will be necessary for us to appoint another member to the Board, and we will need someone who will take part in the duties of the Board, mainly to act as Secretary on the Board to sign correspondence, minutes, etc. This will come up on the next agenda.

The next item was a letter received from Community Services Agency of Washoe County, asking that an alternate be appointed to their Board of Directors to serve in the absence of Mr. Westbrook, who now represents the District on the Board.

Mr. Williams asked if anyone would be interested in serving and Mr. Lobster suggested that Mrs. Vernell Williams be appointed.

Mrs. Williams stated that she would not mind, if the position was only as an alternate.

Mr. Lobster then moved that Mrs. Vernell Williams be appointed to serve as an alternate to Mr. Westbrook on the Board of Directors of the Community Services Agency of Washoe County." The motion carried.

A public hearing on **February 20, 1979** with Regional Planning Commission of Reno, Sparks and Washoe County was scheduled

CHRONOLOGY OF THE 1970'S

between 7:00 & 8:00 p.m. "Change of Land Use District Case No. C-68-79W (STANLEY COOK, ET AL) proposed change from A-1 (First Agricultural) with (Trailer) overlay to Land Use District M-1 (Industrial)..." His request was again denied. Cook appealed the decision again on April 4th.

Deputy District Attorney Edward Dannan sent a letter to the Board of Directors of the Black Springs GID on *February 21, 1979*.

"This letter will serve to notify the Board that a hearing concerning the operation of the Black Springs General Improvement District has been scheduled before the Washoe County Board of Commissioners on March 20, 1979 at 1:30 p.m. as required by subsection 1 of NRS 318.515...

The notification required pursuant to the above-cited subsection of NRS was transmitted to the Board of County Commissioners by the Department of Taxation on January 24, 1979...

At the above-referenced hearing, the Board of Directors will be asked to respond to the allegations made by the Department and, more specifically, to explain why: (1) The records of the District are inadequate, incomplete and do not provide for adequate internal control; (2) a budget was not prepared for the years ending June 30, 1976 and 1977 as is required by the provisions of Chapter 354 of NRS; and (3) cash transactions were not deposited in a bank account in a timely manner. In some instances deposits delayed more than 30 days.

At the conclusion of the hearing, the Board of County Commissioners is required to act pursuant to subsection 3 of NRS 318.515...

In its transmittal of notification to the Board of County Commissioners, the Department of Taxation indicates that it has met with Mr. Al Williams, Chairman of the Board of Directors of the District concerning the District's general operation and financial records Mr. Williams indicates that positive action would be initiated to correct past deficiencies in the District's operation. To prevent the possible adoption of an ordinance pursuant to paragraph (a) or (b) of subsection 3 of the section

A CRY FOR HELP

of NRS, it is advised that Mr. Williams appear at the hearing to respond to the allegations set forth above and to explain what action is contemplated to see that management and organization of the District is revised to correct past deficiencies." A copy was sent the Charles Zeh, Esq.

The Westbrooks, not being entrapped in factions, forged ahead continuing to focus on improving the community of Black Springs.

Ollie Westbrook received a letter from the office of the County Manager's Administrative Assistant Dianne Cornwall dated **March 2, 1979.** The letter was regarding a conversation on February 28, on the status of Washoe County's Community Block Development Small Cities Program for fiscal year 1979/80. Upon Westbrook's request, update on the Black Springs' portion of the pre-application was provided.

"In the 1979/80 pre-application, Washoe County included the following projects for the Black Springs area: Housing Rehabilitation $248,000.00; Water System Improvements $90,000.00; and Curb & Gutter Improvements $110,000.00. The figures do not include monies requested for administrative costs, which will be incurred for the housing rehabilitation program.

The pre-application was scheduled to be reviewed on February 22 by the Department of Housing and Urban Development. To date, we have not received any information on acceptance or rejection of the pre-application.

You will be notified on the status as soon as we receive any confirmation from HUD."

A Public Notice was posted by the Office of the Washoe County Clerk on **March 8, 1979.**

"To Whom It May Concern:

NOTICE IS HERBY GIVEN that the Board of County Commissioners, Washoe County, Nevada, will hold a public hearing on Tuesday, March 20, 1979, at 1:30 p.m., in the Auditorium of the Washoe County

CHRONOLOGY OF THE 1970'S

Administration Building. . ., to consider the future of the Black Springs General Improvement District.

The State of Nevada, Department of Taxation, has advised the Washoe County Board of Commissioners that the Black Springs General Improvement District:

(a) ". . . is not being properly managed;" and

(b) "The board of trustees is not complying with the provisions of NRS 318.515 (1) or with any other law. . ."

Anyone desiring to testify in this regard or to make his views known concerning the district may do so by appearing at the above named location at the time set for the hearing.

A copy of the Public Notice was sent to the Department of Taxation, State of Nevada; Black Springs General Improvement District; and Washoe County District Attorney's Office."

On the Agenda, meeting of Washoe County Board of County Commissioners on **March 20, 1979**, at 1:30 p.m., a discussion of administration of Black Springs General Improvement District and determination regarding board of directors of the District, took place.

The following day, **March 21, 1979** the Reno Evening Gazette reported the County Commissioners actions:

"In an attempt to keep the financially troubled Black Springs General Improvement District alive, the Washoe County Commission approved Tuesday a move to have County Officials help instruct the district Trustees on operating the District efficiently.

The Commission also voted to reconvene the public hearing on June 26 when Trustees will report on their progress towards correcting bookkeeping mistakes and building a larger reserve fund.

The Commission directed the Trustees and helping County Officials to incorporate any recommendations that were suggested to the

A CRY FOR HELP

Commission by Charles Zeh, District Legal Counsel, Deputy District Attorney Edward Dannan and Beatrice Moore, Internal Auditor.

Through the aid of County Officials, yet to be appointed, a policy of accounting and auditing practices and procedures will be established for the Trustees.

The officials will also help develop guidelines for budget and management standards. . ."

District Judge John E. Gabrielli on *May 16, 1979* extended the injunction against Dutch Cook. The original injunction was granted by the Court on the 6th September 1977.

A letter from the Chief Building Inspector on *October 1, 1979* to Mr. Al Williams Chairman of the Board of Directors noted that the division had investigated the Black Springs area for violations of the ordinances and regulations that the Department of Public Works enforces. They specifically checked three properties, one being Dutch Cook, and currently there were no violations. However, this division did not check to determine whether or not individual water services were proved to each unit. It was suggested that if there were violations against the water district and individual services were not being paid for that the Board remedy the situation in the manner prescribed by Ed Dannan, legal counsel.

Helen Westbrook received a letter dated *October 16, 1979* from the office of the County Manager stating, ". . . at the October 9, 1979, Board of County Commissioner's meeting, you were appointed to serve on the Community Block Grant Program Advisory Committee."

The letter was very personable from Dianne L. Cornwall, Administrative Assistant of the Office of the County Manager. It started out "Dear Mrs. Westbrook," then Westbrook has a line through it and in Dianne's handwriting her name "Helen" is written to say "Dear Helen." At the end of the page hand written are the words "See you soon." Also attached, were documents regarding the expectations of the Advisory Committee.

CHAPTER 12
CHRONOLOGY OF THE 1980'S

For the fiscal year of 1980, the community of Black Springs' first priority was sewage. The soil in Black Springs did not absorb. The septic tank system was very inadequate; and the estimated cost to remedy this is $250,000.

The second priority was a multi-purpose room, to be added to the Community Center to be used for Volunteer Fire Department meetings, Black Springs' community meetings, library, classes for arts and crafts, games, etc. The estimated cost would be $110.000.

Third priority would be fire protection. They needed a new or better fire truck, new hoses, nozzles, ladders and fire extinguishers, which were estimated at $100,000.

Fourth priority were street lights, to help eliminate vandalism, burglaries—safer place to live; cost $50,000.

Fifth priority were park improvements; sprinkling system, lawns, shrubs, tennis courts, horseshoe pits and bike paths; estimated cost $30,000.

Sixth priority would be street improvements—resurfacing, etc.

In the Reno Evening Gazette on Wednesday, *January 16, 1980*, the "County gives district deadline.

Washoe County Commissioners said Tuesday; they will dissolve the Black Springs General Improvement District if its water disputes aren't resolved.

A CRY FOR HELP

Commissioners voted to give district officials until April 3rd to solve the problem of illegal water connections.

Commissioner Bennie Ferrari said, he may vote in April to merge the district with Horizon Hills General Improvement District rather than have the county assume total responsibility for Black Springs.

Deputy District Attorney Ed Dannan, who acts as an adviser to the district, suggested the dispute over illegal hook-ups be resolved by gathering a list of those wanting water service. The list would be submitted to State Engineer Bill Newman for approval.

Dannan said, he believes Newman would "look favorably" on the list, and 12 to 15 disputed water hook-ups could be added.

Dannan said, he will ask Horizon Hills' officials tonight if they will agree to interconnect water and sewage systems with Black Springs.

Horizon Hills' sewer plant is capable of handling Black Springs' sewage, he said. Dannan said, waste water is surfacing from septic tanks in some Black Springs locations.

He proposed Horizon Hills and Black Springs wells could back each other up in an emergency.

Black Springs' officials and resident Dutch Cook are embroiled in a dispute about a 2-inch water connection Cook installed.

District officials contend it was installed without their approval. Cook claims it was legally installed.

The matter has yet to be settled in court because the district lacks money to hire an attorney.

District chairman Albert Williams and former chairman Ollie Westbrook both opposed Dannan's suggestion to provide water to Cook or any other alleged illegal hookups.

CHRONOLOGY OF THE 1980'S

"It's the same as if I break into your house . . . and take what you have . . . Do I have a legal right to keep it?" Westbrook asked.

Black Springs' hearings have been held by the commission since last March to evaluate the district's financial status.

But squabbles preventing a solution to the district's problems caused an exasperated commission chairman Bill Farr, to announce the board's "patience is growing thin."

He also said, he would vote to dissolve the district unless the disputes were resolved.

Chan Griswold, Chief Civil Deputy District Attorney, underscored Farr's remarks, by agreeing Dannan's time was being consumed by the district's problems.

"Ed Dannan has spent an inordinate amount of time (on Black Springs) and it is really outside the scope of his function," Griswold said."

There were 18 families who turned in their applications for water service, and where the application asked for a "Date ready for service," all but one responded "now.""

Mrs. Helen Westbrook, relentless in her efforts to improve her community, sent a letter to Washoe County Manager John A. MacIntyre on *February 3, 1980*. Her concern was the lack of street lights in Black Springs.

The letter stated, "that two of the longest streets in Black Springs, namely Medgar Avenue and Westbrook Lane, have only two street lights. The lack of proper lighting in any given area, promotes vandalism, burglaries and molestation of residents," her letter said. Her home was broken into three times in 1979 and the loss was immeasurable.

Mrs. Westbrook's letter ended with, "the residents of Black Springs would surely appreciate some support from the County Commissioners on this issue."

A CRY FOR HELP

Without either of the Westbrooks presence as members on the Board of Trustees, the district appeared lost. After all, the Westbrooks had been pursuing improvements for Black Springs since 1952 and never stopped entering new portals of opportunities that would better the living conditions of Black Springs. Ollie Westbrook was the Black Springs representative on the Board of Directors of the Community Services Agency of Washoe County (CSA), and Helen Westbrook was a member on the Washoe County Community Development Block Grant Citizens' Advisory Committee (CDBG).

While the factious elements squabbled within the district, the Westbrooks kept focused on the current projects. There were three projects under the 1979 Grant in progress; housing rehabilitation—3 homes under construction, 1 out to bid and 2 loans pending; the Black Springs well—engineering was completed and construction was out for bid; and curbs and gutters—under construction with completion expected August 1979.

"A public meeting will be held at the Black Springs Community Building, 300 Kennedy Drive, Reno, Nevada, on Tuesday evening, August 12, 1980 at 7:00 p.m. The purpose of the meeting will be to discuss accomplishments, problems, and any other aspects of Washoe County's Black Springs Community Development Block Grant projects including housing rehabilitation, the curb and gutter project and a new well. We encourage anyone who wishes to comment on any aspect of the CDBG Program to attend." This was a public hearing set by the Washoe County Manager's Office.

With the absence of documentation for the year 1980, the resolutions for the lack of understanding Black Springs GID operations would be speculation. But the changes in 1981 with Ollie Westbrook elected as chairman of Black Springs GID, the district would recover.

February 11, 1981 the Regional Planning Commission of Reno, Sparks & Washoe County (RPC), sent the North Valley Draft Goals and Policies to the Westbrooks.

CHRONOLOGY OF THE 1980'S

The Goals were: Housing—encourage housing which meets the social, economic and aesthetic needs of the North Valley residents. Circulation/Transportation—provides a transportation and circulation system, which will fulfill the mobility needs of the community. Recreation—provides a variety of recreational opportunities for the residents of the North Valley. Environmental Quality—conserves and protects the natural environment of the North Valley. Community Services—expansion and improvement of public services in the valley is desirable. Land Use—preserves and maintains the rural-residential character of the area. Each of the goals was accompanied with multiple policies.

February 27, 1981 the RPC sent a second draft of the North Valley Goals and Policies to the Westbrooks. This draft included the implementation measures to be used. There was an anticipation that the Advisory Board would be able to vote on the goals and policies at the March 25th meeting. They also asked for any comments, questions or suggestions which would be presented at that time.

A public meeting of the Washoe County CDBG Advisory Committee was held *March 19, 1981*.

Tom Purkey gave a report on the final pre-application submitted to HUD. "We should be hearing from HUD on March 27th as to what will be approved," Tom said. "Two public hearings will be required before the final application is submitted." Apparently the Federal government was recommending a CDBG funding increase for 1982.

"Tom gave an explanation of the Housing Assistance Plan, which will be given a lot of emphasis this year. This involves a survey of all housing projects assisting low-income persons."

Tom Purkey, Planner III sent a letter to John MacIntyre County Manager *April 9, 1981* regarding the 1981 CDBG Pre-application Approval. HUD had approved $448,000 for the 1981 Community Development Block Grant program. Black Springs Community Center had requested $80,000 for improvements and was approved. The budget still had to be reworked in cooperation with the CDBG Citizens' Advisory

A CRY FOR HELP

Committee for presentation as part of the final application. Funds would be available in September.

It was quite apparent, that within the last six months significant restructuring took place with county operations and the Black Springs GID.

A regular meeting of the Board of Trustees for the Black Springs GID was held **May 14, 1981.** Those members present were: Ollie Westbrook, William Lobster, Johnnie Stevens and Jackie Supencheck. Shirley Gallian, the fifth member was absent. With the changes in the board, they would become a viable asset to the community once again.

"Chairman Westbrook reported that drilling on the new well was progressing. They have gone down 375 feet and are still drilling in solid hard rock. It has been stated, that drilling would continue until Monday and if solid hard rock is still present, drilling will be discontinued. . ."

Correspondence had been received from Bill Farr's office stating, that the Black Springs GID had been granted a Block Grant which was to be used for construction on a new Community Center.

Correspondence has also been received from the Department of Taxation informing the district of deadlines for presentation of budgets for the various districts. This letter will be forwarded to David Brickley who had agreed to prepare the budget for the district.

A notice of a 'Black Springs Neighborhood Meeting' was posted in May.

"The Washoe County Community Development Advisory Committee will hold a public meeting at the Black Springs Community Center at 7:00 p.m., Thursday, **May 21, 1981.**

"The purpose of the meeting is to discuss the problems and accomplishments of the Community Development Block Grant (CDBG) projects that have been carried out so far in Black Springs, and to discuss what projects the community wants in the future." Past and present

CHRONOLOGY OF THE 1980'S

projects include: Housing rehabilitation; curb and gutter construction; and the new well. "In addition, funding for construction of a new Community Building has been approved for next year." They asked the residents to attend, to hear their ideas, to make Black Springs better!

Fifteen citizens from the Black Springs Neighborhood and Helen Westbrook, who was a member of the committee, were present at a public meeting of the Washoe County Community Development Block Grant Citizens' Advisory Committee held, *May 22, 1981*, in the Black Springs Community Center. The meeting was called to order at 7:35 p.m. with Chairman Mike Katz presiding.

"Tom Purkey passed out a status report as of 4/30/81 which represented all Community Development projects since 1975. This report showed all projects completed thus far as well as the on-going projects. Tom discussed the proposed projects for 1981. The Black Springs Community Building is proposed for $80,000. . .

The results of the March 1981 Vista Survey were presented. The characteristics of Black Springs in regards to Housing, Population, Income and Major Issues were discussed."

During the Public Hearing, regarding performance on previously funded projects; the 1981 CDBG final application and HAP; and future CDBG needs, members of the Black Springs Community commented on the program projects.

"There were no negative comments in regard to the previously completed curb and gutter projects. . .

One community member commented that she was having difficulty reaching the City of Reno housing rehab staff when she was having problems with her contractor. Tom Purkey said that he should be contacted when this occurs. . ."

Another ". . . community member spoke regarding the fact that she and her family were willing to help the contractor to expedite the work. The contractor was not cooperative. He left openings in the home during the winter months. The county's attorney would be looking into eliminating these contractors from any further county projects. This contractor also signed the homeowner's name to the check.

Several community members spoke favorably in regards to the Housing rehab work that was done on their homes.

Helen Westbrook wanted to know why Mrs. Stevens' prospective rehab was unqualified. George Lively, Housing Rehab Counselor spoke regarding qualifications.

Ollie Westbrook asked, if existing lots could be developed and/or subdivided. There are currently no water or sewer connections. Mike Harper, committee member, spoke regarding the trailer overlay and the zone change creating a new North Valley master Plan, etc."

There was a question regarding market value of the lots. ". . . Currently appraisals were in progress for the rehab program. It appears that undeveloped land with no water should not be valued the same as other assessed property because lots cannot be sold for full value. . .

Steve Brown, Washoe County Commissioner, spoke regarding "water bank" trying to pool together all existing water rights stating that it should be controlled by elected officials of the three entities. Washoe County staff feels a strong need to identify problems of water companies. Black Springs lies within the Lemmon Valley ground water basin."

Towards the end of the Public Hearing, there was a discussion on the "design of the new community building to include programs for youth and older citizens. . ." They would have another meeting in Black Springs in the fall to make decisions. "Steve Brown encouraged community members to visit the Lemmon Valley center to get ideas."

Based on the above documentation, the Black Springs GID and community appeared to have re-united under the Chairmanship of Ollie Westbrook. After all, the Westbrooks had almost 30 years of acquired knowledge in community building.

CHRONOLOGY OF THE 1980'S

The *June 30, 1981* document was very interesting to read regarding BSGID financial statements. It was very neatly prepared and very clear as to every penny spent. The report from D. E. Brickley, Certified Public Accountant, was encouraging after such negative reporting in the prior years.

The current year audit recommendations from the accountant stated, "Upon reviewing the budget prepared by the Black Springs General Improvement District, it is evident that the District is still working at a deficit. Revenues are less than expenses. An increase in meter fees is a recommended solution. An approximate increase of $5.00 monthly is recommended." Accounts receivable increased during the fiscal year 1980-1981; any bad debt write offs should be approved by the Board and appear in the minutes; continued outside work by the Board members to serve the District should be compensated in some manner; and Black Springs should engage an attorney.

One of the recommendations from the CPA, that Black Springs should engage an attorney. The question here is, what happened to Charles Zeh Counsel for the Black Springs GID? With no supporting documentation to comment on the separation of Counsel and Black Springs GID, would be evoking without research.

September 1981 a 'Black Springs Facility Plan' initial mini-report was received. The report compiled by the URS Company, Las Vegas, NV in general, provided a preliminary analysis of alternative wastewater collection and treatment options for the Black Springs Study area.

Personally, it's amazing, that in 1981 there was still no sewage system but septic tanks. Having moved back to Reno, I didn't realize that Black Springs was still waiting and working towards obtaining adequate sewage disposal. All the surrounding communities, a lot of them much newer, appeared to have sufficient systems.

All members were present for the regular meeting of the Board of Trustees of the Black Springs GID held *September 10, 1981.*

A CRY FOR HELP

"The minutes of the August 13, 1981 meeting were read. A motion was made by William Lobster and seconded by Shirley Gallian, that the minutes be approved as read with one correction. On Page Two, Paragraph 7, it was erroneously noted that Chairman Williams reported. . . This should be changed to Chairman Westbrook reported. . .

After discussion of bills to be paid, "Chairman Westbrook turned the meeting over to Mr. John Collins, Chief Sanitary Engineer from Washoe County. Mr. Collins introduced Mr. Don Haselhoff of URS Company. URS Company has been requested to draw up a facility plan for the Black Springs District. Mr. Haselhoff explained, that they had been requested to perform the initial tasks in the evaluation of sewering Black Springs. . .

After the presentation, Mr. Collins and Mr. Haselhoff answered questions asked of a number of members of the community.

The initial report is completed by URS Company. It is now up to the District to decide what alternative they wish to proceed with. The District is faced with problems such as water demand to support various treatment alternatives and the high expense which would be incurred. . .

A letter was received informing the Board of a seminar on chlorination which will be held later this week in Elko. A motion was made by Shirley Gallian and seconded by Johnnie Stevens, that Ollie Westbrook represents the Board at this seminar. The Board will pay travel expenses incurred by Chairman Westbrook while traveling to this seminar."

The regular meeting of the Board of Trustees of the Black Springs GID was held ***October 9, 1981***. All members are present except Johnnie Stevens who will be absent for the next 7 months.

"A letter has been received from Douglas W. Hopkins of the Department of Public Works in Washoe County. This letter is in response to the August 11, 1981 letter which the Board sent along with a bill to Granite Construction Company requesting reimbursement for water used during the installation of curbs and gutters in the District. Mr. Hopkins stated, that the bill appeared excessive to him. After

CHRONOLOGY OF THE 1980'S

discussing this matter, the Board voted to send a letter to Mr. Hopkins explaining, that in view of all of the circumstances such as no previous arrangements being made to use the water, the increase in the power bill for those months and the high cost of repairs and maintenance to the pump during this period, it was the decision of the Board, to submit the original request for $1,500.00 as being a fair and reasonable amount.

A copy of a letter to the Washoe County Commissions from W. E. Buck has been received by Chairman Westbrook. Mr. Buck is a general partner in Camino Viejo Investments which owns approximately 373 acres in and adjoining the Black Springs Water District. His letter was inquiring about future water service in the District. John Collins, Chief Sanitary Engineer from Washoe County, responded to Mr. Buck's letter, with a copy to Chairman Westbrook, stating, that the State Engineer has restricted the number of connections which may take place within the District and informing Mr. Buck that his name would be placed on the mailing list regarding any future meetings in which water and sewer service will be discussed.

Bill Lobster reported that all water meters in the District have been located except for the meter of Mrs. Herron and the meter belonging to the Grahams. A complete report on this will be given at a later meeting.

A report was given on the findings of the last year end audit prepared by David Brickley. It was the feeling of the auditors, that the Board should consider a rate increase for water service. After some discussion, William Lobster made a motion that a letter be sent to the State Engineer requesting 30 more water hook-ups. It was seconded by Shirley Gallian... A motion was also made by William Lobster and seconded by Shirley Gallian, that a discussion on a rate increase be held at a future meeting."

The regular meeting of the Board of Trustees of the Black Springs GID was held **November 12, 1981.**

"A letter has been received from John Collins, Chief Sanitary Engineer for Washoe County, requesting to be placed on the agenda

A CRY FOR HELP

for this meeting to discuss the possibility of Washoe County entering into an agreement with the Black Springs GID under which the County would provide the necessary operations and maintenance services for the Black Springs Water Facilities. Chairman Westbrook turned the meeting over to Mr. Collins.

Mr. Collins stated that the Board should file a completion of work on the new well. The final electrical work is nearly completed. The controls for the pump on the new well will be read off the present tank. Mr. Collins then presented the possibility of the Black Springs GID entering into an agreement with Washoe County in regards to maintenance on the water facilities. This would include maintenance on the pump, control panels, etc. This would be done for a fee by Washoe County if this agreement is entered into. A representative from the District will be appointed to represent the Board at the initial meetings on this.

Bill Lobster made a motion that Ollie Westbrook be appointed as the representative from our District. Shirley Gallian will attend if Chairman Westbrook is unable to attend. This was seconded by Jackie Supencheck.

Mr. Collins then discussed the proposed sewage system within the District. It is up to the Board to decide what is best for the community and then to hold a community meeting to discuss the possibilities. . .

William Lobster noted that in the November 10, 1974 minutes of the Volunteer Fire Department, $400.00 was loaned to the District. A motion was made by William Lobster and seconded by Shirley Gallian that $400.00 is returned to the Volunteer Fire Department. Motion carried.

A report was then given on the locating of meters within the District. It was reported that there are three illegal hook-ups within the District. There are 68 meters located within the District including one which has been turned off. This meter is listed as belonging to Frank Robinson. Shirley Gallian made a motion that Bill Lobster be given permission to purchase supplies which are necessary to repair damaged meter boxes and lids for meter boxes. This was seconded by Jackie

CHRONOLOGY OF THE 1980'S

Supencheck. Motion carried. One new meter will need to be purchased for the service belonging to Fate Brown."

The regular meeting of the Board of Trustees of the Black Springs GID was held ***December 10, 1981***.

". . . A letter was received from the Department of Taxation requesting a second copy of the 1980-81 audit of the Black Springs GID. The secretary will check with the auditor to see if they possibly have a second copy to send to the Department of Taxation.

Information was received from the Census Bureau requesting information concerning the District. Chairman Westbrook will check with John Collins to see if he can assist in filling out this form. . .

Chairman Westbrook reported that he had no further contact concerning the maintenance agreement that was proposed between Washoe County and the District." He also stated "that he would contact John Collins and check on the progress on the sewage disposal plan for the District. . .

Chairman Westbrook presented a set of bylaws which he would like the Board to consider. This will be voted on at the next regular meeting. . ."

The regular meeting of the Board of Trustees of the Black Springs GID was held ***January 7, 1982***.

". . . Chairman Westbrook stated that he had still, no word on a meeting with the county to discuss the possible agreement between the District and Washoe County regarding maintenance on the water system.

A copy of a letter, from John Collins to Donald A. Haselhoff regarding the Black Springs Facility Plant, has been received. The Board voted to hold a public hearing, February 11, 1982 at 7:30 p.m., to allow Mr. Haselhoff to present his findings on the most feasible sewer system for the District. John Collins will be notified of this hearing.

A CRY FOR HELP

William Lobster made a motion and it was seconded that the Board pass out flyers within the District and that an advertisement be placed in the Reno Newspaper regarding this public hearing. Motion carried.

A letter has been received from the CPA firm of D. E. Brickley, requesting that a meeting be set up with his firm and the Board of Trustees to explain the new bookkeeping system which their firm has initiated. This meeting will be set-up for February 19th if that is convenient with all parties involved.

A check for $400.00 was given to Chairman Westbrook to transmit to the Treasurer for the Black Springs Volunteer Fire Department. This is to pay back the loan by the Fire Department to the District. This repayment was approved at a previous meeting.

William Lobster made a motion that the Board purchases a copy of the 1981 Edition of the Local Government Syllabus at a charge of $12.50." This was seconded and the motion carried.

"A tax report has been received from the Washoe County Assessor indicating the amount which the District is being taxed for property owned by the District.

A motion was made by William Lobster and seconded . . . that the District adopts a set of bylaws as presented by Chairman Westbrook. Motion carried. These bylaws will be available for signature at the next regular meeting."

"Before the start of the regular meeting held ***February 11, 1982*** Chairman Westbrook turned the meeting over to Mr. John Collins, Chief Sanitary Engineer from Washoe County and Mr. Don Haselhoff of URS Company. They had requested time at this meeting to explain in further detail, the results of URS Company's investigation into alternatives for developing a sewage disposal system within the Black Springs GID. At the end of the presentation, and after extensive participation from members of the community, the Board of Trustees requested that URS Company further investigate the possibilities of hooking into the sewage disposal plant at Lemmon Valley. This will be done and a report will be forthcoming."

CHRONOLOGY OF THE 1980'S

The regular meeting of the Board of Trustees of the Black Springs GID then commenced...

"A bill in the amount of $329.57 from D. E. Brickley was deferred until further clarification was received... There is a $60.00 charge on the statement which appears to be for auditing the accounts payable for the District.

A letter was received from Dianne Cornwall, Registrar of Voters, stating that all candidates for the Board of Trustees must file through her office. The first date for filing was January 4, 1982, and the last day to file is July 21, 1982, 5:00 p. m. There are three seats on the Board of Trustees up for election this year. The Board will inform members of the community of this information...

Correspondence was received from the Department of Taxation informing the Board of a public hearing which will be held at 1:30 p.m. on Monday, March 15th. The purpose of the hearing will be to receive comments from all interest persons regarding the adoption of Local Government Regulation No. 22 concerning the ad valorem taxes, service charges, license fees and permit fees...

William Lobster reported that the delinquent notices, for water services over two months delinquent, had been sent. The time period granted will expire Friday, February 12, 1982. All services not brought current at this time, will be turned off.

Another discussion was held regarding the disposal of the old tank which is located on the site of the new well. Several suggestions were made. This will be discussed further at a later date."

The regular meeting of the Black Springs GID Board of Trustees was held ***March 11, 1982***.

"After February's minutes were approved, Chairman Westbrook turned the meeting over to John Collins from Washoe County who wished to bring the Board up to date on the Black Springs sewer proposal. Mr. Collins stated that there are some criteria which must be

A CRY FOR HELP

taken into account when deciding on a sewer system. Among these was: The most cost effective method, what the environmental impact might be and can the project be implemented. Some of the options discussed were: Designing a collection system within the District and putting in its own treatment plant and bringing collection system to Lemmon Valley. Possible potential cost savers could be having Horizon Hills and C-Mor Trailer Park hookup to the sewer line going into Lemmon Valley.

The possibility of obtaining grant money for this project was discussed. John Collins indicated that the District might be eligible for grant money if some other project dropped out or if the District could prove that there is a definite health hazard. Mr. Collins indicated that he will have another report in approximately 60 days..."

Correspondence has been received regarding beneficial use on the new well. John Collins will check into this matter.

Willie Stevens then requested that his second meter be put on standby. This should have been done for the entire year of 1981. The bookkeeper will be informed of this and Mr. Stevens will receive a corrected statement. Also, Mr. Stevens agreed to sell the tank that is presently located on the site of the new well. This will be done on a 20/80 commission basis."

The Department of Public Works sent a letter **March 24, 1982** along with the Preliminary Draft Request for Proposals for Operation and Maintenance, to Ollie Westbrook, Chairman of the Black Springs GID.

Chief Sanitary Engineer John Collins was asking for a review and comments as appropriate for the proposals to supply contract utility services. He stressed that this was a preliminary draft and was scheduled to be finalized by the end of March, with final distribution by April 5th. Accordingly, any revisions needed are to be made as soon as possible and sent to his office.

The regular meeting of the Black Springs GID Board of Trustees was held ***April 8, 1982***.

CHRONOLOGY OF THE 1980'S

". . . It was reported that nothing further had been reported by Willie Stevens on the sale of the tank, which sits on the site of the new well.

A tentative budget for the District has been prepared by D. E. Brickley. A motion was made by William Lobster and seconded by Jackie Supencheck that this tentative budget be approved as prepared. Motion carried.

A motion was made by Shirley Gallian and seconded by William Lobster stating that the Board should write a letter to Johnnie Stevens inquiring as to whether she will be able to continue as a member of the Board of Trustees or if she wishes to resign her seat. Motion carried. The secretary will write such a letter. . ."

Tom Purkey Community Development Planner sent a notice to the Black Springs Community Center Architect Selection Sub-Committee which was received **May 11, 1982**. Some committee members were residents of Black Springs; they were: Mae Ella Carthen, Frank Vignon, Helen and Ollie Westbrook. The other members were: Tom Purkey and Bob Olson.

Tom Purkey had set up an appointment schedule with the four architects that were selected for personal interviews at the meeting on May 6th.

The Parks Department would provide a county vehicle for transportation. They planed on meeting at the County Manager's office, at 9:30 a.m. Wednesday, May 12th. Expecting each interview to take about an hour, which would leave them time to go look at some of each architect's buildings.

The regular meeting of the Board of Trustees of the Black Springs GID was held **July 9, 1982**. Roll call was taken and all members were present.

". . . John Collins of Washoe County was unable to attend this meeting. He has requested that the Board appoint a representative to

A CRY FOR HELP

attend meetings in connection with meeting contractors, who have submitted bids for maintenance and other services within the District. The Board decided not to rate the material submitted by these firms because it would be necessary to go with the lowest bidder but that estimate is still out of our price range.

A letter has been received from Thomas Purkey, Community Development Planner stating, that Washoe County is preparing to carry out three Community Development Block Grant projects which require environmental assessments. Construction of a community center in Black Springs was one of the three...

A motion was made by Shirley Gallian and seconded by William Lobster that the secretary be authorized to call the CPA firm of Gordon Douglas (formerly David Brickley), to determine what the charge would be for performing the audit for the district for 1981-82. If this amount is reasonably inline with what has been charged in the past, the secretary is instructed to write a letter giving authorization to do this audit. Motion carried.

The maintenance man for the District has encountered some problems with gaining access to meters within the District which require repairs. A motion was made by Shirley Gallian and seconded by Johnnie Stevens that he be given a letter which he can show to the property owner explaining what work is being done and that the maintenance man has been authorized to do the work."

In reviewing the documents, Ollie Westbrook's words of December 1968, ring out loud, when in front of the County Commissioners he stated, "...we are continually trying to build and live within your rules..." The Westbrooks became educated in the processes of running a General Improvement District over the years. The struggles were immense, yet they persevered to establish a place to call home, a community.

The regular meeting of the Board of Trustees of the Black Springs GID was held ***August 12, 1982***.

After the business portion, Chairman Westbrook introduced Mr. Gordon Douglass, CPA who has taken over the CPA practice of

CHRONOLOGY OF THE 1980'S

D. E. Brickley. Mr. Douglass introduced Mr. Malcom Greenlees who would be acting as consultant to his firm.

"... Mr. Douglass explained that if the Board decides to retain his firm, that there would be no increase in rates for their services. He also stated that his firm could do the yearly audit for the District for $1,200.00 which would be approximately the same as last year. He would also check into the possibility of having the District being exempt from having a yearly audit and possibly present the information in the form of financial statements. He stated that his firm would continue doing the billing for the District water bills at a price of $95.00 per month. He would also ensure that the Board of Trustees is informed as to time limits the Board must meet when submitting various forms to the State, County, etc. In summary, his firm would provide the following services for the District: preparation of financial statements, audits, monthly billing and cooperation in providing information for various aspects in the activity of the District. This work would not exceed $100.00 per month plus postage..." It was motioned and carried.

"A letter has been received from John Collins concerning contract utility services. This letter was sent to John MacIntyre, County Manager from John Collins. There was no action taken on this by the Board..."

The regular meeting of the Board of Trustees of the Black Springs GID was held *September 16, 1982*.

"... There was some discussion on the $31.00 owed to Nevada Bell." A motion was made and second that Chairman Westbrook be given a check. "He will check on the bill from Nevada Bell personally and when it is clarified, he will pay this bill.

A letter has been received from the Department of Taxation asking for an indebtedness report for the District. The secretary will write a letter stating that the District has no indebtedness and anticipates none for the future.

Copies of the various permits for wells within the District have been received. All of these permits state that the District shall be limited

A CRY FOR HELP

to 63 hook-ups. The totalizing meter will be read regularly to determine the actual amount of water that is being used by the District. . .

Jackie Supencheck reported that the auditor has received all the material necessary, for the audit which is in the process of being completed. . ."

The regular meeting of the Board of Trustees of the Black Springs GID was held *October 14, 1982*.

". . . A bill from Nevada Bell for $31.00 was ratified. This bill was paid by Chairman Westbrook. He explained that this was for the rental of equipment to turn on the switch on the new well when it is necessary. This will be done automatically when it is needed.

The bill from Jensen Electric was explained. This was for repairs that were made to the water system. This problem was causing the water pressure to be very low at various times. . .

A letter will be sent to the CPA firm indicating that there is some serious concern as to the way in which our requests for changes in the billings are being handled. In several cases, there seems to be no response to our requests. . ."

January 6, 1983 John MacIntyre, County Manager sent a brief history of the Black Springs Community Center Project and a timetable for completion. The main highlight was showing an August 1983 completion of construction date for the Community Center.

The regular meeting of the Black Springs GID was held *January 13, 1983*.

". . . A letter has been received from Belie Williams, Chairman of the Washoe County Commission stating, that he is looking forward to working with the Board and requesting our support and input on any problems which may occur. . .

Under old business, William Lobster stated that Mr. Brown had paid $60.00 towards his water bill and he also stated that Mr. Brown has

CHRONOLOGY OF THE 1980'S

refused to set a date to meet with the Board to discuss payment for the meter which has been placed on his property.

At this point in the meeting, Chairman Westbrook expressed the Board's appreciation to William Lobster for his service on the Board. Mr. Lobster stated that he would be available to serve in the capacity of maintenance man for the District if the Board so desired.

After some community participation, Chairman Westbrook stated, that the members of the community should feel free to bring suggestions or information to the Board.

At this point, the newly elected Board members were seated and nominations for officers were opened. . ." The new members were Ollie Westbrook, Chairman; Barbet Bufkin, Vice-Chairman; Jackie Supencheck, Secretary; Shirley Gallian, Treasurer; and Johnnie Stevens, member.

The regular meeting of the Board of Trustees of the Black Springs GID was held *February 10, 1983*.

". . . The outstanding bill from Western Nevada Building Supply has been corrected. The correct customer will be billed for the supplies and the District does not owe anything.

A motion was made by Barbet Bufkin, seconded by Jackie Supencheck that the Treasurer is granted authority to pay the bill from Nevada Bell when it is received and it will be ratified at the next meeting. This will avoid being listed in arrears. Motion carried.

Correspondence has been received from Judy Bailey's office, requesting the name of a representative from the District to serve on the General Obligation Bond Commission. Since the deadline had already passed, no action was taken.

Correspondence has been received from Bill Berrum, requesting the District's support for Leonard Mays as the representative to serve on the General Obligation Bond Commission. Mr. Mays is now serving on the Board for Sun Valley Water and Sanitation District. . .

A CRY FOR HELP

There has still been no response from Mr. Brown in regards to payment of the bill for the meter which was installed at his residence.

An editorial from the Reno Gazette Journal 2/1/83, was read regarding the County controlling water and sewage services for all the GIDs. There will be a meeting of the Washoe County Commissioners next Tuesday, February 15 at 1:30 p. m., to explore this further. All interested persons were urged to attend. . .

There was a discussion of delinquent water bills. It was agreed that the Board will draft a notice of possible discontinuance of service if these bills are not taken care of. All Board members will be asked to sign these notices before they are distributed. . ."

The regular meeting of the Black Springs GID Board of Trustees was held *10th March 10, 1983*.

". . . A note has been received from Fate Brown, stating that he intends to start paying on the bill for the meter which was installed on his property. He will do this as soon as possible.

A letter has been received from John Collins, enclosing a request for extension of time for beneficial use on the new well. The fee for this extension is $25.00." A motion was made and seconded that this application be made. Motion carried.

"A new form was signed by each Board member requesting payment for delinquent water bills. Account numbers have been assigned to each water account. The name on the property may change but the account number will stay the same. This is the number listed on the property through the Washoe County Assessor's office. Dutch Cook has a question on the number assigned to one of his properties. Chairman Westbrook will check into this."

A motion was made and seconded "that the initial budget for the District be approved as prepared by Gordon Douglass, CPA. Motion carried."

CHRONOLOGY OF THE 1980'S

The regular meeting of the Black Springs GID Board of Trustees was held *April 14, 1983*.

". . . Mr. Fate Brown was present at the meeting. Mr. Brown paid $50.00 on the amount due on the meter on his property and $30.00 on his monthly water service. At this time, he agreed to pay $50.00 per month on the meter until it is paid off. If he has difficulties with this payment schedule, he is to come before the Board to make other arrangements.

A motion was made and seconded that William Lobster be assigned to work with Forrest Miller as maintenance man. He will be working on repairing water meters and meter boxes within the District and other required work in connection with the maintenance of the water system within the District. This will be done on a job order basis. Motion carried.

A motion was made by Barbet Bufkin, seconded by Johnnie Stevens that the members of the Board of Trustees receive $30.00 per month to help compensate for services performed on behalf of the District. This will commence May 1, 1983. Motion carried. . ."

The regular meeting of the Black Springs GID Board of Trustees was held *May 12, 1983*.

". . . Mr. Fate Brown has paid the balance on his meter. His water bill is now current.

On the Higgins bill, we received another note saying there is one less hook-up. A discussion was held on accepting the $150.00 payment for 2 months on 5 meters. Mr. Bufkin made a motion to make proper adjustments on this bill. It was seconded. This motion would remove $70.00 from this bill and make account current. Motion carried.

The Block Grant chairman has the final plans for the new Center for consideration. Nothing has been decided on what to do with the building we now have.

We received a letter dated April 20, 1983, stating that we had not filed the 1983-84 tentative budgets.

A CRY FOR HELP

We received a letter on May 2, 1983, stating that they had received the budget. It said that we had done something wrong when filling out the form, Mr. Westbrook will talk to the accountant about this matter. We received a new form for the budget. June 3, 1983, is the last date for sending in this form. Mr. Westbrook will talk to the accountant about this matter. . .

Bill Lobster reported on the meter repairs. Jackie's meter can't be shut off. Bill is to go ahead and fix what ever is wrong with the meters. He will give a report on what is needed and what he has done. He will also notify the people whose water is to be shut off. This will be done 2 days before the shut off. . ."

A letter date *June 8, 1983* was received from Gordon Douglass & Co., Ltd. Apparently the district will again be operating at a loss unless revenues are increased.

". . . All budgeted expenses have been reviewed, and have been reduced wherever possible. The remaining expenses represent amounts necessary to continue the minimum operation of the district.

We would recommend, as we have previously, that the district increase its monthly meter fees by $5.00 from $15.00 to $20.00 from regular service, and from $5.00 to $7.50 for standby service.

Failure to implement this change will result in a deficit in operations, and would require further budget adjustments, including reductions of maintenance on the water system."

The regular meeting of the Black Springs GID Board of Trustees was held *June 10, 1983*.

". . . The District has received a Tax Number which should be used when reporting all information to the Internal Revenue Service. . .

The secretary was asked to report any money paid to individuals for services to the district. This should be reported to the bookkeeper, so that the District will have a record of these transactions.

CHRONOLOGY OF THE 1980'S

The final budget prepared by Gordon Douglass, CPA was approved by the Board of Trustees. A transmittal letter stating that in order for the District to function effectively, it will be necessary to raise the fees for water service from $15.00 monthly to $20.00 monthly was attached to the budget. If this is not done, it will not be possible to maintain the system in the proper way. It was decided that a Public Meeting will be held on August 11, 1983 in regards to this increase in fees. Notices for this meeting will be advertised in the Reno newspaper and individuals living within the District will be notified. Gordon Douglass, CPA will attend this meeting if the Board wishes him to do so.

Shirley Gallian was requested to check on the different bank accounts available so that the District can be earning interest on the money now carried in the treasury. There is also a check which was returned (to Mrs. Fitch for $100.00) that was never picked up. This should be placed in an account so that it can be earning interest.

William Lobster reported that there are some dead-end caps within the water system that need to be repaired. Some of this line is now under asphalt. Chairman Westbrook requested that he check into the approximate cost for these repairs.

The bids for the new Community Center will be held June 15, 1983 at 4:00 p.m. in the Washoe County Purchasing Department. Chairman Westbrook will check with the County to see what can be done with the present building now serving as the Community Center. Inquiries will be sent to individuals within the District asking if anyone would be interested in acquiring this building. . ."

The regular meeting of the Board of Trustees of the Black Springs GID was held *July 14, 1983*.

". . . In regards to maintenance, a question arose as to what kind of insurance coverage was available for people doing work for the District such as maintenance. The secretary will check with Capurro & Voss to find out what coverage is available. A question also arose regarding any injuries which might occur as the result of work being done by the District. This will also be checked.

A CRY FOR HELP

W. Lobster reported that the flush-out valve located at the end of Medgar needs to be located and repaired. It might be possible that the street will have to be cut. If this is done, a permit may be required. William Lobster will check into this and obtain a work order to proceed with this work. Several meters in the District are not working properly. This will also be checked. Chairman Westbrook also reported that the pressure pump valve needs to be repaired. He will check into getting this repaired.

Funds have been requested from HUD for the completion of the new Community Center. Per this request, funds will be transferred from the monies available for home improvement loans. We should be hearing back on this soon. Money has been received for drawing up the plans for a sewer facility within the District. Work should begin approximately July or August of 1984.

Mr. Greenlees from the firm of Gordon Douglass, CPA was present at this meeting. Permission has been received from the Nevada Tax Commission not requiring an annual audit from the Black Springs" GID. . .

Chairman Westbrook stated that his term on the North Valley Board is up. A representative from the District is requested. These meetings are held on the second Tuesday night of each month at the Community Center in Lemmon Valley. Anyone interested in serving on this board, should contact Tom Purkey from the Washoe County Commissioners office. . ."

The regular meeting of the Black Springs GID was held **August 11, 1983**.

". . . Chairman Westbrook introduced Mike Lucchesi from Washoe County. Mr. Lucchesi reported on the progress for the sewage disposal system within the District. He reported that the District was short of funds for this system, and that he made application to the Farmers Home Administration for a farm loan to make up for the short-fall. He requested that the Board approve this application. It was motioned and seconded the Board approve this application." Motion carried.

CHRONOLOGY OF THE 1980'S

At this point, Chairman Westbrook introduced Malcolm Greenlees representing the accounting firm of Gordon Douglass. The Public Meeting concerning the increase in water fees was then opened.

"Mr. Greenlees explained that due to the increase in maintenance costs, professional services and utility costs that his accounting firm was recommending the water fees be increased. . . This would enable the District to function properly and the District would not show a loss at the end of the fiscal year. If this increase is not approved, the District could not afford maintenance costs to keep the water system in proper condition. After extensive public participation, a motion was made by Barbet Bufkin and seconded. The motion carried and the increase will go into effect September 1, 1983. . ."

The regular meeting of the Black Springs GID was held *September 15, 1983* in the Fire House.

"Correspondence has been received from Thomas Purkey, Community Development Planner for Washoe County, indicating that all of the projects submitted on the 1978 priority list for Black Springs have been completed or are underway. In a few months they will be starting the next CDBG application cycle and his office is requesting that the GID develop an updated list of needs in Black Springs so that these needs can be addressed. An updated list will be provided, and it is hoped that the Board will receive input from members of the community in general.

Notice of a Public Hearing before the State of Nevada Board of Health concerning amendments to public water supply regulations has been received. Due to the lack of time to respond to this, the Secretary was requested to request a copy of these proposed amendments, so that the Board can remain up to date on these regulations.

The following items were reported by William Lobster, maintenance man for the District.

The meter on the property belonging to Graham has been raised. Several of the meters that was not registering properly having been cleaned, that this seems to improve the condition. Shirley Gallian will

A CRY FOR HELP

assist William Lobster in checking out the water service on the property belonging to Wendt to see how many services are actually being used. All of the meters currently in the pump house are dirty and not working properly. Chairman Westbrook will check with Sun Valley as to what meters they are using and report back to the Board. John Collins will be asked to forward information on the purchase of new meters. The meter located on the property belonging to Cecil Washington, needs to be cleaned and moved out further to the street. William Lobster will report at the next meeting on the cost of insurance for himself; while he is performing work for the District."

An addition to the minutes, "It was noted the Mr. Dutch Cook is the representative for Black Springs on the North Valley Board. Members of the community were urged to attend these meetings which are held on the second Tuesday of each month, in Lemmon Valley."

This ends the documentation for 1983 with no minutes for the months of October thru December.

The regular meeting of the Board of Trustees of the Black Springs GID was held *January 12, 1984*.

". . . Mr. Walker was present at this meeting. He presented proof-of-purchase documents for the property. The Board approved his application for service since there is currently a meter located on this property. . .

Chairman Westbrook indicated that he had not had the opportunity to contact an attorney in regards to researching the original water rights within the District.

Shirley Gallian will check into setting up a slush fund for the District. They will need to know the District's tax number. . ."

A letter dated *March 16, 1984* to the Community Support Review Board and Community Development Advisory Board, which Helen Westbrook was a member was regarding reorganization. Both boards review and make recommendations on funding applications

CHRONOLOGY OF THE 1980'S

from many of the same organizations, and combining the two boards would provide all board members with a better overall understanding of the human service needs and resources in Washoe County. The combined boards would be called "Community Support and Development Advisory Board."

Per Ollie Westbrook, Chairman's request, John Collins, P. E. Chief Sanitary Engineer, sent data relative to water consumption in Black Springs. This showed a breakdown of water consumption history of the main well, as well as the supplemental well for 1983.

The regular meeting of the board of Trustees of the Black Springs GID was held *April 12, 1984*.

There was a change in the Boards membership. William Lobster was on the Board now replacing Barbet Bufkin. The change is unknown due to lack of information.

According to April's minutes, an application for Extension of Time under Permit No. 42225 had been paid for the new well. This amount was $25.00. Notice had been received that this was the last extension that the Board may apply for. Chairman Westbrook would discuss this with John Collins as to how the Board should proceed and report back to the Board.

A motion was made by William Lobster and seconded, that a letter be drafted to send to prospective water users within the District who own vacant lots. This letter will state that the Board is prepared to consider applications for beneficial use of water within the District. Motion carried.

"A motion was made by Johnnie Stevens and seconded, that block grant money for the community be used to proceed with work on the new sewer system. Motion carried.

The Board will check into getting a federal tax number for the District in order to open an account in which excess monies will be deposited.

A CRY FOR HELP

Chairman Westbrook reported that the new community center is ready to be opened..."

The regular meeting of the Black Springs GID was held ***June 14, 1984.***

"... Realtors present at the meeting, asked Chairman Westbrook to explain what the situation is on getting new hook-ups within the District. Chairman Westbrook gave a brief history of the problems which the Board is facing in receiving additional new hookups. Chairman Westbrook gave a brief history of the problems which the Board is facing in receiving additional new hookups.

Mr. Gary Dawson and Mr. Richard Koepnick were present at the meeting. They came to explain possible action that is presently being considered by the County. This would possibly involve directing the excess surface water from the northern valley to such areas as Golden Valley and Lemmon Valley for the purpose of putting the water back into the earth. It was the concern of certain people within the District who are on wells that this might cause their wells to dry up. This matter will be investigated further and discussed at the next meeting as to what action the Board of Trustees could possibly take to protest this action..."

The regular meeting of the Black Springs GID Board of Trustees was held ***July 12, 1984.***

"... The financial statements for the District have been received from Gordon Douglass. These financial statements cover the periods ending December 31, 1983 and March 31, 1984.

It was reported that a North Valley Water Conservation Committee has been formed and a petition has been filed by the District requesting a public hearing on the matter of capturing the surface water in the area and channeling it to other areas such as Golden Valley. Nothing has been heard on this matter as of this date.

It was reported that there has been some illegal transportation of water from the District. A motion was made by William Lobster and seconded, that a brochure be sent to residents within the District alerting them to this illegal use of water and requesting that they report any information on persons using this water. They will be asked to notify the Sheriff's Department or one of the board members if they suspect that water is being transported illegally from the District. . .

The Board authorized Jackie Supencheck to offer up to $100.00 for someone to clean up around the District's water tank. Jackie will check with Richard Neidweid to see if he might be interested in doing this.

Correspondence has been received from CT Leasing & Financial Corporation. This corporation offers lease-purchase agreements on various equipment and services. The District is interested in pursuing this in regards to office equipment. The Secretary will obtain further information. . ."

July 16, 1984 the following order was sent to Gene Sullivan, Director of Department of Parks & Recreation:

"I, Judi Bailey, County Clerk and Clerk of the Board of County Commissioners, Washoe County, Nevada, do hereby certify that at a regular meeting of the Board held on July 10, 1984, Chairman Williams issued the order:"

RESOLVED, that the Washoe County Parks Department is designated to have primary responsibility for operating and maintaining the Black Springs Community Center. Operation and maintenance includes scheduling building use, controlling key issuance, ensuring that necessary cleaning and maintenance is performed and any other activities needed to guarantee effective management of the building; and be it further

RESOLVE, that with the concurrence of the Parks Department Director, the Black Springs General Improvement District Chairman or his designee shall be provided a set of keys to the facility to assist the Parks Department in carrying out its responsibilities for operation and maintenance of the facility. It is intended that the General Improvement District

A CRY FOR HELP

Chairman will assist the Parks Department in providing keys to properly scheduled groups, operate the heating system and other utilities as needed, and ensure that the building is left clean and undamaged after each use.

"It was further ordered that the invitation to the grand opening and dedication party on July 28, 1984 be acknowledged and that annual funding for the operation and maintenance of the new Black Springs Community Center be provided. It was noted that annual operating funds for the Center were inadvertently not included in the Parks Department 84/85 budget, that the department will attempt to absorb the costs, and that if later in the year the Parks Department has a shortage of funds, the Department of Budget & Analysis has agreed to recommend an augmentation from contingencies."

The regular meeting of the Black Springs GID Board of Trustees was held ***August 9, 1984***.

". . . Notice has been received from the office of the Washoe County Clerk regarding the use, responsibility for and scheduling of the new Community Center within the District. In response to this notice, a motion was made by Shirley Gallian and seconded, that the following agreement be drawn up for approval by Washoe County. "The Board of Trustees of the Black Springs Water District is hereby requesting, that the Board be granted permanent office space within the Community Center. In return for the permanent office space, the Board will in turn agree to supply water for the maintenance of the Martin Luther King Memorial Park located within the District, at no charge." Motion carried. . ."

The regular meeting of the Black Springs GID Board of Trustees was held ***September 13, 1984***.

". . . It was expressed that the increase in the power bill for the new well was due to excessive water use which causes the new well to kick into action. It may be possible that there is illegal use and transportation of water within the District. People were urged to keep an eye open for this water misusage and report it to the Sheriff's Department or to a member of the Board. If possible, they should try to obtain the license number of vehicles transporting water illegally.

CHRONOLOGY OF THE 1980'S

A memo has been received from John Collins indicating that the Sanitation Division within the County has been changed to the Utility Division.

The agreement drawn up for permanent office space for the Board of Trustees in the new Community Center is in the hands of the attorney for the County.

There was some discussion among the Board members about the interpretation of certain regulations set up by the County regulating water districts. Perhaps at some time, the Board should request clarification from the County.

Applications for water service were distributed to interested persons. These applications will be considered by the Board at the next Board meeting. . ."

The regular meeting of the Black Springs GID Board of Trustees was held *October 11, 1984*.

". . . At this time Chairman Westbrook introduced Mr. Jack Craner of the Washoe County Engineering Department. Mr. Craner reported on the progress of the sewer facility. The design and financial aspects of the facility were explained. It was reported that Washoe County has purchased the Lemmon Valley sewer plant and that when the sewer facility is completed in the Black Springs District, there will be no initial hook-up fee at that time. Hook-ups requested after the initial hook-ups are completed, will be charged $1,500.00. The customers within the District will be charged approximately $18.45 per month for sewer service. The bids for construction of this sewer facility will go out in January 1985. Construction should begin around March of 1985, and the completion date is expected to be approximately six months from the starting date. There are some authorizations for easements for the sewer line still outstanding. These will all have to be completed before construction can begin. . ."

The regular meeting of the Black Springs GID Board of Trustees was held *December 20, 1984*.

A CRY FOR HELP

"... A copy of a memo to John A. MacIntyre, County Manager from John M. Collins, Chief Sanitary Engineer regarding the Resolution concerning financing of water and sewer improvements in the Lemmon Valley, Black Springs, Horizon Hills, and the C-Mor areas was read.

The Board of Trustees has received the financial statement for the District for the year ending June 1984. Additional copies will be requested for submission to the Department of Taxation.

A notice has been received that the water being served in the District has received a clean bill of health from the County Health Department..."

As we begin to end the chronology of Black Springs, the documents are very limited. Ollie Westbrook does not appear to be on the Board after 1984 and Helen Westbrook is on the Board once again in the 90's. The history of this strong and determined community, as you know, is based upon the documents archived by my grandparents, the 'Westbrooks.'

March 3, 1986 a Notice of County Ordinance was issued. The notice stated:

"NOTICE IS HEREBY GIVEN that Bill No. 854, Ordinance No. 680, entitled "An ordinance amending Washoe County Ordinance No. 624, Washoe County Ordinance No. 638, and Washoe County Ordinance No. 663 by adding provisions requiring mandatory connection to the sanitary sewer collection system in the Black Springs General Improvement District and adjacent areas and redefining connection charges," was adopted on February 25, 1986, by Commissioners King, Lillard, McDowell, Ritter and Williams."

We had a sewer system up and working from what I can tell. It would cost $1,500.00 for the sewer connection, and a per quarter fee of $55.35 for sewage disposal.

There was a regular meeting of the Black Springs General Improvement District held *September 17, 1987.*

CHRONOLOGY OF THE 1980'S

"The meeting was called to order at 7:30 p.m. at the Black Springs Community Center. Minutes were read and approved on a motion by Thurman Carthen, 2nd by Mae Carthen.

Old Business, Jackie Supencheck stated that Commissioner Larry Beck was out of town and would not return until Monday, September 21, 1987. And we could look forward to the letter lifting the water moratorium, and we can hook-up more customers as the District is badly in need of more revenue. The Board also decided to raise the standby rate to $10.00. Jackie Supencheck will go to the bank and find out the best way to invest money to gain more revenue.

The Board also decided to charge a late fee of $15.00 if any account is more than 60 days delinquent on a motion by Thurman Carthen 2nd by Honey Williams. The motion passed.

The Secretary is to send out letters to all customers stating that as of October 1, 1987, all bills three months behind will owe a $15.00 late fee. Failure to pay this fee will result in your water turned off without further notice with an added fee plus a deposit.

Mae Carthen is to notify the Bookkeeper, Phillip Osborne and Larry Evans is to pay for 2 units in full use.

Ernestine LeRoux, 103 Westbrook, will be charged with one stand by unit as of 9-1-87.

The meter at Roy Remsen's should be placed on standby. Ollie Westbrook should be paying for 2 units in full use. Also, how much extra would be charged to add $15.00 to every 60 days of late payment.

The Secretary is to get the Board on the agenda with the County Commissioners. The 2nd reading of the by-laws were read and approved.

The adoptions of the new rules are on the agenda of the September 17, 1987 meeting.

The treasure report was $25,368.81.

A CRY FOR HELP

There being no further business, the meeting was adjourned at 10:00 p.m."

Based upon the minutes of September 17th, the Board members were, Chairman Al Williams, Secretary Honey Williams, Thurman Carthen, Mae Carthen and Jackie Supencheck.

Now, there appears to be inaccuracies and thoroughness in the recording of minutes. In a portion of the minutes it stated that, "The Board also decided to charge a late fee of $15.00 if any account is more than 60 days delinquent." This was motioned and seconded and carried. In the next paragraph, "The Secretary is to send out letters to all customers stating that as of October 1, 1987 all bills three months behind will owe a $15.00 late fee." There is the possibility, that the minutes were corrected but there is no documentation to state such. This alone shows a limited amount of knowledge in the operational procedures in running a GID. Even in viewing the document shows a lack of professionalism that should have been used in composing the minutes.

The ending document is a letter to the Washoe County Building Department dated **September 18, 1987** from Al Williams, Chairman of the Black Springs GID. The letter reads as follows:

TO WHOM IT MAY CONCERN:

As of the above date, the Blacksprings General Improvement District will no longer honor any of its old Will-Serve letters.

There will be no water issued in this district at all.

I must point out before closing, that the spelling of Black Springs above, is not by accident on my part. The document was sent out as such, which once again shows a lack of professionalism.

CHAPTER 13
CHRONOLGY OF THE 1990'S

The final decade of the chronology of Black Springs, begins in 1990 with a name change for Black Springs General Improvement District. The official name now is Grand View Terrace General Improvement District. Personally like most old time residents, the community will always be Black Springs. You're able to read about the name change at the Nevada Historical Society. You'll be able to review and research about the different views of residents and the history of the Black Springs community in its entirety.

Minutes of Grand View Terrace Water District dated *November 21, 1991:*

"The meeting was called to order at Black Springs Community Center, 301 Kennedy Drive, Reno, Nevada by chair Al Williams at approximately 7:30 p.m. A roll call showed the presence of Al Williams, Honey Williams and Carrie Fitz. Absent from the meeting were Thurman Carthen and Mae Carthen. Also present were John N. Schroeder, attorney to the District, bookkeeper Roberta Stedfield, Douglas Coulter of the Washoe County Health Department and members of the public.

The first order of business was the reading of the minutes of the October 17, 1991 meeting, which were read and approved as read.

Douglas Coulter of the Washoe County Health Department reported on the current status of the District's compliance with the Safe Drinking Water Act and other applicable rules, regulations and statutes. He reported he would check on water contamination within the District and report back to the Board. District representatives reported to Mr. Coulter the status of Washoe County's completion of a block grant.

A CRY FOR HELP

Furthermore, Mr. Coulter told the District representatives about compliance with the chloroform rule, chlorination of the system, if needed, the Volatile Synthetic Organic Chemicals Act, the cost of tests, $80.00 per well every quarter, and the prospective effect of random testing. In conclusion, he reported he will make an inspection, take samples and let the Board know what Washoe County's concerns are, if any.

A financial report was distributed by bookkeeper Roberta Stedfield and she reported the financial standing of the District. The bills were submitted and approved for payment by unanimous vote of the Board... The total amount paid out was $1,448.89.

The matter of Mr. Cuillard was discussed.

Upon motion being made and carried unanimously by the members of the Board, bookkeeper Roberta Stedfield was instructed to write a letter to service connection customers, to advise each customer that if full payment or arrangements for payments are not taken care of, then they will be given a 5-day notice to be disconnected from service because of non-payment of bills.

Upon motion being made and carried unanimously by the members of the Board, Attorney John N. Schroeder was directed to contact Tom Purkey, Washoe County, pertaining to the block grant. Also, Attorney Schroeder was instructed to send a letter to H. Cuillard to invite him to the next meeting. Placed on the agenda for the next meeting was the Dutch Cook matter as well as the selection of a new bookkeeper.

Upon motion being made and carried unanimously by the members of the Board, it was decided not to hold a meeting in December 1991, and defer any meeting to the third Thursday in January 1992. Placed on the agenda for the January 21, 1992 meeting are the block grant, H. Cuillard, Dutch Cook, compliance with the Safe Drinking Water Act, block grant application, and selection of a bookkeeper.

There being no further business, the meeting adjourned at approximately 9:15 p.m."

CHRONOLGY OF THE 1990'S

A letter ***December 3, 1996*** was sent to Helen Westbrook from the Office of the Washoe County Clerk, Judi Bailey. The letter was congratulating her on being elected as Trustee of Grand View Terrace Water Board.

"Swearing-in ceremonies for all newly-elected officials have been scheduled for Monday, January 6, 1997 at 9:30 a.m. in the Washoe County Commission Chamber at 1001 East Ninth Street, Reno, Nevada and will be administered by the Washoe County Clerk."

This would be Helen Westbrook's last stint as an active member of the Board. Helen and Ollie Westbrook would continue striving to improve conditions within the community through advising their grandson Joseph Townsell, Chairman, Grandview Terrace/Horizon Hills Task Force.

The regular meeting of the Grand View Terrace GID was held ***January 16, 1997.***

The new members were Thurman Carthen, Chair; Roy Moore, Vice-Chair; Shelley Moore, Secretary; Mae Carthen, Collector; and Helen Westbrook, Depositor.

General information was given regarding new hook-ups--$1500.00, there must be signed a will serve letter and go through the proper paperwork with the Board. No new hook-ups at this time; Monthly service, $30.00; and standby service, $15.00.

"Shelley will put together an introduction letter to go with the next billing. This will show the members of the Board, and how to contact them if needed."

Black Springs' name change, took time for State and Local officials to get accustom to. A letter to the Black Springs GID dated ***February 4, 1997*** from Hugh Ricci, P. E., Deputy State Engineer was sent.

"Enclosed please find a copy of the State Engineer's Order Number 1100, allowing Domestic Well Credits in Lemmon Valley. The order gives public water systems credit for customers who are added to their system.

If the subject parcel meets the criteria set forth in State Engineer's Order Number 1100, the public water system will receive the domestic well credit.

In exchange for the domestic well credit, the owner of the parcel must voluntarily cease to draw water from an existing domestic well (the lot owner will be required to plug the existing domestic well) or must give up the right to drill a domestic well for the particular parcel. As long as the subject parcel falls within the criteria set forth in order number 1100, credit will be given to the water system. . ."

A letter from 'The White House', Washington, to Helen Westbrook dated **January 7, 1998** who had been nominated for the Golden Rule Award, was received. I recall seeing the plaque on her kitchen wall above the dining table. That's where my grandparents displayed their awards, recognitions and plaques they received throughout their years of service in their community, Black Springs, as well Washoe County. The letter reads as follows:

"I am delighted to congratulate all those who have been nominated for this year's Golden Rule Award.

If we are to make our world a better place, each of us must take responsibility for solving the problems around us. We must be interested not just in getting, but also in giving; not just in looking out for ourselves, but also in looking out for others. Each of you has led the way in this endeavor.

Your leadership is helping to strengthen families and communities, setting an example of compassion across America and around the World. I commend you for working to solve the problems of today and to meet the challenges of the future. You represent America at its best, getting things done and reinforcing our nation's fundamental values of community, responsibility, and compassion.

CHRONOLGY OF THE 1990'S

Hillary joins me in extending best wishes for continued success."

The letter was signed Bill Clinton.

I must say what an honored recognition to receive from the President of the United States of America. God bless America.

Another grant was in the making. This was through the Alturas power line mitigation funds, and my brother JoJo was the spearhead of this project. My grandparents were getting up in age. They were tired and needed and wanted the young people to get involved again. It was their final project, mostly done through JoJo.

While conversing with my bother I learned that when he had gone to apply for funding for his organization MEFIYI Foundation, he was approached by a lady asking him if he knew anyone in the Black Springs area. He informed her that he grew up in Black Springs. She informed him there were monies allotted for Black Springs. Quite a bit of money was just sitting in a pot waiting for someone to come and claim it.

In *February 1999* a grant proposal was written under the guidance of Ollie and Helen Westbrook to the Alturas Mitigation Fund:

Priority 1 – Black Springs Community Building Expansion project cost (funded by Alturas Funds): $320,000.00, to add approximately 3,000 sq. ft. to the existing Black Springs Community Center. The new addition would have tutoring and mentoring programs, fitness and recreation programs, parenting classes, continuing education classes and a children's break program.

Priority 2 – Grandview Terrace Water System Improvements project cost (funded by Alturas Funds): $100,000.00, to connect proposed water service line in Seneca Drive to Kennedy Drive and connect to Grandview Terrace's GID water system. Service line would be from Sierra Pacific Power Company's North Virginia/Stead water line.

Priority 3 – Install street lights in Grandview Terrace area – cost $1,750.00, to add 5 lights on existing Sierra Pacific poles in Grandview Terrace on Kennedy Drive, Westbrook Lane and Medgar Avenue.

A CRY FOR HELP

March 2, 1999 a town hall meeting was hosted at the Black Springs Community Building (Martin Luther King Park) regarding disbursal of the Alturas Intertie Power Line Mitigation Funds. The discussions of proposed projects (in priority) were the expansion of the Black Springs Community Building and Martin Luther King Park ($320,000); improvements for water service through the Grandview Terrace General Improvement District ($100,000); completion of Heindel Road (total project cost is $200,000; however, mitigation fund contributions is $70,000). Remaining funds would be directed toward projects in the North Valleys Regional Sports Complex.

You may wonder the out come of the street lights. Well, on *April 9, 1999* a letter to Helen Westbrook from Gail Jackson, Project Utility Coordinator for Sierra Pacific Power Company stated:

"This letter represents Sierra Pacific Power Co's proposal to provide and install five street lights at the above referenced locations. The cost portion for these lights is $1,750.00 for the installation and is due 30 days prior to construction. Sierra Pacific will provide and install all materials and labor associated with the lighting installation. For your information, these lights are being designed as 100 watt bulbs.

Following the installation, and with their approval, Washoe County will assume the monthly charge of $7.23 for each light totaling $36.15. A one time charge of $15 will be placed on the "master" street light billing to the County to process the paperwork with these new lights."

You can read the Grants in there entirety at the Nevada Historical Society.

The above was the biggest project in the 90s, completed in the new century. As you can see, things have calmed considerably. It seems like each decade ended with a major accomplishment through non-violence, and dedicated perseverance to enhance the quality of humankind and a down-trodden people. Black Springs/Grandview Terrace had become a neighborhood, a community. We have trees, nice big ones; lawns verses dirt; gardens; a park, playground; paved roads; sewage

CHRONOLGY OF THE 1990'S

system; very good pressure and good tasting water; 2 churches in the community; stop signs; divide lines on the streets; and the most important of all, was Mama Helen's street lights. A place anyone would be proud to call home. Oh yes! One more thing, it is now a Historical Site. Who would have ever thought Black Springs would be a Historical Site.

And as Big Daddy always quoted: "I must work the work of Him that sent me while it is still day, because when night comes no man can work."

THE END

A CRY FOR HELP

Mon, 22 February 2010, 10:30:38 AM

Helen: I wish Carol and I could be there for your reading and discussion this Sunday. We would love to read your manuscript. Also, will someone be recording or videotaping the evening?

I'm so very impressed that you've taken your passion about this era so very far. By sharing it with the Nevada Historical Society and the community you've made sure that the lessons and good from it all are preserved and passed on. Clearly, the name and motto of the 1960's Black Springs youth group survives, **P.O.W.E.R - People Organized to Work for Equal Recognition.**

Mama Helen so loved that name. The last time I saw her before her passing, Ollie and I were in their living room on Westbrook Lane -- he and I were on the couch and Helen was in her chair. Although a lot had changed in three decades, I felt at home in the warmth of the room that was almost frozen in the times. We had spent so many, many hours there planning, organizing, and sharing our passion for life, Black Springs and justice for all. A lot of laughter and tears were left in that room and, in some ways; your book probably captures what I thought only the paintings on the wall would say, if they could speak. That day, Mama Helen was not able to communicate much and I wasn't sure if she recognized me. But, when I showed her the P.O.W.E.R logo on a old t-shirt I had saved since the 1960's, and brought with me, her eyes lit up, she crossed her fisted forearms and, as only she could do with her soft but ever so powerful voice, she said with conviction only one word ... "POWER". I still hear her today. Although the three of us shared part of the afternoon that day together, Ollie and I conversed about old times, the present and the future, that was really all that Mama Helen had to say. I know she was thinking about a lot more.

Please give our love to all: **Andy Gordon**

Made in the USA
Middletown, DE
13 March 2025